Praise for the Mysteries Featuring
Senior Sleuth Fred Vickery

NO PLACE FOR SECRETS

"Fred's quite a character, and he's sure to charm the reader . . . Ms. Lewis has kept the clues subtle and the tension tight."

—*Rendezvous*

"Delightful . . . quirky . . . exciting . . . Ms. Lewis has developed a hero that readers cannot help but admire."

—*The Paperback Forum*

"[Fred Vickery is] fiercely independent, instinctively loving."

—*The Salt Lake Tribune*

NO PLACE LIKE HOME

"Well-written and believable . . . Ms. Lewis knows just how to keep the reader guessing."

—*Rendezvous*

"Entertaining, gently witty and cozy . . . [with] a maximum of heart."

—*Tower Books Mystery Newsletter*

NO PLACE FOR DEATH

"A clever story by a gifted writer . . . This won't be the last Fred Vickery mystery."

—*Rendezvous*

"[As] refreshin[illegible] orcher of a day."

—[illegible] *Magazine*

N[illegible]

"This cohesive [illegible] pon itself to an exciting e[illegible]"

—*Rendezvous*

"Mesmerizing . . . dynamic . . . a tantalizing read."

—*Affaire de Coeur*

MORE MYSTERIES FROM THE BERKLEY PUBLISHING GROUP . . .

FORREST EVERS MYSTERIES: A former race-car driver solves the high-speed crimes of world-class racing . . . "A Dick Francis on wheels!" —Jackie Stewart

by Bob Judd

BURN
CURVE
SPIN

THE REVEREND LUCAS HOLT MYSTERIES: They call him "The Rev," a name he earned as pastor of a Texas prison. Now he solves crimes with a group of reformed ex-cons . . .

by Charles Meyer

THE SAINTS OF GOD MURDERS
BLESSED ARE THE MERCILESS

FRED VICKERY MYSTERIES: Senior sleuth Fred Vickery has been around long enough to know where the bodies are buried in the small town of Cutler, Colorado . . .

by Sherry Lewis

NO PLACE FOR SECRETS
NO PLACE FOR DEATH
NO PLACE FOR SIN
NO PLACE LIKE HOME
NO PLACE FOR TEARS

INSPECTOR BANKS MYSTERIES: Award-winning British detective fiction at its finest . . . "Robinson's novels are habit-forming!" —*West Coast Review of Books*

by Peter Robinson

THE HANGING VALLEY
WEDNESDAY'S CHILD
GALLOWS VIEW
PAST REASON HATED
FINAL ACCOUNT
INNOCENT GRAVES

JACK McMORROW MYSTERIES: The highly acclaimed series set in a Maine mill town and starring a newspaperman with a knack for crime solving . . . "Gerry Boyle is the genuine article." —Robert B. Parker

by Gerry Boyle

DEADLINE
LIFELINE
BLOODLINE
POTSHOT

SCOTLAND YARD MYSTERIES: Featuring Detective Superintendent Duncan Kincaid and his partner, Sergeant Gemma James . . . "Charming!"
—*New York Times Book Review*

by Deborah Crombie

A SHARE IN DEATH
LEAVE THE GRAVE GREEN
ALL SHALL BE WELL
MOURN NOT YOUR DEAD

NO PLACE FOR SIN

SHERRY LEWIS

BERKLEY PRIME CRIME, NEW YORK

NO PLACE FOR SIN

A Berkley Prime Crime Book / published by arrangement with the author

PRINTING HISTORY
Berkley Prime Crime edition / December 1997

For information address: The Berkley Publishing Group, a member of Penguin Putnam Inc., 200 Madison Avenue, New York, NY 10016.

The Putnam Berkley World Wide Web site address is
http://www.berkley.com

ISBN: 0-425-16113-7

Berkley Prime Crime Books are published by The Berkley Publishing Group, a member of Penguin Putnam Inc., 200 Madison Avenue, New York, NY 10016.

PRINTED IN THE UNITED STATES OF AMERICA

10 9 8 7 6 5 4 3 2 1

one

Fred Vickery stormed down Cutler, Colorado's, Main Street toward the Bluebird Café, muttering under his breath. He'd just spent half an hour on the telephone, arguing with his oldest son, Joseph. Long distance. Now, Fred needed coffee. Lots of it.

He loved all four of his children. Really. But sometimes they put his sunny disposition to the test. Joseph had called, worried, because Fred's last checkup showed his cholesterol level had taken a slight jump. He'd informed Fred that he'd found a senior center near his New Hampshire home where he thought Fred should live out the rest of his days.

Fred didn't want or need to move, and if he did, it wouldn't be into a retirement home. But he'd listened to Joseph's nonsense as long as he could stand to. Then, he'd pointed out—quite reasonably, in fact—that Joseph's idea was the biggest bunch of hogwash he'd ever heard.

Of course, Joseph had flown off the handle. Even as a child, he'd hated the mildest reproach. So, he'd argued louder until, in the end, Fred had done the only thing possible. He'd slammed down the receiver in Joseph's ear, grabbed his keys, and walked out the door to avoid a repeat call.

There was only one way Joseph could have known about Fred's checkup—Fred's only daughter, Margaret, must have called her brother and given him a full report. Well, Fred would have a thing or two to say about that the next time he saw her.

But right now, he needed to soothe his jangled nerves. And

he intended to do so by treating himself to one of Lizzie Hatch's country-fried steak lunch specials at the Bluebird Café. Even the thought of Lizzie's cooking made his mouth water and nearly brought a smile to his lips. He'd order mashed potatoes with extra gravy and a steaming pot of coffee. Real coffee. Positively no decaf.

A light breeze whispered across his cheek and ruffled the aspen leaves overhead. The rich scent of new pine needles filled the air. Somewhere nearby a chipmunk chattered at an intruder, and birds squawked down at Fred from the treetops. If Joseph hadn't called, Fred would have enjoyed his walk through town on this sunny afternoon in May. But Joseph had called, and Fred wasn't in the mood to enjoy anything. And that, he thought, was that.

He stepped off the boardwalk and started across Aspen Street, but someone gripped him by the shoulder and yanked him backward a step.

"What in the—" he snarled and pivoted on his heel to stare straight into the deputy sheriff's badge pinned to Grady Hatch's chest.

"Whoa, Fred. Watch out. You could have gotten yourself killed."

Fred turned to look at Bessie Marshall piloting her 1968 Oldsmobile toward the intersection. She peered up over the steering wheel and kept her gaze firmly locked on the pavement.

"By Bessie?" Fred demanded. "She can't drive fast enough to hurt a fly on the road."

Grady released Fred's shoulder and took a step away. "Sorry. Instinctive reaction, I guess."

He looked so apologetic that Fred's anger faded a bit. "That's all right. No harm done. I may not have been paying close enough attention." Checking for traffic, he started across the street again.

To his surprise, Grady fell into step beside him. "Are you going to the Café?"

Fred nodded.

Grady stuffed his hands into his pockets. "I'll walk with you. I'm catching a late lunch myself."

Fred stole a glance at Grady's profile. Did he have an ulterior motive for coming along? Had Doc Higgins flapped his big mouth to everyone in town about Fred's cholesterol level? If so, Grady wouldn't be the only one in town keeping an eye on Fred's diet. Even Lizzie had been known to tinker with his orders from time to time. But she wouldn't get away with it this time. Fred had had enough for one day.

Besides, she'd think twice about annoying Fred when he walked in with her son. She knew Fred had a soft spot in his heart for Grady, in spite of the boy's occasional bouts of bullheadedness. Always had, though he didn't show it often.

Years ago, the unexpected death of Lizzie's husband left her with a teenaged son to raise and a load of bills to pay. The very minute the previous owners retired to Florida, she'd put parts of her insurance settlement as a down payment on the Bluebird Café and set to work putting her own stamp on the place.

She and Grady had done most of the work themselves, and Fred had soon recognized the wisdom in her decision. The physical labor had helped young Grady release his anger and frustrations and work through his grief. Fred suspected it had done the same for Lizzie. Secretly he thought Lizzie had done a fine job of raising her son alone under trying circumstances. Grady had turned into a fine young man.

They put another block behind them before Grady spoke again, and he made a valiant effort to sound casual. "So . . . Is something wrong?"

Fred started to shake his head, then changed his mind. He'd feel better if he could hear someone under the age of seventy tell him Joseph had behaved like an idiot. "I just had an argument with Joseph."

Grady nodded slowly. He was a good twenty years younger than Joseph, but they knew each other slightly. Everyone with a connection to Cutler knew everyone else, at least by sight and reputation. "Doesn't he live back east somewhere?"

"New Hampshire."

Grady pursed his lips, as if Fred had said something he needed to remember. "How's he doing?"

"Stubborn."

Grady nodded again and let a few more steps fall on the boardwalk. "You want to talk about it?"

Fred slowed his pace. "This isn't a new argument—we've been over this before. And I felt the same way last time he brought it up. I don't know what makes him think I'll change my mind now."

"About what?"

"A senior center." Fred stopped in his tracks and glanced up at Grady as the young man ground to a halt beside him. "He thinks I need to move into a dad-blasted retirement home and live out my days near him."

"Why?"

"So he can keep an eye on me during my waning years," Fred growled. "That's exactly what he said—my *waning years*."

Grady bit his bottom lip and glanced away, probably to avoid saying something foolish.

Fred jabbed him in the chest with his index finger, anyway. "He thinks just because I have a touch of arthritis and because my cholesterol level took a slight jump, that I'm too old to take care of myself. Now isn't that the most ridiculous thing you've ever heard?"

"Well, you did have that heart attack a few years ago," Grady said.

Fred glanced at him. "It wasn't a heart attack. It was a blip. And I'll tell you the same thing I told Joseph. I've lived in Cutler for seventy-three years, and I'll die right here in my own bed—not in some dad-blasted retirement home clear across the country."

"What did Joseph say to that?"

Fred's glare slipped into a deep scowl. "What do you think he said? I don't know how I ever raised such a fool."

Grady let out an uncomfortable laugh.

Pulling in a deep breath, Fred tried to calm himself. "Don't misunderstand me—I love my son. But I know why he wants me to move. It's because he doesn't want to feel guilty about never coming home to visit. Well, that's not my problem. And I'm *not* leaving my home just so he can justify his decision to work sixty hours a week."

He broke off and stared around him, studying the place he'd called home his entire life. Aspen trees and Englemann spruce towered over the buildings. High mountain peaks shielded the valley. Dense pine forests scrambled up the hillsides, and Spirit Lake sparkled through the foliage in the afternoon sun.

Fred's heart ached at the mere thought of moving away. He could never do it. Cutler held his childhood memories safe and preserved the memories of life with his late wife, Phoebe. His sister and most of his brothers lived nearby. So did all of Phoebe's family. And he resented Joseph for even suggesting that he leave it all.

Grady remained silent for a long time, and Fred could tell he chose his next words carefully. "What do the other kids think?"

"I haven't talked to Jeffrey or Douglas, but Margaret has to be the one who called Joseph and started this whole mess." Fred frowned, but he had to struggle to maintain his sour expression.

Margaret looked so much like her mother that it hurt sometimes. When her brothers had raced away to pursue careers, she'd stayed in Cutler to raise her family, and she'd been invaluable in helping Fred nurse Phoebe through the last stages of her cancer. He tried to remember that when she grew overanxious about protecting him—like now.

"I'm sure she's just worried about you," Grady said.

"Well, she doesn't need to be," Fred snapped. He sighed heavily and reached up to clap Grady on the shoulder. "I think I'll put Joseph out of my mind for the rest of the day. Let's get lunch."

Grady smiled and looked relieved. "Sounds like a plan to me."

They covered the remaining distance to the Bluebird in companionable silence. Grady stepped forward to open the door, and Fred sighed with pleasure as the comforting aromas of fresh coffee, roasting beef, and rich gravy rushed out to meet him.

Lizzie's most recent piece of Elvis memorabilia, an Elvis painted on black velvet, gazed down on Fred as he stepped inside, and last notes of "In the Ghetto" died away on the jukebox.

Grandpa Jones and Arnold Van Dyke sat at the counter, but the rest of the stools were empty. Perfect. Fred could eat in peace and take plenty of time to pull himself together.

Grandpa looked up from his plate and wagged a french fry to say hello. Arnold stopped stuffing his sandwich into his mouth long enough to nod. Lizzie checked the new arrivals and smiled when she saw Grady. She reached for the coffeepot on the warmer, and Grady took a step away as if he intended to sit in his usual spot near the kitchen.

"Aren't you going to join me?" Fred asked.

Grady glanced back over his shoulder. For some reason, he looked astonished. "Well, I . . ." He shrugged and turned around. "Sure."

Fred led the way to his favorite corner booth beneath the *Kissin' Cousins* poster, pleased to see a customer at only one other table in the dining room.

Hannah Irvine sat with her red head bent over a book, so engrossed she didn't even look up when Fred and Grady entered. He'd never known Hannah well. She was young—no more than seventeen. Just about the same age as his grandson Benjamin. She was a quiet girl. Shy. Fred didn't often see her with kids from school, and he suspected her stepmother had a lot to do with that.

Lenore Irvine was an unpleasant woman, at best. She'd grown up in Cutler and remained single until about six years earlier, when she'd met and married Kent Irvine and taken in Hannah, Kent's youngest daughter, for an instant family. Fred knew Kent had another daughter, older than Hannah, but he couldn't remember ever seeing her.

One way or another Lenore had managed to offend almost everyone in town, and he often wondered whether Hannah paid the price for her stepmother's attitude. As a matter of fact, Fred could think of only one person who truly liked Lenore—Janice Lacey. In Fred's opinion, having Janice as a friend was worse than having no friends at all, but he never said so aloud.

Slipping into the booth, he turned over his coffee cup while

Grady worked his long legs under the table. But before Fred could even enjoy a moment's peace, the bell over the door tinkled again and George Newman stepped inside.

Fred tried not to groan aloud. Of all people to come in when Fred needed peace and quiet. George could rattle on for hours and still say absolutely nothing. Fred wasn't in the mood to listen. Not today.

He started to look away, but a younger version of George stepped inside and held his attention. This time, Fred didn't even try to hold back his groan or hide his dismay.

George's son, David, had moved away years ago. He hadn't been back to Cutler in so long, Fred thought he'd forgotten how to get here. But today, of all days, he'd come home.

Both men stood nearly six feet tall, both let their shoulders stoop forward slightly, both had prominent roman noses and narrow-set eyes. George had more wrinkles on his face and a lot more gray in his hair, but within a few years, David would be his father's double.

Fred had never cared for David, even as a boy. But that didn't stop George from telling Fred about David's every boring achievement—real or imagined. Fred had never been able to stop George from raving about David's law practice somewhere on the east slope of the Rockies—Boulder, if Fred remembered right—and he'd probably expect Fred to admire the boy in person.

Grady followed Fred's gaze and looked back quickly. "Is that George's son?"

"Unfortunately."

"He's an attorney, isn't he? Like Joe?" The second Joseph's name left his lips, Grady caught himself and sent Fred a guilty smile.

Fred nodded and refrained from pointing out that no one could consider Joseph and David in the same league.

He watched as David took a few seconds to renew acquaintances with Grandpa and Arnold and dreaded the moment George would spot him. He wondered whether country-fried steak and mashed potatoes were worth spending even five minutes with George and David.

Before he could reach a decision, Lizzie reached in front of him to fill his cup. Without looking away from her task, she jerked her chin toward the counter. "Home for a visit."

"So I see."

She placed a hand on Grady's shoulder while she filled his cup. "Brought his wife with him."

Fred had heard talk about David's wife over the years. He couldn't remember details, but he couldn't imagine anyone very impressive taking up with a man like David. "Have you met her?"

"Once," Lizzie said.

"What is she like?"

"Once was enough." Lizzie lowered the coffeepot to the table. She must have said all she intended. "Ready to order?"

"I'll have a cheeseburger and fries," Grady said. "And a large Coke."

"Bring the special for me," Fred said. "With mashed potatoes and extra gravy."

Lizzie stared at him with narrowed eyes. "I can't bring you that."

Fred ignored her. "And a roll—with two pats of butter."

"Doc hasn't been in yet," she warned.

Fred waved away her concern with one hand and pretended not to understand. "Doc can order his own lunch."

"With your cholesterol up, Doc will have something to say if I feed you like that."

What remained of Fred's good humor evaporated. He folded his hands on the table and met her gaze with a harsh one of his own. "I refuse to eat salad or sprouts or that ridiculous diet plate you try to pawn off on me," he warned. "I'm having country-fried steak. If you won't give it to me, I'll drive down to Granby and get it there."

Fred thought he saw a hint of a smile tug at the corners of her mouth, but she turned away too quickly for him to be certain.

He called his order after her for good measure, then looked back as George and David left the counter and started into the dining area.

Just as Fred feared, George made a beeline toward his

table. "You remember Fred Vickery, don't you, son? And Grady?" George said over his shoulder as he clomped toward them.

David nodded at his father's back, sent a halfhearted smile in Fred's direction, and focused on Grady. "You're Lizzie's son?"

Grady half-stood, bumping the table and sending coffee sloshing over the rim of Fred's cup. He offered his hand to David. "Grady Hatch."

"I don't believe it. You were a scrawny kid about ten feet tall last time I saw you."

Grady's smile faded. He'd been overly sensitive about his height as a boy, and Fred suspected thoughtless remarks could still affect him. Trust David to offer one right off the bat.

George dropped onto the bench beside Fred, groaning as if he were about to keel over. "David showed up last night out of the blue. He's stayin' around for a few weeks—isn't that great?"

Great.

George beamed up at his son. "That fancy law office down in Aurora finally decided they could do without him for a bit, didn't they?"

David sent his father a tired smile, then perched on the bench beside Grady. Pushing up his glasses, he rubbed the bridge of his nose as if strolling through town had worn him out.

"He was just commentin' as to how things've changed." George said. "Myself, I don't see it. It being gradual, and all. But David—he can really tell."

Fred took a bracing sip of coffee and made an effort to hide his irritation. "My boys always say the same thing."

David lowered his glasses and focused on Fred slowly. "Hard to believe things change at all in this sleepy old place. The town looks better than I thought it would, considering everything Dad's been telling me."

Grady started to lift his cup, but he lowered it quickly and looked from George to David. "Like what?"

"Oh, you know," George said, with a casual wave toward

the window. "I mentioned those old clay water pipes that are crumblin'. And how the Civic Center needs to be refurbished. And the way the Historical Society's raisin' such a fuss about preservin' those old buildings along Main Street . . ."

A fleshy ridge formed between David's eyes. "You said something about the education system, too. You'd know about that, wouldn't you, Fred? How's the school district's funding?"

"I was the buildings and grounds supervisor," Fred said. "Not the accountant. Besides, I'm retired."

David turned to Grady before Fred even finished speaking, as if he hadn't really expected Fred to help. "How about you, Grady? Any idea how many computers the school district owns? How's the funding for the sports program? I was a letterman, you know."

Everybody knew. George didn't let anyone forget about David's less than illustrious career warming the bench in every sport for three years.

"I don't know," Grady said. "But I'm sure someone at the district offices could tell you."

Fred leaned his elbows on the table. "Why the sudden interest in Cutler after all these years?"

David smiled slowly. "What would you say if I told you I knew how the city could pull itself out of this slump?"

"It's not in a slump," Grady insisted. He looked offended.

David flashed a half smile. "All right. Put it this way, then. I know how the city can get the money it needs to repair those water pipes, restore the historic buildings, and supplement the education budget."

Grady lifted his eyebrows. "How?"

"Cutler isn't the only small Colorado town to face money problems, you know. But it is one of the last to take action to fix them." David gestured toward the window. "We can turn Cutler's economy around in just a few months. We can bring in money and jobs and our fair share of the tourist trade. *And* we can put money into the pockets of Cutler's citizens."

We? Fred stared at him and tried to fight down his mounting outrage. "What are you doing? Running for political office?"

David laughed, but he didn't sound amused. "Political office? No." He leaned back in his seat, hitched his thumbs into the waistband of his trousers, and smiled as if he knew the effect his next words would have. "I'm here to build support for a petition to bring legalized gambling to Cutler."

two

Fred reared back in his seat as if David had gut-punched him. "Gambling?" Of all the blasted silly ideas—

He must have spoken too loudly, because Hannah Irvine jerked her head up and away from her book. He didn't want Hannah to overhear their conversation and say something to her step mother. Lenore considered it her personal obligation to see that everyone followed her personal moral code, and she'd steamrolled the citizens of Cutler more than once over issues less threatening than this.

Cursing himself silently, he clamped his lips shut and tried to pull his already ragged temper under control.

Grady didn't say anything, but his eyes narrowed, his lips thinned, and his forehead creased.

Fred glared from David to George and back again, but he didn't speak again until Hannah returned her attention to her book. Lowering his voice, he tried again. "That is the stupidest idea I've ever heard. We don't want gambling in Cutler."

"Dad said you'd feel that way," David said with a tight smile. "But if you'll just listen for a minute, you'll be as impressed with the idea as I am."

"Never in a million years," Fred assured him.

George wagged a hand in Fred's direction. "You're wastin' your breath on him, son. That's one thing about Fred. He's stubborn. Too stubborn for his own good half the time."

Stubborn? Fred humphed a response. He wasn't stubborn, but neither was he easily manipulated.

David went on as if neither of them had spoken. "You know they've got gambling in Central City, Blackhawk, and Cripple Creek . . . Right?"

"Of course I know that," Fred snapped. Only a fool could have missed the hubbub that had rocked the state at the time.

Grady nodded, but he looked even more wary.

David smiled, apparently satisfied with the level of their understanding. "Well, in 1990, Central City's general funds revenue was only three-hundred fifty-thousand dollars all year. In 1995, it was just under six million—the direct result of legalized gambling."

George nudged Fred's foot with his own. "Did you hear that? Six *million*."

Fred heard. "We don't need six million dollars," he snapped.

"You need revenue," David insisted. "You can't argue with that."

"We don't need it *that* badly," Fred insisted.

"Or the increased crime rate that comes with it," Grady said.

David laughed. "That's bunk."

"It is not." Grady leaned his elbows on the table. "You might have statistics to support your argument, but what about the stats that prove the other side? Population has increased in those towns so rapidly they can't keep up with everything. Crime rates rise. Divorces skyrocket. People are gambling away their paychecks and everybody ends up in trouble."

"That's a bunch of bull," David insisted.

"You can't just decide to bring slot machines and casinos into Cutler," Fred reminded him. "It takes an amendment to the state's constitution, and *that* has to be provided in a statewide election."

"I know that," George said. "I also know there'll be *some* who are too closed-minded to even consider the idea." He raked his eyes over Fred as if he had a point to make.

"Gambling's been defeated in every election since 1990," Fred said. "What does *that* tell you?"

George opened his mouth as if he might have an answer.

Fred didn't want to hear it. "It tells you that Colorado learned its lessons after it approved gambling the first time."

David waved his hand in front of his face as if Fred's argument annoyed him. "Yeah, yeah, yeah. That's what they all say. The truth is, they blow a couple of horror stories totally out of proportion in the newspapers, and all the anti-gamblers run around saying I told you so. You can't believe everything you read."

"You can't discount everything you read, either," Fred argued.

David ignored him. "It'll take some work to get the petition together, the signatures verified, and the proposal in front of the legislature."

"And money," Grady pointed out.

David flicked a sharp glance at him. "And money."

"How much are we talking about?" George asked. "Bottom line."

David shrugged. "I talked to some folks in Central City. They said they'd figured somewhere between four hundred fifty and five hundred thousand, but that was a few years ago." He kept his voice lazy and unconcerned, as if he were discussing pocket change.

"If we can raise that much money," Fred suggested helpfully, "why don't we just use it to fix everything and forget gambling?"

"It may sound like a lot," David said with an impatient scowl. "But even that much money won't fix everything."

"This is ridiculous," Fred insisted. "Gambling would be the ruin of Cutler."

George's wrinkles folded in on each other. "That's *your* opinion."

Grady shook his head slowly. "He's not the only one who feels that way."

David glared from Grady to Fred and readjusted his position in the seat. "You're both afraid of change. You're so isolated from the real world up here, you don't even know what's going on anymore."

"It seems to me," Fred said, not caring who heard him now, "the people who live here ought to be the ones who decide what's done and what's not. You've ignored this town for years, and the only reason you're back now is because you can smell a way to put a profit in your own pocket."

David thumped his palm on the table and shot to his feet. "I don't have to sit here and listen to you insult me. This has nothing to do with me. This town will die if someone doesn't take some action."

Fred snorted his response.

David used his palm on his chest next. "Well, I intend to be that someone. I'll do whatever it takes to pull Cutler into the 21st century, and I'll do it with or without you—makes no difference to me." He caught his father's gaze and jerked his chin toward the door. "We're wasting our time on these two. Let's get out of here."

Tossing an indignant look in Fred's direction, George stood. But instead of leaving, he leaned his fists on the table. "You're nothin' but an old fool, Fred Vickery. A stubborn old fool." Without waiting for a response, he pivoted away and clomped toward the door a step behind David.

Grady expelled his breath on a heavy sigh and flicked a glance at Fred. "Well?"

Fred couldn't make himself speak until the door slammed shut with the Newmans on the outside. Then he managed a weak smile. "I don't suppose you can arrest them for being idiots?"

Grady laughed softly. "I don't think so."

Fred shook his head. "I ought to know better than to argue with George. It doesn't accomplish a blasted thing. He's as mule-headed as they come, and David is obviously cut from the same bolt of cloth."

"Think they'll succeed?"

"No."

Grady stared at him for a second. "What makes you so sure?"

"I don't know," Fred admitted, taking a sip of lukewarm coffee. With a grimace, he put the cup back on the table and stared out the window at the businesses across the street and the receding figures of George and David Newman.

"They can't bring gambling into Cutler," Grady insisted. "It'll ruin everything."

Fred nodded. "I know." But their conversation left him worried and a little sick. He knew how excited many of the folks in Central City, Cripple Creek, and Blackhawk had been to turn their town over to casinos and slot machines, and he worried many of Cutler's citizens would react the same way.

He didn't know how to stop George or his stupid son. But he had to do something. He couldn't sit idly by and watch while someone barged into town and ruined his way of life.

three

The minute Fred finished his lunch, he left the Bluebird and hotfooted it to Margaret's house. First things first, he'd decided. First he needed to alert a few of Cutler's more intelligent citizens to David and George's scheme. Get the opposition up and running before the Newmans swayed too many people to their side.

If Fred did say so himself, Margaret was one of the brightest people in Cutler. She'd have a few ideas about how to fight back.

He hurried up the sidewalk to Margaret's front door, relieved to see stray grass clippings on the walk and two garbage bags sprouting dead weeds and twigs near the driveway. Obviously she was home and in the middle of yard work. Good. Fred didn't want to wait.

He glanced next at the driveway. Empty. Perfect. That meant Margaret's husband, Webb, had gone to work. Fred tried to avoid Webb whenever he could, and he especially wanted to avoid him today. Webb was always looking for a way to make an easy buck, and Fred would be a fool to mention gambling anywhere near him.

He climbed the steps, knocked lightly on the screen door, and rocked back on his heels to wait. For a split second he thought he heard the low rumble of a man's voice, then immediately decided he'd been mistaken. A moment later, a whisper of sound announced Margaret's approach.

She wore jeans cut off just above her knees and a faded blue T-shirt, and she'd slipped on her Keds without socks—

her one continuing act of rebellion against her mother. Brushing back a strand of dark hair, she peered out at him and pushed open the screen door. "Dad? This is a surprise. What are you doing here?"

Fred stepped inside, pausing just long enough to brush a kiss to her cheek. "I just came from the Bluebird, sweetheart. Ran into David Newman there. Did you know he was in town?"

Margaret's eyes widened. "David's in town? Why? Is something wrong with George?"

"No. But David is here for a reason, and that's what I want to talk to you about. You'll never guess what that blasted fool wants to do—" He stepped into the living room, then stopped when he realized Margaret wasn't alone.

Too late to make an escape, he recognized Lenore and Kent Irvine smiling up at him from Margaret's couch. What on earth were they doing here? Hannah couldn't have told them about the conversation at the Bluebird already—Fred hadn't wasted even a minute getting here.

"I didn't realize you had company," he said. "Why don't I come back later?"

Lenore patted the back of her blonde hair, which she'd kept clipped in the same style her entire adult life. "Nonsense. You don't need to leave. In fact, you might just be able to help."

The high pitch of her voice set her already frayed nerves on edge. "No," he said quickly and took a tentative step backward. "I just stopped by to say hello to Margaret."

Lenore readjusted her position on the couch and made a vain attempt to tug the hem of her blouse to meet the waistband of her pants. "We need your help convincing Maggie to chair a project for us."

Fred didn't have to look at Margaret to know how she felt about that idea. She'd never been overly fond of Lenore.

Lenore went on, patting her hair again. "You probably know Kent and I are the founders of PFAAD."

Fred didn't know. He didn't care. In fact, he had no idea what PFAAD was. But one look at the frantic expression on Margaret's face convinced him to stay. He sank into an easy chair and made a noncommittal noise.

"Parents Fighting Alcohol and Drugs," Kent added with an almost apologetic smile. He took up a full third of the couch—a barrel of a man, with thinning brown hair, massive shoulders, and a prominent belly. He wore a suit that might have fit him once, but which had to strain to reach across him today. His broad face and swollen lips looked even larger underneath a too-small pair of horn-rimmed glasses that perched on his generous nose and splayed across his temples to lodge on his ears. "Lenore believes we should provide alternatives to the youth of America."

"I see." Fred tried not to look relieved. He understood better the expression on Margaret's face, but at least they weren't here to discuss gambling.

"You can help us talk some sense into Maggie," Lenore insisted. "Don't you think she'd be a wonderful chairperson for our Dry Cutler campaign?"

Fred would rather not know more about Lenore's causes than absolutely necessary. But when another flash of irritation flicked across Margaret's face, he tried to look interested. "Dry Cutler?"

Lenore frowned at him and ticked her tongue against the roof of her mouth. "The campaign to outlaw the sale of liquor within Cutler's city limits," she said as if she'd personally explained it to Fred a thousand times.

That certainly didn't surprise him. It fit right in with the campaign she'd led to prohibit dancing at the schools because it led to immoral behavior and the one to ban books containing material she found questionable.

Margaret perched on the arm of Fred's chair. "I've already told you, Lenore. I can't do it."

Lenore brushed her words away with the wave of her hand. "Nonsense. Who could possibly do it better?"

Kent's thick lips puffed into an embarrassed smile. "What Lenore means to say—"

Lenore shushed him with an impatient noise and a glower. She leaned forward, drawing her blouse a bit further up her back and exposing a broad, white section of skin. "Maggie, I don't want to offend, but you *know* the effect alcohol can have on a family. You know how destructive it is. People would listen to you."

Wanting to offer support, Fred placed one hand on Margaret's back. She jerked away from his touch, then immediately flashed an apologetic smile. She was obviously wound tighter than he'd imagined.

"Lenore—" Margaret began again.

But Lenore barrelled on, wagging her hands to help make her point. "I don't have to tell you about the moral decay in our society. I don't have to tell *any* of you about the kinds of crimes children are committing these days. They're fueled by alcohol and drugs—*and* by parents who don't care enough to do anything about it." She accomplished this last statement with a meaningful glance at Margaret.

Kent tried to stop her. "Really, Lenore—"

She evaded his gaze with skill and kept her attention riveted on Margaret. "This downward spiral has to *stop* before our entire country is ruined. We're self-destructing, and you know it."

Margaret sighed so softly in reply, Fred suspected he was the only one who heard her.

Lenore certainly didn't. "We have to *do* something. We need to create a wave of moral decency that will eventually roll across the country. And we can—*if* people will support us. But the effort begins *right here*." She pounded her knee in rhythm with her last few words.

Margaret held up both hands in a self-protective gesture. "I know there are a lot of kids in trouble these days. They're angry. They're confused. They're frightened—"

Lenore snorted a laugh. "*They're* frightened? We're the ones who are frightened. Good, law-abiding, God-fearing folk like us. We're at the mercy of kids who are on the streets without proper supervision. They're smoking and doing drugs and drinking anything they want. They're having sex and spreading disease and producing illegitimate children who'll pay the price for their parents' stupidity. But I ask you, Maggie. Where do they learn it?" She pointed an accusing finger at the living room floor. "They learn from parents and other irresponsible adults who refuse to take a stand."

Fred waited for the walls to stop ringing. Lenore had never been able to see beyond her own point. She pushed her opinions too hard, embellished facts beyond belief, and tossed around blame like confetti.

"You're going to have to find someone else," Margaret said again. This time, Fred heard more than a touch of impatience in her voice.

To give Kent credit, he seemed to realize Margaret wouldn't change her mind. He slapped his palms on his thighs and hoisted himself off the couch. "Well," he said on a loud groan, "you can't blame us for trying. Thanks for your time, anyway."

But Lenore refused to give up. "Maggie, I'm not going to take no for an answer. PFAAD needs you." She watched for Margaret's reaction, then drew in a deep breath and plunged on again. "All right. I didn't want to say this, but you've left me no choice. You have a moral obligation to counteract the negative influence your husband has on the children of our community." She parked her hands in her lap and nodded. "There. I've said it. As clearly as I know how."

Fred waited for Margaret to explode. To tell Lenore to mind her own business. Instead, she opened her mouth to speak, then stopped and tipped her head to listen. In the distance, a vehicle approached, slowed, and finally turned into the driveway.

Fred checked his watch. Webb? What in blazes was he doing home at this time of day?

For Margaret's sake, Fred didn't want Webb to find Lenore Irvine in his living room, discussing alcohol abuse. Webb and Lenore had butted heads more than once over the years, and Webb had ranted about her on a regular basis.

He worked back to his feet, cursing the arthritis that made him move so slowly. "Lenore, you're going to have to find someone else." The words came out a bit stiff, but he smiled pleasantly and held out a hand to help her to her feet.

Before she could accept, Webb burst into the room through the kitchen door. A wide smile stretched his face and excitement widened his bleary eyes. The smell of beer and old cigarette smoke drifted from him, and he walked with the slightly unsteady gait brought on by a diet of alcohol that had increased over the years.

He swept the room with his gaze, but when he saw Lenore and Kent his smile evaporated like morning mist. "What's this?"

Margaret crossed to him and took his arm. "Lenore and Kent are on their way out, and Dad just got here."

Making no effort to mask her disapproval, Lenore finally pushed out of her seat and joined her husband, but she kept her gaze riveted on Webb. "He's been drinking again," she muttered to Kent, but Fred knew she intended Webb to hear. Her voice carried easily across the room.

"What'd you say?" Webb demanded.

Kent made a vain attempt to get Lenore to keep her big mouth shut, but again she ignored him. "I said, you've been drinking again."

Webb's eyes narrowed and his lip curled. "I might have had a beer. So what? It's none of *your* business."

Lenore rolled her eyes in exasperation and managed to look at everyone before she spoke again. "Your alcohol abuse is everyone's business who lives in this town. Everyone who walks these streets while you're driving them in that condition. Everyone with young and impressionable children." She drew herself up and hitched her pants to her waist. "You are a menace."

Kent put a restraining arm around Lenore's waist, but he held her so loosely he might as well have done nothing. Fred tried to draw his attention, to send a silent message to get Lenore outside before she could set a match to the fire she'd kindled. But Kent didn't look at him, even for an instant.

Lenore shook off her husband's arm. "You're a drunk and you're a hazard, Webb Templeton. If I had my way, you'd be locked up just to keep you from killing someone."

Fred groaned aloud. Of all the fool things to say. He had no doubt how Webb would react to *that*.

Sure enough, Webb's temper flared. "Get outta my house," he demanded and pointed toward the door as if Lenore needed help to find her way.

For one horrible moment, Fred thought Webb intended to

strike her. Pushing past Kent's bulk, he caught Lenore by the arm before Webb could move any closer. "I think you'd better leave, Lenore."

She tried to tug away from him, but Fred held fast.

Kent came up behind them. "Fred's right, dear. We should go."

Eyes a little wide, Lenore rounded on him. "Don't you *dare* take his side against me."

"I'm not taking sides," Kent said, struggling to sound patient.

"*You,* of all people, should know how important this is," she shouted, as if he hadn't spoken. "Do you want men like *him* running loose around Hannah?"

Webb made a noise like a low growl and lunged toward her. "Get *out.*"

This time, Lenore jerked her arm out of Fred's grasp. "I'm not here to see you. I'm here to see Maggie."

"I don't give a rat's ass *who* you came to see," Webb bellowed. "Get the hell out of my house. *Now*. Before I call the sheriff." It was an empty threat, and everybody knew it. Webb had always been jealous that Margaret and the sheriff, Enos Asay, had almost married shortly after high school. He'd never voluntarily invite Enos into his home.

When Lenore didn't budge, Webb turned on Kent next. "Get her out of here. Can't you even control your own wife?"

Kent didn't say a word. Everybody knew the answer to that, too.

"If anybody's a menace to this town, *she* is," Webb shouted with an angry flick of his hand in Lenore's direction. "Get her out of my house. You're trespassing."

As she always did, Margaret tried to placate Webb's foul temper. She touched one hand to his shoulder and spoke in a soothing voice. "Don't blow this out of proportion. Please."

Swallowing his annoyance, Fred tried to hand Lenore over to her husband, but Kent might as well have been a thousand miles away. Frustrated, Fred released Lenore's arm and grabbed Kent by the front of his shirt. "This is getting out of hand. Either you get her out of here, or I'll drag her out myself."

Kent stared at him for what felt like an eternity. At long last, he came back from wherever he'd been, gripped his wife's shoulders, and propelled her toward the door. "Let's go, Lenore."

Lenore jerked away from him again and struck his shoulder several times with the flat of her hand. "Don't *touch* me. I'll go when I'm ready."

Kent flushed an angry shade of red and gripped Lenore again. This time, he pinned her arms to her side and dragged her toward the door. "We're leaving. Now."

"Maggie needs help," Lenore insisted. "She's setting a bad example for all the girls in Cutler—"

"Be quiet, Lenore," Kent warned. "You've done enough damage here. If Maggie doesn't want help, there's nothing you can do."

Lenore struggled against him, but she didn't stand a chance against her husband's determined bulk. Kent pushed open the screen and wrestled her onto the porch.

And Webb chased after them. "Maggie doesn't *need* help," he shouted. "Especially not from hypocrites like you."

Lenore tried to turn, and she might have responded, but Kent didn't give her a chance. He twisted her around to face front and hustled her down the steps.

Webb propped one arm on the door's frame and leaned his forehead against the mesh. "I'm warning you, Irvine. Keep that meddlin' bitch away from my wife." Acting very much like a dog who thinks it's chasing away a speeding car, he shouted again. "Do you hear me? Keep her away from me and my family, or you'll both be sorry."

four

In the sudden quiet following Lenore Irvine's departure, Fred tried to pull himself together and calm his shattered nerves. The day had started badly and had quickly gone downhill. He didn't even want to speculate on how much worse it could get.

Margaret slowly approached Webb, touched the small of his back, and used her soothing voice again. "It's okay. She's gone."

Fred watched, wishing more than anything he dared turn away. He'd always hated watching her placate Webb after one of his tantrums, and he had no more taste for it today than usual. But he didn't trust Webb not to turn his drunken hostility on Margaret now that Lenore had disappeared.

To his relief, Webb faced Margaret and trailed his fingers across her cheek, then turned to glare out the screen door again. "A man *oughta* be able to come home to a little peace and quiet."

Margaret led him a few steps away from the door. "I didn't invite them, but I couldn't be rude and refuse to let them in." She patted his shoulder and worked up a hopeful smile. "Let's forget about them, okay? What brings you home so early?"

Webb scowled for a minute more, then brightened as if Lenore and Kent had never existed. "I've got great news."

Fred couldn't imagine any news Webb could bring home that would be great for Margaret.

But Margaret obviously didn't share his doubts. "You do?" she asked. "What?"

Webb worked his arms around Margaret's waist and twirled her. "We're out of the woods, Maggie, my gal. Out of the woods and sailin' clear." He grinned over at Fred as if he expected Fred to shout for joy.

Fred didn't.

"I know you've always thought of me as a loser," Webb told him. "But this time, I'm going to prove you're wrong about me."

Fred could only hope he would, but he wouldn't hold his breath while he waited. He made a noncommittal noise.

Webb laughed and flapped a finger loosely in Margaret's face. "I found us an investment opportunity, Margaret Irene. We're gettin' in on the ground floor and we're goin' to be filthy, stinkin' rich. My ship has finally come in."

Fred's heart skipped a beat. Margaret's expression sobered. "How?" she asked. "What?"

Surprisingly, Webb pecked a quick kiss to her cheek, more affectionate than Fred had seen him in years. "All's we need is some investment capital, and we're set. And I know exactly where to get it."

Margaret narrowed her eyes. "Where?"

Fred fought back the dread that threatened to engulf him. He knew without being told that Webb had been talking to David Newman. He could feel it in the air.

Webb slanted a sideways grin in Fred's direction. "Gambling, Maggie. Right here in Cutler." He paced a couple of steps away. "They're looking for investors to get a petition up and running and get it on the ballot. We'll put a little money in now and use the rest to go in on a casino."

"What money?" Fred asked. He couldn't remain silent.

Pride filled Webb's face. "I'm gettin' a second mortgage on the house."

Margaret shot Fred a frantic look before she turned back to her husband. "A second mortgage? Webb, we're having enough trouble making ends meet. How could we ever pay off a second mortgage?"

"Let me worry about that," Webb insisted.

That would be the second biggest mistake Margaret ever

made, Fred thought. The first had been marrying Webb in the first place.

To Fred's relief, Margaret didn't look happy about the idea. "I don't know—"

"You don't need to know," Webb insisted. "This is *my* house. It's not your decision."

Margaret flushed, and a knot formed in the pit of Fred's stomach. Margaret had been young and foolish and too much in love to have understood the repercussions of letting Webb and his father set up the mortgage to exclude her. Fred had found out too late to talk sense into her, and he'd always prayed she wouldn't find herself in a situation like this.

"You're not listening," Webb said with exaggerated patience. "We'll pay it off and have money to spare."

Margaret shook her head slowly.

"Okay." Webb's voice grew louder. "I'm gonna explain it again. See if you can understand it this time."

Fred had tolerated a lot from Webb over the years. Too much, if you wanted his opinion. And he refused to stand idly by while the jerk spoke to Margaret in that tone. "It seems to me you're the one who doesn't understand," he said, moving to Margaret's side. "If you take out a second mortgage on this house, chances are, you'll lose it."

Webb turned on him. "Can't you ever keep your nose out of *anything?* I'm not talking to you."

"You're talking like a fool," Fred said, determined to keep Webb's hostility focused away from Margaret. "What are you going to do? Lose this house and leave my daughter and grandchildren homeless?"

"Nobody's gonna lose nothin'," Webb shouted. "I guarantee it." He paced a step away, then turned back. "Why in the hell are you always so sure I'm going to fail?"

Fred didn't offer the answer that rose to his lips.

"Well, I'm *not* goin' to fail," Webb insisted, making a broad sweep with his arms. "No matter what you think. No matter what it takes. This time, I'm going to make it."

"When? Even if your investment does pay off, when do you think you'll have the money? It won't be in time to make two mortgage payments next month. And what will you do if the petition fails? If the amendment isn't approved in a general election?"

"It won't fail," Webb insisted stubbornly. He held up his index finger and used it to site in on Margaret. "And you'd better not even think about fighting me on this. This is my chance. Finally. And I'm not going to let anybody take it from me. Not even you." He pivoted away and started toward the kitchen door muttering, "If this is the way a man gets treated in this house, I'm leaving."

Margaret shot a frustrated look at Fred and followed. "Where are you going?"

"To the bank, if it's any of your business. To get my money."

Fred rubbed his forehead and tried to think of some way to convince Webb not to take this step. He certainly couldn't count on Kirby Manning not to give Webb the loan.

"Webb, wait—" Margaret reached toward him, then jerked her hands back and steepled them under her chin. "Can't we talk about this?"

Webb backed away from her. "No. There's nothin' to talk about."

"Okay, you've made up your mind. But won't you wait until tomorrow? Stay, and let's talk about it tonight."

"No!" Webb plowed through the kitchen to the back door. "You just want to talk me out of it, but you're not goin' to." He yanked open the door and stepped halfway through. "I can't believe my own wife is against me."

"I'm not against you," Margaret reasoned. "I just want to make sure this is the right thing."

Obviously unmoved, Webb turned to leave.

"Webb, please—" She broke off and muttered, "Dammit," then raced toward the door. "When will you be home?"

Webb glared at her. "When you see the whites of my eyes." He slammed the door behind him hard enough to rattle the window over the sink. A few seconds later the door to his truck banged shut, and the truck's engine roared to life.

Fred stood in Margaret's kitchen, too angry to even comfort his daughter. He clenched his hands into fists, ignoring the stiffness of his joints and almost welcoming the pain while the screech of Webb's tires on the driveway provided background music for Margaret's quiet tears.

Fred started his morning constitutional nearly an hour behind schedule the next day. He hadn't slept well at all. He'd spent the night worrying about Margaret, when he wasn't fuming about Joseph or fretting about David Newman.

Some time well after two o'clock, he'd finally drifted into an uneasy sleep and awakened late as a result. His arthritis had flared again, making him move slowly as he dressed. He'd spent far too long fumbling with his shirt buttons and struggling to tie the laces on his work boots. After battling to separate a coffee filter from the stack for at least five minutes without success, he'd tossed the whole blamed bunch of them back into the cupboard and stomped outside.

He didn't fare any better there. The weather had turned cool overnight—cooler than usual for mid-May—and his knees protested every step he took. His finger joints throbbed. His eyes scratched and burned from fatigue. And his temper simmered somewhere just short of the boiling point.

Out of necessity, he walked slowly and tried to find his usual pleasure in the clear mountain air, the sun sparkling off the surface of Spirit Lake, and the scent of the forest. But his head pounded, and even his back felt slightly out of whack.

Phoebe used to tell him he worried too much, and he'd argued that he didn't worry for the fun of it. But she'd climbed out of bed in the middle of more than one night and found him sitting in the dark, fussing about one of the kids or grandkids. She'd told him adversity made people strong and urged him to let the kids work things out for themselves. He'd tried, but he'd never been able to stop stewing while they did it.

At the moment, he worried more about Margaret and the kids than he did about Joseph. No matter what Joseph thought, Fred was still his father and more than capable of making decision for himself. But even under the best circumstances, Margaret had her hands full with Webb. She didn't need this on top of his ever-increasing drinking.

Fred glared around him, wishing he could throttle David

Newman for putting such foolish ideas into Webb's head. Webb didn't need help with foolish ideas. He had plenty on his own.

He sighed softly, pushed aside the new growth on a chokecherry bush that threatened to overtake the path, and made his way carefully along the narrow spot where the trail fell away to the water below. The sunlight played games with him, alternately gilding the aspen trees with golden light, then hiding deep behind an Englemann spruce and plunging the trail into shadow. The thought of losing all this to increased population, hotels, restaurants and casinos made his stomach churn.

When he reached the far edge of Doc Huggins's property, he turned and retraced his steps home, just as he did every morning. He wanted desperately to believe he could stop the change he felt coming on the wind, but he supposed that made him a fool. His way of life wouldn't be the first that had been lost to "progress" along these shores.

By the time he caught the first glimpse of his back deck through the trees, he'd already decided he needed to do something to relieve the depression settling over his heart before he gave in to it. On a normal day, he'd have gone straight inside to make breakfast—a real breakfast with sausage and eggs, hash browns and toast. He'd have eaten it quickly and tossed out the evidence of contraband food before Margaret came to check on him. But this morning he had little appetite. More than that, he didn't want to be alone.

But what could he do? Where could he go? He couldn't visit Margaret—not this morning. Seeing her with Webb and witnessing the sorrow on her face would make him feel worse, not better. Neither did he want to chance calling his other sons. Joseph would have called Jeffrey and Douglas by now, and they'd each have an opinion about Fred and the retirement home. But Fred didn't want to discuss it. Not today.

He walked a few more steps, contemplating the idea of going to the Bluebird and ordering breakfast there. But that wouldn't help, and he knew it. He needed a friend. Someone with a level head on his shoulders and a dose of common sense. Someone like his friend Sheriff Enos Asay.

Other than his own three boys, Fred didn't know a man he liked better than Enos. Or one he trusted more. Glancing at his watch, he battled disappointment. Only a little before nine—too early for Enos to be at work since he never arrived before ten o'clock. Said he didn't see any sense in getting there earlier since everyone in town knew where to find him. If you asked Fred, it was nothing more than an excuse to sleep late.

Now what? Fred briefly considered walking all the way up the hill to Enos's house and talking with him there. But Enos's wife, Jessica, always made Fred slightly uneasy. She watched television as if it were a religion and kept the volume so loud Fred couldn't hear himself think above it. Besides, he didn't want to discuss Margaret's problems in front of her.

Enos and Margaret had dated all through high school. In fact, everyone had expected them to marry when they reached an age for that sort of thing. Fred had never understood exactly what happened to split them up, and neither of them ever talked about it.

Whatever the reason, Margaret had married Webb before Enos even knew what hit him, and Enos had countered by marrying Jessica less than six months later. Margaret's marriage had soured almost immediately, and Enos's had been shaky from the beginning.

It was obvious to Fred, and probably to anyone else with two eyes, that they'd never lost that spark of interest. He understood both of them well enough to know they'd never act on their feelings, but they'd been mooning silently over each other for nearly thirty years.

No, he couldn't talk to Enos about Margaret. Not with Jessica anywhere near. He'd just have to find some way to occupy himself until ten o'clock.

Ducking off the path onto Lake Front Drive, he strolled slowly up the tree-lined road the half mile to town. He waved halfheartedly at Arnold Van Dyke, who roared past in his Ford Taurus as if he had somewhere important to go. He spent a few minutes exchanging pleasantries with Loralee Kirkham outside her big, ugly cabin at the top of the hill. He moved some dead branches to the side of the road, shooed the Parkers' dog toward home, and cleared away a broad patch of gravel that had somehow found its way to the middle of the southbound lane. But he still reached Main Street well before ten o'clock.

Shielding his eyes with one hand, he stood on the corner and looked up the street toward the east end of town. A few cars clustered in the parking lot outside Lacey's General Store. Less than a handful of others were parked on the street, where they reflected bright morning sunlight off their windshields.

When he looked toward the lake, he noted with surprise that Enos's truck was parked in its usual spot in front of the sheriff's office. Fred checked his watch again and lifted it to his ear to make sure he could hear it running. No sense looking a gift horse in the mouth, he decided, and crossed the street. He climbed the steps onto the boardwalk and followed it to the sheriff's office.

He found Enos behind his battered wood desk with his fingers clasped in front of his mouth. His old black cowboy hat and a half-empty box of doughnuts sat on the desk beside him. He looked as if he had a million things on his mind.

Fred worked up a hearty smile and started to close the door behind him. "Morning."

Enos glanced up, but instead of smiling back, he rolled his chair away from the desk and frowned until his sandy eyebrows knit together in a solid line across his ridged brow. He waved one arm as if they were already in the middle of a conversation. "Ask me why I'm even *slightly* surprised to see you here."

Without releasing the doorknob, Fred glanced over his shoulder to see if anyone stood behind him. Nobody. He turned back with a hesitant shrug. "Why are you surprised to see me?"

Enos ignored the question. "So, who told you this time?"

"Who told me what?"

"Oh, come on, Fred. Just tell me how you found out. I thought I had all my bases covered."

Fred closed the door and crossed to Enos's desk. "What in heaven's name are you talking about?"

Enos laced his broad fingers across his duty belt and snorted in response.

Stifling a groan, Fred lowered himself into one of the wooden visitors' chairs. He glanced around the office, hoping to find some clue to Enos's behavior and trying not to let it offend him. "I feel like I've walked into the middle of something," he said at last. "Do you mind starting over?"

Enos brought his chair upright so fast that Fred jerked back involuntarily. "It won't work, Fred. This time, you can't even *try* to claim there's a reason for you to get involved."

Fred stared at him as his words slowly began to make sense. "This time? What are you trying to tell me? Has somebody been killed?"

Enos barked a laugh. "Are you trying to tell *me* you didn't know?" He rocked back in his chair again. "Spare me the innocent act. I know that's why you're here."

Fred abandoned his efforts to keep from being offended. He leaned across the desk and held Enos's gaze. "I didn't know anything, so quit accusing me of something I didn't do."

Enos shrugged.

"Who died?" Fred demanded.

Enos didn't answer immediately. He stared deep into Fred's eyes for what felt like an eternity before he finally said, "Are you serious?"

"I had no idea," Fred snapped. "Now, tell me who died."

"If you didn't know, why did you stop by?" Enos looked so honestly confused that Fred couldn't help forgiving him.

He pulled in a steadying breath. "To talk."

"About what?"

"About David Newman and his blamed fool idea. I suppose you've heard about it."

Enos nodded. "Oh, Lord, yes. The boys and me had to clear up that disturbance at the Copper Penny last night."

Fred's turn to look surprised. "What disturbance?"

Enos pushed the box of doughnuts at Fred, then pulled them back again when Fred declined the offer. "Lenore Irvine got some of her PFAAD members together to protest our drinking laws," Enos said. "Apparently, they decided to make a fuss about that gambling petition, too. It started out peacefully enough, but for some reason, everything turned sour. One thing led to another, and we ended up with a full-scale confrontation between the customers and the protesters."

Fred's headache chose that moment to double in intensity. "Was Webb there?"

Enos nodded unhappily. "Right in the thick of it." He turned the doughnut box slowly and stared at it as if he suddenly found it fascinating. When he spoke again, he sounded incredibly sad. "I had Grady give him a ride home. He wasn't in any shape to drive himself."

Fred closed his eyes for a second and cursed his son-in-law silently. Focusing on Enos again, he asked, "So, what happened? Who died?"

Enos looked away from the doughnuts, met Fred's gaze and held it for a long moment. "Lenore Irvine."

five

Fred didn't know what he'd expected, but he hadn't expected that answer. He stiffened in his seat and tried to steady his breathing. "Lenore? Dead? Are you serious? How? What happened? Where?"

Enos shifted in his seat and rested one elbow on the arm of his chair. "After we broke up the mess at the Copper Penny, we sent her home with Kent."

"Kent was there, too?"

Enos nodded. "Actually, he was there before she was, but I still don't know why. It's not like Kent to hang out in a bar." He shoved the doughnut box away and leaned his elbows on the desk. "Kent says they went home and ended up arguing for a while. Apparently, Lenore had been pissing people off all around town for two days. He says she got so angry with him she decided to head into Denver in the middle of the night so she could start first thing this morning rounding up support for her new anti-gambling movement. Kent says he was too irritated to even try to stop her. About six o'clock this morning, I got a call from Kirby Manning on his cellular phone. He was coming to work early and noticed a section of guardrail missing near the summit. He stopped to check and saw Lenore's car way down in the trees at the bottom of the cliff." He dragged his gaze to meet Fred's again. "Doc says she died on impact, so she didn't suffer."

Fred stared at his friend, scarcely able to believe what he'd just heard. "Did she lose control of the car? Did her brakes go out? What happened?"

Enos shook his head, wiped his broad face with the palm of his hand, and let his shoulders droop. "It's looks like another vehicle pushed hers off the road."

Nausea welled in Fred's throat. Mountain cliffs rose like a wall on one side of that highway and left a sheer drop on the other. He'd always felt as if the road had been laid on top of the rocks with nothing to hold it in place. He could easily imagine Lenore's terror at having an accident there. He forced himself to ask, "Who was in the other car?"

"We don't know."

"You don't know? What was it, a hit-and-run?"

Enos met his gaze steadily. Too steadily to suit Fred. "No," he said at last. "We're almost positive Lenore was murdered."

A cloud skittered across Fred's vision, and his pulse roared in his ears. "Murdered?"

Enos nodded miserably. "Grady could see it the minute he got to the scene, and our preliminary data verifies his call."

"What data?"

"I'm telling you this in confidence," Enos warned. "It can't go any further."

"Of course."

"We've run a couple of tests at the scene—Grady measured the skid marks and checked Lenore's vehicle after the county boys pulled it up from the bottom. It's pretty obvious somebody drove up behind her and then sent her car over the side."

"Couldn't it have been an accident?"

Enos shook his head. "There's skid marks from one vehicle, not two. The other car must have eased up behind her and then accelerated to send her over the cliff that way."

"But—" Fred began again, then broke off, confused.

"If somebody had rammed her car, both vehicles would have lost control. There's no way you can hit someone else's car hurtling down the mountain at even thirty miles an hour and keep your own vehicle under control. The skid marks indicate that Lenore was traveling a lot faster than that—probably around fifty. And that's way too fast for that stretch of highway."

Fred couldn't even form a response.

"We've found some paint transfer on Lenore's car," Enos went on after a brief pause, "and some broken glass on the road. It looks as if the other driver had a dark-colored truck or maybe an all-terrain vehicle—something with a fairly high bumper. The lab's working on the paint samples now."

Fred studied his knees for several long seconds and struggled to comprehend it all. Lenore had been a pest. Fred would have been the first to say so. But he couldn't imagine anyone hating her enough to do such a thing.

"Now, all we have to do is find a dark-colored Jeep or Bronco or Blazer or pickup with a broken headlight, smashed grillwork and some white paint—" Enos broke off with a shrug.

"Any possibilities?"

"We've got it narrowed down to a few dozen people who were at the Copper Penny last night and the people Lenore managed to offend during her tirade yesterday."

"So, basically, you suspect everybody. Including me."

Enos narrowed his eyes. "You? Why?"

Fred explained in a few words about Lenore's visit to Margaret and about the scene with Webb at the end. "I guess that adds us all to your list."

Enos lifted one shoulder and tried to smile. "I'll send Grady over to look at the bumper on your Buick right after we talk to everyone else she managed to aggravate."

Fred looked away. "She wasn't a very popular woman."

"No, she wasn't. But we'll find her killer."

"I'm sure you will," Fred assured him. "You've obviously seen Kent already. How's he taking it?"

"Real hard. His first wife died, too, you know."

Fred had almost forgotten, but he remembered now. In fact, Lenore and Kent had married so soon afterward, there had been speculation about the nature of their relationship. In the end, everyone had reluctantly admitted that Lenore wasn't the type to indulge in premarital anything. In fact it had been almost universally decided that Kent had merely been anxious to find a mother for his two daughters, even though Hannah had been the only one left at home.

"It's only a matter of time before we find the murderer,"

Enos said. "And I don't seriously consider you a suspect, so you can't use that as an excuse to interfere."

"What about Margaret?"

Enos's expression softened. "Maggie? No."

Fred shrugged and forced a smile. "Then I don't see any reason to get involved."

Obviously relieved, Enos locked his fingers behind his head and leaned back. "Good. Then, let's change the subject. What did you say you came in for?"

Fred studied his fingernails. "It's nothing really. Not by comparison—"

"Something's troubling you—I can see it on your face."

Fred pushed to his feet and paced a few steps toward the window. "All right. I'm worried about Margaret."

Enos's expression grew guarded. "Why? What's wrong?"

"Webb's decided to take out a second mortgage and give the money to David Newman to finance that gambling petition."

Enos made a visible effort to hide the anger that flashed across his face. "How does Maggie feel about that?"

"She doesn't like the idea, but if Kirby Manning gives Webb the loan, there's nothing she can do to stop him."

"I can't imagine Kirby doing that," Enos said, but he didn't sound convinced.

"Considering Webb's current income and his track record, I keep telling myself Kirby'd be a fool to give him more money," Fred said. But he hadn't been able to convince himself. Kirby might have been book smart, but he didn't have much horse sense.

"Maybe it won't come to that," Enos said. "Maybe David won't get the backing he's expecting."

"I hope not, but that won't make any difference. Not really. Even if David doesn't move forward with the petition, once Webb gets the loan, he'll spend the money. Margaret and the kids will suffer."

Enos's shoulders sagged. "And if David does move ahead, Webb won't be the only one to do something like this."

"I know."

A muscle in Enos's cheek jerked a second before he shot to

his feet and slapped his palm on the desktop. "I had no idea people would jump on the idea so fast. What in the hell does David think he's doing? Doesn't he know what this'll do to a town like Cutler?"

"He claims it will save the town from ruin."

"Oh, does he?" Enos barked a disbelieving laugh. "Good billy hell." He pivoted away, then turned again and shook his index finger in Fred's face. "You and I both know what'll really happen. We'll end up with more people than we can handle, we'll be deeper in debt than we are now, and we'll lose all the good stuff we've got."

It did Fred's heart good to realize how strongly Enos felt. "I know."

"Crime rates will go up. Forgeries, thefts, fraud, counterfeiting. We'll have bankruptcies and divorces—and *suicides.*"

"Is there anything you can do to stop him?"

Enos stopped pacing and faced Fred slowly. "Nothing. Not a blasted thing."

Fred crossed back to his chair and sat. "Any law against me throttling Webb with my bare hands and running David out of town on a rail?"

Enos flicked a glance at him and managed a sad smile. He dropped back into his seat and let silence fall between them. He sat that way for several long minutes, letting the clock on the wall keep Fred company.

Fred waited until he could stand the silence no longer. "Joseph called yesterday."

Enos pulled himself back from wherever he'd been and made a vain attempt to keep his face stoic, but Fred watched a wary expression creep into his eyes. "Oh?"

"He's making noises again about moving me to New Hampshire."

Enos made a noise like a low growl. "The hell you say. What'd you tell him?" That kind of reaction was exactly what endeared him to Fred.

"I told him no. What in blazes do you think I'd say?"

In spite of the tension in the room Enos grinned, then ducked his head quickly.

"Well?" Fred's tension started to diminish for the first time in two days. "It's not as if I can't dress myself, for hell's sake. Or feed myself. Or get around on my own."

Enos struggled to wipe the smile from his face. "I didn't say a word."

"Blasted kid thinks I need someone to look after me," Fred groused, "just because I'm a few years older than him and living on my own."

Enos clamped his lips together.

"Well, I don't," Fred insisted.

"I know you don't."

"I'm doing fine on my own."

Enos held up both hands in mock surrender. "I know. I know. So you told him no. What did he say?"

"I don't know," Fred admitted, then allowed himself a tiny smile. "I hung up on him."

Enos chuckled. "You did?" He rubbed his face again and grinned at the ceiling. "I can imagine the look on his face."

His laugh was infectious, and Fred felt a bit more tension slip away. He met Enos's gaze and smiled slowly. "It's been a strange few days, son."

Enos sobered. "It sure has."

"You want to walk down to the Bluebird and get some coffee or something to eat?"

Enos shook his head reluctantly and pointed at the box of doughnuts. "I'd like to, but I've got too much to do here. I'm still waiting to hear from the lab, and I need to be here when Ivan comes in from the crime scene. Are you going to be okay?"

Fred nodded and stood. "Sure. Just needed to spout off for a minute."

"You can spout off to me any time."

"I know that, son. The offer works in reverse too, you know." He took a couple of steps away, then turned back when Enos called after him.

"You'd better mean what you say about not getting involved this time," Enos warned.

"I mean it."

"You won't start asking questions?"

"No need to, is there?"

Enos narrowed his eyes. "No. So, tell me why I think I ought to get that in writing?"

Fred mock-frowned at him. "You're a very untrusting soul, do you know that? It can't be good for you."

Enos chuckled. "I'm pretty sure it's not. I wonder how I ever got this way."

Fred crossed to the door and gripped the knob. Pulling the door partway open, he glanced over his shoulder one last time. "Relax, Enos. As long as Margaret and I aren't suspects, I can't imagine anything about Lenore Irvine's death that would make me want to get involved."

"I'm going to hold you to that," Enos warned.

Fred allowed himself a tight smile and pulled the door shut behind him. He walked to the corner and stepped off the boardwalk. But within seconds his relief began to fade, and concern slowly took its place.

He wondered whether Margaret had heard about Lenore Irvine yet. No doubt, she'd be having a rough time this morning. Webb would be in a foul mood after being delivered home, drunk, in the middle of the night. An early morning visit from Fred probably wouldn't go over well with him, but after yesterday's confrontation with Lenore, Fred didn't feel right keeping the news from Margaret.

Walking quickly, he put the first few blocks behind him, but he couldn't put aside the mental picture of Lenore and Kent Irvine as they'd been yesterday. And he couldn't stop imagining Kent's grief this morning. His second wife, dead. This time, tragically murdered. At least he wasn't alone. Hannah was there, and surely the older daughter would come to help him get through this.

As he rounded the corner onto Arapaho, the sound of someone starting a vehicle nearby caught his attention. A second later, Webb's truck shot out of the driveway and onto the street half a block away.

Good. Fred could talk to Margaret alone. Without Webb and his hangover.

With a soft squeal of tires, Webb started toward the corner where Fred stood, driving too fast as usual. Fred lifted his hand in a halfhearted wave just as Webb reached the intersection, but Webb screeched around the corner without even a sideways glance. Gunning the engine, he sent gravel skittering across the road and roared away up the street.

Fred stood rooted to the spot, trying to catch his breath. The sun suddenly felt too hot on his face and neck, and the birds overhead seemed to taunt him. He stared after Webb's truck as it disappeared around the next corner, his pulse throbbed steadily in his ears, and his heart clipped a staccato rhythm.

Fighting back the bile that threatened to make his retch, Fred kept his eyes riveted on the corner long after Webb disappeared and the sound of his engine faded away. And he struggled to convince himself he hadn't seen the broken headlight, smashed fender, and damaged grillwork on Webb's truck.

six

Fred stood on the corner for what felt like an eternity before he could make himself move. The damage to Webb's truck was a horrible coincidence—nothing more. No matter how much he disliked his son-in-law, he wouldn't let himself believe Webb had been responsible for Lenore Irvine's death.

Surely, if he asked Margaret about the truck, she'd tell him some story about Webb and a tree or a pole at a drive-through window somewhere. Something. *Anything* but the horrible thoughts that raced through his mind as he stood there.

Hurrying the remaining distance to Margaret's house, he pounded on the door once, then again. She answered after the second knock and smiled sadly when she saw him. Her feet were bare, and she still wore her bathrobe. Her face looked waxy and pale, her eyes dark and shadowed.

She pushed open the door and stepped aside to let him enter. Just as Enos had done, she launched into the middle of a conversation. "I guess I shouldn't be surprised to see you here. Let's hear it."

Fred blinked in response. "Hear what?"

"You're here to tell me about the argument Webb had at the Copper Penny last night, aren't you?"

He hesitated for a second. "Not exactly."

"No?" She narrowed her eyes in disbelief. "Then what, exactly?"

Fred didn't like to see her so suspicious. But with a husband like Webb, he supposed she'd come to it naturally over the years. He forced a smile and kept his voice casual. "I just saw Webb driving away."

"And you stopped by to tell me about it?"

"No." He glanced over his shoulder through the open door. "I hadn't noticed the damage to his truck before. Has he been in an accident recently?"

All at once, Margaret's expression changed. She looked surprised for half a breath, then infinitely weary. "What damage?"

"A broken headlight and smashed fender." He could hear the hope in his voice, almost begging her to suddenly remember.

She shook her head slowly. Her jaw clenched and her eyes flashed with that peculiar golden light that had always signaled a fine temper in her mother, but her voice sounded steady when she spoke again. "I guess he forgot to mention it to me."

Fred's stomach knotted and his shoulders tensed. Touching the small of her back, he guided her into the living room. "Let's sit down for a minute. Are the kids in school already?"

She nodded without taking her eyes from his face. "What is it?"

He couldn't think of any easy way to tell her, and he didn't say a word until she lowered herself onto the couch. He sat beside her and held her gaze. "Lenore Irvine died early this morning."

Margaret's entire body tensed. "*Died?* How?"

"Her car went off the road near the summit."

Margaret sucked in a quick breath and touched her fingers to the hollow of her throat. "My God. What happened? Did she fall asleep at the wheel?"

"No," Fred said slowly. "Enos says someone pushed her car off the road."

To Fred's surprise, she scowled at him. "Are you sure that's what *Enos* says, or have you decided that on your own?"

Fred didn't appreciate the implication behind the question, but he tried not to let it bother him. "There's no question about it. There's evidence."

"Who else was involved?"

"They don't know yet," Fred admitted.

"They don't know? Was it a hit-and-run?"

"No. Enos says they can tell from the length of the skid marks and the damage to her car that she was intentionally rammed from behind."

"You're saying she was murdered?" She drew back and stared at him. "Is that why you asked about Webb's truck?"

Fred forced himself to nod and reached for her hand. "They found dark-colored paint on Lenore's car and broken glass on the highway from the killer's headlight. They figure it was a truck or all-terrain vehicle because the point of impact from the bumper was high."

Jerking her hand from his grip, Margaret shot to her feet and glared down at him. *"What?"*

He struggled out of the soft couch to stand beside her. "Sweetheart—"

She shook her head and backed a step away. "Are you accusing *Webb* of killing Lenore?"

"I'm not accusing anyone."

"Yes, you are." Her voice rose several decibels. "You think Webb's capable of murder."

"His headlight *has* been smashed," Fred reasoned. "And his fender is dented pretty badly. You didn't know about that?"

"No." She backed another step away.

"You didn't see his truck when he came home?"

"No," she said again, more firmly this time. "He parked right up by the garage, the way he always does. I don't even notice the truck most of the time."

"Webb was pretty upset yesterday afternoon," Fred reminded her. "And he had another argument with Lenore last night at the Copper Penny."

Shoving her fingers through her hair, Margaret pivoted away and crossed to the front window. "That doesn't mean anything."

"He hated her, Margaret."

She wheeled back to face him, and her eyes snapped. "*Everybody* hated her. She was a mean, vicious, vindictive, spiteful, *hateful* woman."

Fred closed the distance between them, but when he would have taken her into his arms, she pulled back again to avoid his touch. "Webb needed that gambling petition to make it onto the ballot," he said.

"You think he killed Lenore over *that*?"

"I hope not—" he began.

But she didn't let him finish. "Yes, Webb's excited about legalized gambling, but he's not so gung ho over that petition that he'd kill somebody just to make sure it gets on the ballot."

"Now, I never—"

"David Newman has more at stake than Webb," she insisted, waving one hand in the general direction of the Newman house. "He's got *everything* riding on that petition." She paced a few steps away. "And what about Lenore's husband? Did you see the way they acted yesterday? Things were strained between them, I could tell." She turned to glare at him again. "Why do you immediately think the worst of Webb?"

Because that's the side Webb always showed. Everyone except Margaret saw it, but Fred refrained from pointing that out to her. "I didn't come here to accuse Webb of murder."

She answered with an unladylike snort.

"I came here so you'd set my mind at ease."

She snorted again and flicked an angry glance at him.

Fred didn't want the conversation to disintegrate into a full-fledged argument. "No matter what you think, I don't want Webb to be guilty."

"He *isn't* guilty," she insisted.

"I hope you have proof of that," Fred muttered. "You'll need it after Enos sees Webb's truck."

She glared at him. "As a matter of fact, I do."

"What proof?"

Her expression hardened again. "Why are you asking? Are you trying to find out if I can provide an alibi for my husband?"

Fred didn't see any advantage in denying the truth. "*Can* you? Was he here with you all night? Did he stay here after Grady brought him home?"

She wrapped her arms around her waist and took a step away. "No," she admitted at last.

Fred's heart dropped.

"But I know where he was."

That was something, Fred told himself. "Did he go back to the Copper Penny?"

"No. He stayed in the back room at the shop."

Fred couldn't imagine Webb staying in the back of Tito's shop without a television and a six-pack of beer, but he didn't comment. "Did he stay there all night?"

"He was at the Copper Penny until one o'clock or so. Grady brought him home a few minutes after that. We had another argument," she confessed. "He stormed out of here about half an hour after Grady dropped him off."

"What did you argue about?"

She didn't answer immediately but studied him for an uncomfortably long time, as if she had to decide whether to tell him.

Fred forced himself to wait patiently while she made up her mind. He sent her a reassuring smile and tried to convey with his eyes that only fatherly concern prompted him to ask.

"I tried to talk him out of getting that damned second mortgage," she said at last.

"He's still determined to go ahead with it?"

She nodded miserably. "I think so. He's absolutely convinced it's his ticket to financial freedom, and he won't listen to a thing I say."

That didn't surprise Fred at all. When had Webb ever listened? "So, he left—"

Margaret nodded. "But he called when he woke up this morning and told me where he'd been. He walked over to the Copper Penny, got his truck, and then came home to shower and change before work."

Fred supposed that sounded believable. After all, Webb had managed to hold onto his job at Tito Romero's Auto Repair for over a year now. And Tito *had* given him a set of keys several months back to use when he opened or closed the shop alone.

Margaret paced another step away. "Be reasonable, Dad.

Yes, Lenore was making noises about gambling, but Lenore was *always* making noises about something. She was a pest and a nuisance, but she never actually stopped anything, did she? The school still has its dances. Albán still sells alcohol at the Copper Penny . . ."

Fred nodded slowly. "You're right."

"So why would Webb suddenly find her such a threat that he'd kill her?"

"I don't know," Fred admitted. But he intended to find out. "Well, then," he said. "There's nothing to worry about, is there?"

"No, there isn't."

"Is that where Webb was going when he passed me—to work?"

Margaret's entire body froze. "Yes. Why?"

"For heaven's sake, Margaret, I just wondered."

"Why?" She looked wary.

"I'm curious."

She narrowed her eyes and wagged a finger in front of Fred's nose. "Don't you *dare* go to the shop to check on him."

Fred drew himself up and fixed her with a stern glance. "Did I say anything about checking on him?"

"No," she admitted. "But that doesn't mean you aren't thinking about it."

"For heaven's sake, Margaret, why would I want to do that?"

"Because you still think he's guilty."

"I just saw him driving down the street in the truck that may have been used to kill someone," Fred reminded her.

Margaret huffed out an impatient sigh.

"I'm not the only one who'll wonder about that," he warned.

"I'm sure there's a perfectly innocent explanation for what you saw."

Fred wished he could believe that. But one glance at the angry glint in her eyes, the set of her jaw, the thin line of her mouth convinced him to drop the subject for the time being. Obviously she wasn't going to listen to anything he said.

He gave her one of his most sincere smiles. "So," he said

hopefully. "Were things better between you two this morning?"

She nodded, but her expression didn't relax. "A little. He didn't mention the second mortgage this morning, and neither did I."

"Well, good. That makes me feel better."

"Me, too." Drawing a deep breath, she straightened her shoulders and sent him a wary smile. She let another short silence hang between them, then cocked her head and eyed him curiously. "You never did tell me why you came over yesterday."

"No," he said. "I didn't, did I?"

She dropped onto the couch and crossed her legs. "So? What was it?"

"Two things," Fred said and lowered himself to the opposite end of the couch. "The first was the silly gambling petition." Not so silly now. It had taken on a far more serious outlook.

"And the second?"

"When did you talk to Joseph last?"

Just as he suspected it might, guilt darted across her expression. "A few days ago. Why?"

"What did you talk about?"

"This and that." She smiled weakly and tried to look innocent, but Fred could tell she knew why he asked.

"Did you mention me?"

She pretended to think about that for a few seconds, then nodded slowly. "We probably did. I don't know. I don't remember. Why?"

"Because somehow, your brother's gotten the notion that my cholesterol level's ready to soar through the roof. And he's decided I need to move into an old folks' home in New Hampshire."

"He's *what?*" The surprise on Margaret's face looked genuine. She held up both hands in a gesture of surrender. "All right, I'll admit we talked about you. We always do. And I mentioned what Doc said at your last checkup about your cholesterol." She smiled weakly and leaned toward him. "But the minute I said that, I knew I'd made a mistake. I tried to tell Joseph it wasn't as bad as I'd made it sound, but you know how he is—"

Fred knew Joseph, all right. Once he fastened on an idea, nothing could shake him from it.

"You've got to believe me, Dad. I had no idea he was going to suggest something like *that*."

"It's not necessary to discuss my checkups with Joseph, you know."

"He's just concerned about you, Dad."

"Concerned?" Fred barked an annoyed laugh. "He ought to be concerned about himself. He works too much. One of these days, he's going to start having trouble with *his* health."

"I'm sure he'll calm down in a few days," she said.

"I certainly hope so."

"He will. You'll see." She tried to look convincing, but they both knew Joseph could be like a pit bull when he fastened on an idea. Fred couldn't tell whether she was trying harder to convince him or herself.

"I suppose I could call him again and tell him it's not as bad as it sounds."

Fred tried to smile, but the offer didn't make him feel a whole lot better. He didn't think Joseph would pay much attention to his sister, anyway. He scarcely paid attention to his father.

"If you worry too much," Margaret said, "you'll cause trouble for yourself. Just put Joseph out of your mind."

Easy enough for her to say. Joseph wasn't trying to ruin *her* life. But Fred didn't point that out. Pushing to his feet, he leaned to kiss her cheek.

"I'm serious, Dad. And forget about Lenore Irvine's murder. Webb didn't have anything to do with it."

Fred wished he could share her optimism. He smiled softly, patted her shoulder, and crossed to the door. But after he stepped outside and the door closed between them, his expression sobered. He wanted to believe Margaret was right—that Webb wasn't involved with Lenore's death.

He walked slowly down the sidewalk to the corner and tried to find some pleasure in the late spring weather, the light green of the leaves, the scent of lilacs and the bright reds and yellows of spring bulbs in neighbors' lawns.

But he couldn't help wondering whether others would make the same connection he had between Lenore Irvine's death and the damage to Webb's truck. If they did, the resulting gossip would hurt Margaret and her children.

He made it all the way to the corner of Porter Street before he stopped walking again. He didn't want to go home—not yet. The events of the past two days had left him too keyed up to relax. Besides, if he went home, Joseph might call. And he was in no mood to talk to Joseph.

Maybe he should go to the Bluebird instead. Peace, quiet and a nice hot cup of coffee—that would make him feel better. It always did.

Turning toward town, he walked quickly until the sign above Tito's Auto Repair caught his eye. He slowed his step again and studied the small building and its even smaller parking lot. He really should give Webb the benefit of the doubt, but he couldn't. For Margaret's sake, if nothing else, Fred ought to take a closer look at that truck and give Webb a chance to explain how he'd crunched his fender and broken the headlight.

Webb wouldn't be happy to see him—Webb never was. But since Tito didn't come to work before eleven these days, they'd have plenty of time to talk alone. Webb wouldn't be able to accuse Fred of starting rumors or jeopardizing his job.

Before he could change his mind, Fred checked for traffic and crossed the street toward the garage. He pushed aside a niggling uneasiness and told himself that, once word of Lenore's death leaked out and the gossip started, Webb would thank him for his concern. And so would Margaret.

seven

Fred pushed open the grimy front door to Tito's Auto Repair and glanced inside. With minimal structural changes, Tito Romero had converted the old Shell filling station into an auto repair shop almost ten years ago. The office still had its two wide windows overlooking the parking lot, complete with what looked like the original dirt caking the glass. A long, grease-stained counter stretched half the length of the room in front of a cheap metal desk, two cracked Naugahyde chairs formed a tiny waiting area, and a soda machine leaned against one wall and hummed softly in the silence.

To Fred's surprise, Tito sat behind the desk, scribbling something on an invoice. He was a stocky man whose oversized head, thick salt-and-pepper hair, and pointed beard left him with an unfortunate resemblance to a buffalo.

He glanced up with an automatic smile that changed to a smirk when he saw Fred. Dropping his pencil, he pushed the invoice away and leaned back in his chair, which creaked in protest. "Fred? Well, this is a surprise. I thought you swore you'd never bring your car back to me after I told you there was nothing wrong with your brakes."

"I'm not here about my car," Fred assured him. "I'm here to see Webb."

A splotch of color crept into Tito's cheeks, and he stiffened almost imperceptibly, a movement so subtle that Fred wondered if he'd only imagined it. "Webb?" He sent an uneasy glance toward the back of the building. "He's not here."

Fred stuffed his hands into his pockets, rocked back on his

heels, and tried not to look disappointed or curious about Tito's reaction. "Do you know when he'll be back?"

Lifting one shoulder, Tito fiddled with a pack of cigarettes in his shirt pocket. "He's not working today."

That would be news to Margaret. What in the hell was Webb up to now? Fred tried not to look overly surprised. "I didn't realize he had the day off."

"Yeah?" An emotion Fred couldn't read flitted across Tito's face. "Well. He's not here," he said again. "What did you need?"

"Nothing important," Fred lied. "I just stopped by to say hello."

Tito narrowed his eyes and stared at him. "You're here for a friendly visit? With *Webb??*" He shook his head slowly without taking his eyes from Fred's face, and a disbelieving smile crept across his face. "Okay. If you say so."

Fred didn't let himself rise to Tito's bait. It was none of Tito's business, anyway. "I'll just catch him later."

Tito leaned back in his chair studied Fred with undisguised curiosity. "What's going on? Why are you so friendly toward Webb all of a sudden?"

"Can't a man pay a visit to his son-in-law?"

Tito threw back his buffalo head and laughed aloud. "Usually. But not you. You don't like Webb. Everybody knows that. So, what do you want?"

Impudent whelp. Scowling, Fred tugged open the door to leave. "It's personal. A family matter."

Tito's expression sobered. "Is everybody okay? Maggie? The kids?"

His obvious concern made Fred feel slightly better. He nodded. "They're fine. As a matter of fact, Margaret's the reason I'm here."

Tito's brows knit in confusion. "You're here for Maggie? Why? Did she send you?"

"As a matter of fact, she did."

The red splotches returned to what little Fred could see of Tito's cheeks. "*She* sent you here?" He stood and paced past Fred to the door, leaned against the frame and lit a cigarette. "Do you mind my asking why?"

Under normal circumstances Fred might have resented the question. But these weren't normal circumstances, and Tito's reaction made him more than curious. "She asked me to stop by and pick up the blanket he left here this morning."

"Blanket?" Again that unsettled expression flickered in Tito's eyes.

"He spent the night in your backroom," Fred said, dropping his voice before he went on. "He and Margaret had a little spat."

"In my backroom?" Tito glanced at the door again.

Fred nodded slowly. "I suppose we could check in back. If the blanket's there, I'll take it home to her now."

Tito glanced down at his cigarette and watched the smoke curl away for a second or two. "I didn't see a blanket back there when I came in."

"Well, then, I suppose he must have taken it with him when he left."

"When he left this morning?"

Fred studied him for a few seconds before he answered. "That's right."

Tito rubbed his forehead, and the cigarette left a trail of smoke in front of his eyes. "Aw, hell."

Fred tried to push aside a surge of uneasiness. Obviously, Tito didn't like hearing that Webb had spent the night here. "Is something wrong?"

"No." Tito met his gaze and tried to hold it, but he glanced away, rubbed his forehead again, and laughed uncomfortably. "Aw, hell," he said again. "You know, as a favor to Webb, I've been trying to keep this quiet. But I don't feel comfortable lying to Maggie—even indirectly."

Fred's mouth dried. "Lying? About what?"

"Webb couldn't have left a blanket here this morning, Fred. He hasn't been here in days. He's . . . uh . . . not working here anymore."

Not again. Margaret didn't need this on top of everything else. "What did he do? Quit?"

Tito wagged his head slowly and inhaled deeply from his cigarette. "No. I had to let him go."

The answer didn't surprise Fred, but he almost wished it

had. This wouldn't be the first job Webb had lost, and it probably wouldn't be the last. "How long ago?"

"Last week. Thursday, to be exact."

Webb had been unemployed for a week, and Margaret still didn't know? Fred pulled in a steadying breath and leaned against the counter. "What happened?"

Tito flicked ash out the door. "I know you don't like Webb, but he's a good mechanic—at least, he used to be. But the past few months, he's been making mistakes—careless ones." He dragged in another lungful of smoke. "Honestly? I think he's drinking more than he used to."

Fred didn't trust himself to respond, so he nodded for Tito to go on.

"Until last week the mistakes were relatively minor. But last Thursday he did a shoddy job reconnecting the brake lines on a car after he finished it. I don't have to tell you, a mistake like that could have caused a fatal accident, especially up here in these mountains." Tito managed a tight smile. "Luckily, I caught the mistake before we released the vehicle, so we were able to fix it, but I couldn't take any more chances. I have several customers who are already fed up and threatening to take their business somewhere else. A mistake like that would have ruined me."

Fred's heart dropped to somewhere near his feet as he pieced together the events of the past few days. No wonder Webb was so eager to invest in the gambling petition. No wonder he'd taken Lenore Irvine's opposition to the petition so seriously. "Did Webb ask you to keep it secret?"

Tito nodded and shrugged at the same time. "Just until he could find another job." He managed a rueful smile. "It's not that I don't like Webb, you know. And I don't want to make it any harder on him than it has to be. He was pretty upset when it happened. Said I was ruining his life and that he'd lose everything if I let him go, but I didn't have a choice." His tone pleaded with Fred to understand.

And Fred did. In fact, if he'd been in Tito's shoes, he'd probably have fired Webb long ago. "Has he found another job?"

Tito answered with a quick shake of the head. "I don't

think so. At least, not that I've heard about. I gave him a month's severance pay—just to tide him over, you know? I like the guy, but I couldn't let him drive me out of business."

"No," Fred said. "You couldn't."

Tito smoked thoughtfully for a few seconds, tossed the butt of his cigarette out the door, and cocked an eyebrow at Fred. "So, what's going on? Why did he tell Margaret he stayed here last night?"

Fred didn't like discussing Margaret's troubles, so he only shrugged. "I don't know the whole story."

Tito dug another cigarette from his pocket and clamped it between his lips. "Does it have anything to do with that business at the Copper Penny last night?"

Fred's expression grew more guarded. "What do you know about that?"

"Not much," Tito admitted as he lit up again. "Just that there was some trouble over that gambling petition."

"Were you there?"

"Me? Hell, no. But I heard about it."

Of course, he had. Fred would have been surprised to find someone in Cutler who hadn't.

"This *is* about last night, isn't it?" Tito asked again. "I heard Webb was there and that he got into an argument with Lenore Irvine again."

Word certainly got out quickly. "Where did you hear that?"

Tito shrugged an I-don't-know. "Can't say I blame him, really. You know what a pain in the ass she can be. She's always harping on Webb about his drinking, as if that's going to make him stop. Personally, I think she does more harm than good, you know?"

Fred knew, but he didn't say so.

But now that Tito had started, he didn't seem to want to stop talking. "Just like last week. That was a prime example."

"What happened last week?"

"Oh, Lenore started in on him as usual last Thursday when she dropped off her car, so Webb was already pissed when he started working on her brakes. Add a few too many nips from the bottle while he was stewing about it . . . To be honest,

I'd say the problem with the brakes was at least as much her fault as it was his."

Fred's stomach gave a sickening lurch. "You mean, the car he left the brake line loose on was Lenore Irvine's?"

"Yeah," Tito said, as if he thought Fred already knew that. "That's the reason I finally fired him. Like I said, I was just lucky I found the mistake. I mean, can you *imagine* what would have happened if she'd driven out of here with the brake line loose?"

Fred had no difficulty imagining. Lenore would have driven her car for a while, blissfully unaware that she was losing brake fluid each time she slowed down. At some point, the brakes would have given out completely. If she was lucky, she'd have merely run a stop sign or been involved in a fender bender. If not, she'd have plummeted off one of the rocky hillsides surrounding Cutler—without a second vehicle to help hers over the side.

He breathed slowly, trying to rid himself of the nausea that left him slightly dizzy. Shaking his head slowly, he tried to rub away the sudden pain that shot from his neck into the back of his head.

Tito's eyes narrowed. "What's going on, Fred?" He crossed to Fred's side and touched his shoulder. "Are you all right?" Fred tried to wave away his concern, but Tito hovered a bit closer. "Sit down. You're white as a sheet. You want me to call Doc or something?"

"I'm fine. I don't need Doc."

"You're not having another heart attack, are you?"

Fred didn't even try to hide his irritation. "No, I'm not having a heart attack."

Tito pulled back a little, but his dark eyes still looked worried. "I think you'd better tell me what's going on."

Fred hesitated. He didn't want to voice his suspicions aloud, but he was realistic enough to realize it was only a matter of time before word of Lenore's death got out. Once it did, Tito would put two and two together on his own.

He pulled in a steadying breath and met Tito's gaze steadily. "Lenore Irvine was killed this morning."

Tito's face paled. He took a step backward and perched on the corner of his desk. "Are you serious?"

"Unfortunately."

"How? What happened?"

"Her car went off the road near the summit."

"Sweet Jesus." A second later his eyes flew wide, and he shot to his feet again. "You're not trying to tell me her brakes gave out, are you?"

"Enos didn't seem to think her brakes were the problem," Fred said truthfully.

Tito seemed to relax slightly, but Fred could almost see his mind racing. "That's why you're here, isn't it? Not to visit Webb or pick up a blanket. You think Webb's involved somehow." His eyes widened a bit further. "You think Webb killed her."

"I don't know what to think."

Tito looked away for a long moment, dragged another cigarette from his pocket, and lit it with an unsteady hand. "Did Webb really say he spent the night here?"

"That's what he told Margaret."

Tito took a deep drag, flicked ash, and looked into Fred's eyes again. "I know this sounds selfish. I don't want to get dragged into the middle of this, but I'm going to, aren't I?"

Fred couldn't say he blamed him, really. "It looks that way."

"After everything I did to help him out, he'd do this to me." Tito wagged his head as if he couldn't believe what he'd heard. "I kept him on here *long* after I should have let him go. I gave him money to see him through—" He inhaled again and sent Fred a sideways glance. "Where do you think he really was?"

That, Fred thought, was the million dollar question. "I don't know."

"Maybe he went back to the Copper Penny."

"Maybe," Fred said, but he didn't believe it.

Tito paced a couple of steps away and waved the cigarette over his head. "What about Quinn Udy's place? Have you checked there?"

"No." Fred hadn't even thought of checking with Webb's

best drinking buddy, but he wouldn't be surprised to find Webb there. He didn't stay out all night often, but he had been known to disappear for a day or two during one of his binges. "He might have stayed with Quinn, I suppose. It wouldn't be the first time." But if so, why had Webb lied to Margaret this time?

"What about his old man?"

Webb's father? Another definite possibility. Lamar Templeton was an older, drunker, angrier version of Webb. He probably would have given his son a place to stay, but again, why lie to Margaret?

Tito paced back to Fred and held his gaze. "Listen, Fred. You've got to find out where he really spent the night before words gets out that he was here."

"*I've* got to—?" Fred began. He broke off with a quick shake of his head. "I'm not getting involved in this one." He could justify asking a few questions of Tito but didn't need to take an active role in a murder investigation when his son-in-law might be guilty. Margaret would never forgive him.

"What do you mean, you're not getting involved?" Tito's expression tightened and his eyes narrowed.

"I just don't think it would be a good idea. I'll take what I know to Enos and let him figure out what to do next."

Tito stared at him for a moment, then brayed a laugh. "Sure, you will."

"I'm serious," Fred insisted. "That's exactly what I'm going to do."

The smile slid from Tito's face. "Why?"

"Because . . ." Fred paused, at a loss for words to explain. "Because."

Tito leaned closer. "You're going to just sit back and let Webb waltz around town when he might be guilty of murder? You're going to let him go home to Maggie tonight and pretend like nothing's happened? Eat dinner at the table? Watch TV? Climb into bed with her at the end of the day?" He wagged his big head right in front of Fred's face. "I don't think so."

Fred could only blink in response. He pushed to his feet

and started for the door, but when he'd opened it, he turned back to face Tito once more. "When was the last time you saw Webb?"

"Yesterday afternoon. He came by for his check."

"Did you notice his truck?"

Tito nodded. "He parked right in front of the building, just like he always did."

"Did you see any damage to it? A broken headlight? A smashed fender?"

Tito shook his head slowly. "No. The truck was fine."

"You're sure? Maybe you missed it?"

"I'm sure," Tito said. "I stood right by it and talked to him for half an hour. If there'd been something wrong, I would have noticed."

Of course, he would have. Murmuring thanks, Fred shut the door behind him and closed his eyes. No matter how much he wanted to believe the damage to Webb's truck was nothing more than a horrible coincidence, he couldn't pretend any longer. In his heart he knew Webb was guilty. And he couldn't ignore the possibility that Webb had plotted Lenore's murder for a week or more. That maybe he'd tried at least twice to kill her.

If Webb could do that, were Margaret and the kids safe? Fred didn't know, but the ball of spurs in his stomach told him Tito was probably right. Fred wouldn't be able to rest knowing Webb was alone in the house with Margaret and the kids.

eight

Lost in thought, Fred walked slowly away from Tito's. Maybe things would work out, he told himself. Enos might surprise him and rush right out to arrest Webb, which would keep Fred from having to get any further involved. Margaret might never have to know he'd been the one who'd turned Webb in to the authorities.

But he wouldn't count on Enos. Fred had no hard evidence to support his theory, and he knew from past experience how Enos would react to speculation.

He considered briefly going back to Margaret's and telling her everything. But she wouldn't believe him, either. Not without something concrete to back up his suspicions. He needed proof. Something nobody could dispute. But what? And where would he find it?

Pausing at the intersection with Main Street, he shielded his eyes against the spring sunlight and stared at the store-fronts as if they'd give him an answer. But they remained stubbornly silent.

With a sigh, he turned toward home. Less than two hours ago his biggest problem had been Joseph's ridiculous idea about that blasted retirement home in New Hampshire. But now his entire world had been turned upside down, all because he'd watched Webb careen around the corner in his truck.

The thought pulled him up short and made him turn around in his tracks. Staring, he replayed the scene and his earlier conversation with Enos in his mind.

If Grady drove Webb home last night, when had Webb picked up his truck from the Copper Penny? If he'd gone back last night, maybe someone had seen him. If Fred could prove Webb had his truck at the time of the murder, Enos might pay more attention.

He crossed the intersection, quickstepped along the boardwalk toward the bar, and hurried across the parking lot. To his relief, a white Isuzu stood near the front door and the neon beer signs had been turned on in the blackened windows, which meant the bar's owner, Albán Toth, was on the premises and open for business.

Fred liked and trusted Albán. He'd known him nearly forty years, since Albán—then just a boy—and his mother first came to town after escaping the Hungarian revolution. If anyone at the Copper Penny could answer questions honestly and keep his mouth shut, Albán could.

Tugging open the bar's door, Fred stepped inside and stood for a moment, letting his eyes adjust to the dim lighting. The place smelled of stale cigarette smoke and something spicy—probably some Hungarian concoction Albán planned to serve for lunch. None of the stools at the bar were occupied, and most of the tables were blessedly empty. Best of all, Albán himself stood behind the bar slicing something with a butcher knife.

He watched Fred stroll across the room and hoist himself onto a stool. Flashing a broad smile, he pushed a lock of blonde hair out of his eyes with the back of a hand. "What brings you in here?"

Fred didn't want to jump in with questions too quickly, so he forced a friendly smile of his own. "I was just passing by and thought I'd stop in to say hello."

But Albán knew him too well to believe that, even for an instant. His hazel eyes narrowed almost imperceptibly, and his broad forehead creased. "Really? Well, imagine that."

Fred glanced casually over his shoulder to make sure nobody had moved within earshot. "Really."

Still looking unconvinced, Albán tossed a towel over his shoulder and moved away from the counter. "Okay. What can I get for you?"

"Coffee. Black."

Albán poured a cup, settled it on the bar in front of Fred, and leaned a hip against the counter. "What's really up?"

Working to keep his expression casual and his voice light, Fred sipped the scalding coffee and glanced around once more. "I don't see Webb. Has he been in this morning?"

Just as Fred suspected, Albán's expression sobered. "Not yet." Albán might serve Webb, but that didn't mean he liked watching him drink his life away.

"He wasn't here earlier?"

Giving a quick shake of his head, Albán glanced at the clock over the bar. "I just opened ten minutes ago. Why?"

"I'm trying to catch up with him. I understand Grady gave him a ride home last night. I thought maybe he'd stopped in when he came after his truck."

Albán shook his head slowly. "No. I thought he got his truck last night. At least, it was gone when I left."

Fred hadn't really expected any other answer, but he didn't like hearing Albán say the words aloud. "What time was that?"

"A little after two."

"Did you see him when he came back?"

"No."

"He just picked up his truck from the parking lot some time between, what . . . one and two in the morning?"

Albán eyed him steadily. "I guess so."

Fred sighed, took another bracing sip of coffee, and readjusted his position on the uncomfortable stool. "Were you here when the fight broke out last night?"

Albán crossed his arms on his chest. He didn't look happy. "I was."

"What can you tell me about it? What happened?"

"I can't tell you much. I was in the office taking care of some paperwork when the whole thing started. By the time I heard the noise and came out, things were pretty well out of control."

"But you saw Webb. Was he drunk?"

"He was in pretty bad shape," Albán admitted. "Drunker than usual. Ornery. Ready to fight with just about anyone."

"What about Lenore Irvine?"

A flicker of something danced through Albán's eyes. He shifted position and slanted closer to Fred. "That woman is a born troublemaker. She had everybody, including Casey Daniels, so upset it's a wonder somebody didn't hit her."

Somebody had done worse than that, but Fred didn't say so. "Casey was tending bar last night?"

Albán nodded. "He *was* until Lenore and that idiot David Newman got started. Then, he forgot about everything but wanting to join the fight. If he'd stayed behind the bar and exercised some authority, things wouldn't have gotten so far out of hand. As it was—" He broke off, shook his head as if the rest defied description, and shoved a lock of hair out of his eyes.

"Did you hear any of the argument between Webb and Lenore?"

"Between Webb and Lenore?" Albán thought for a second. "Not really. Why?"

Fred considered telling Albán about the murder but decided against it for now. "I'm just trying to piece together what happened. Do you know how the argument started?"

Albán frowned slightly. "All I know is, David Newman and Lenore started arguing about that stupid gambling petition, and the next thing anyone knew, the whole bar was involved. This gambling thing . . ." He picked up his knife again and shook his head slowly. "I know and understand all the arguments in favor, but I'd sure hate what it'd do to Cutler."

Fred couldn't say he understood the arguments, but he agreed with the rest of Albán's sentiment. He stared into his coffee cup for several seconds before Albán's first words hit him. "David Newman? I thought—"

"You thought Webb started the argument?"

"Yes."

Albán shook his head, and his lips tightened into a sad smile. "From what I've been able to pick up, the argument started between David and Lenore. Webb got involved eventually, like everyone else, but not at first."

"He must have gotten pretty upset if Grady escorted him out of the bar."

"Yes, but he wasn't the only one who was escorted away last night. David was lucky he didn't leave in handcuffs. Kent and Hannah were here, so they hauled Lenore away." His smile hardened a little. "To tell you the truth, I think Grady took Webb home because he was far too drunk to drive, nothing else. Why? What's going on?"

Fred hesitated before he spoke again. He didn't like lying to Albán, and he just might learn more if Albán understood why he needed to know. "This isn't common knowledge yet, but Lenore was killed this morning. Someone helped her car over the side of the road just outside of town."

Albán's face froze in an expression of disbelief, but it thawed slowly and enlightenment filled his eyes. "And they think Webb did it?"

Fred nodded and excused the tiny lie by reminding himself they'd think so soon.

Albán processed the news for a few seconds, then shook his head. "Why Webb? If it were me, I'd check out David Newman long before I'd consider Webb a suspect. Or Kent. I've never heard him speak to Lenore the way he did last night."

"What happened here wasn't the only trouble between Webb and Lenore," Fred admitted.

"No. But it wasn't the only trouble between David and Lenore, either. And it didn't sound like the first argument between her and Kent, either."

Fred moved around on his seat again. "Maybe not. But there's other evidence."

"Such as?"

"Damage to Webb's truck."

Albán gave that some thought, but he still didn't look convinced. "I'm sorry, Fred, but I don't see it. I know Webb's a disappointment to you, but I don't think he's capable of killing anyone."

"Unless he was drunk," Fred pointed out.

"Maybe."

Fred's frustration level rose a notch. "Everyone's capable of killing someone if they're provoked enough."

"I suppose that's true," Albán said thoughtfully. "But I saw Webb last night. He was upset, I won't deny that—"

"And drunk," Fred reminded him.

"True. But that's the trouble. He was *so* drunk, I don't believe he was capable of driving his truck anywhere."

"He's driven drunk more than once," Fred said.

"Maybe," Albán agreed. "But I was here, remember? Webb was upset, but he wasn't *that* upset."

Fred pulled in a steadying breath and fiddled with the handle on his coffee cup. "Did you know he lost his job?"

Shock flitted across Albán's face, followed by resigned understanding. "That explains it, then."

"Explains what?"

Albán shrugged lightly. "He's been in here more than usual the past week or so. Different hours than usual. He's here during the day more. I figured Tito would eventually let him go."

Fred leaned across the bar to shift the weight from his hips. "He was fired a week ago. After he *accidentally* left the brake line on Lenore Irvine's car loose."

Albán stared at him for a long moment, straightened his shoulders, and checked the surrounding tables as if he feared someone might overhear. "You think Webb did that on purpose?"

"Sure sounds that way to me. I think Tito thinks so, too."

"No." Albán said it slowly, as if he needed time to make sure that's what he meant. He shook his head and repeated. "No. I don't believe it."

He sounded so certain that Fred wondered if he knew something he hadn't mentioned yet. If so, Fred wanted to hear it. "Why not?"

Albán leaned across the bar again, this time on both elbows in a mirror of Fred's posture. "Because I saw the way he acted last night. Sure, he was angry with Lenore, but there's no way he wanted to kill her."

"How do you know?"

"The look on his face. The tone of his voice." Albán

scowled and threw his hands in the air. "I don't *know* how I know. I just do."

That didn't help.

"I'm telling you," Albán went on, a bit more certain now. "If I'd been behind the bar, the whole thing would have been handled quickly. Quietly. The sheriff's department wouldn't have been involved. But Casey is a fool." He pulled another carrot from the pile and attacked it with his knife. "People get drunk in bars. They fly off the handle all the time. Casey's trouble is, he takes every damned thing so literally. And now, here you are, asking questions like *this*."

Fred waited until Albán stopped thwacking the carrot and the noise level faded. "Who said what last night?"

Albán stopped in the act of positioning another carrot. "What?"

"I said," Fred repeated more slowly, "who said what? What did Casey take literally? Why *did* he call the sheriff's department?"

Albán's gaze narrowed and his hand dropped to the counter. "You're kidding, right? I thought you knew. I thought—"

Fred's stomach started to churn again, and the hairs on the back of his neck prickled with foreboding. He knew the answer, even before he asked. "It was Webb, wasn't it?"

Albán didn't answer.

"What did he say?"

Sighing as if he had the weight of the world on his shoulders, Albán wiped his hands on a towel and tossed it onto the bar. "I thought you knew," he said again. "Webb told Lenore that if she didn't stop fighting the petition and causing so much trouble, he'd . . ." His voice trailed away and his gaze faltered. "He said he'd kill her."

nine

Still huffing from walking back across town as quickly as his legs would move, Fred pushed open the door to Enos's office and clutched the door frame for support. "Sit down. I've got something to tell you." His voice came out nearly as shaken and unsteady as he felt.

Raising both eyebrows nearly into his hairline, Enos closed a file folder on his desktop. He looked at his backside in his chair and back up at Fred. "What's the matter? Are you sick or something?"

Fred shook his head and tried to catch his breath. "No. I'm fine. But I've found your murderer."

"You've *what*?" Didn't you just promise me less than—" He checked his watch and scowled. "Good billy hell, Fred. It hasn't even been two hours since you promised you'd stay out of this investigation, and you're back with the murderer already? This must be a record—even for you."

Fred didn't have the time or the patience to play this game with Enos today. Given a few hours head start, Webb could destroy the evidence before Enos ever saw it. With a few drinks under his belt, he could fly off the handle and hurt Margaret or one of the kids—or worse.

He crossed to the younger man's desk and leaned his fists onto its cluttered top. "I saw your murderer driving his truck this morning, and I've already learned enough to put him behind bars. Now, do you want to know who it is or not?"

Enos pushed the file out of his way and leaned back in his chair. "I suppose you just *happened* to see it—"

"Dammit, Enos. I was on my way to Margaret's, and the blasted thing passed me on the street."

"All right." Enos leaned a little further back. He tried to look serious but failed. The corners of his mouth twitched as if he were waiting for the punchline of some grand joke. "I'll bite. Whose truck was it?"

"You won't like it when I tell you."

"No? Tell me, anyway." Enos let his smile grow and cocked an ankle over one knee. "Whose truck was it? Who's our murderer."

"Webb."

"What?" The irritating smile evaporated, his ankle uncocked, and his chair sprang back into position with a pop.

Fred held back a satisfied smile, but he couldn't deny Enos's reaction made him feel a bit better. "Webb's truck," he said and ticked off points before Enos could interrupt again. "Dark body, dented fender, smashed headlight, damage to the grillwork—"

Laughing through his nose, Enos seemed to relax. "For a minute there I thought you were serious."

"I'm dead serious. Webb's your murderer."

Enos scowled at him and let his eyes flick rapidly across Fred's face as if he still suspected he'd uncover a joke if he looked hard enough. But after several seconds, the flicking slowed and his eyes clouded. "You're serious?"

Fred propped his fists on Enos's desk and leaned across it. "For hell's sake, Enos. I wouldn't lie about a thing like that. I know what I saw." When Enos looked as if he might interrupt, he rushed on. "Did you know Webb lost his job last week?"

Enos's reaction gave him the answer, even without words.

"No? Well, neither did I until this morning. Do you know why Tito fired him?" He didn't wait for an answer this time, either. "Because he *accidentally* left Lenore Irvine's brake line loose after he fixed her car."

Enos's expression sobered even further.

"I'm assuming you already know he threatened to kill her last night," Fred pressed. "In front of witnesses."

"I knew that. He was drunk."

As if that made it all right. In spite of Enos's reaction, Fred knew he'd hit a nerve. He didn't let himself gloat, but he could tell Enos was listening hard. "He's probably got the truck locked up somewhere right this minute, destroying the evidence."

Enos let out a heavy sigh and leaned back in his chair. "Destroying the evidence?"

"Hammering out the dent in his fender. Fixing the grill—"

"Even if he is," Enos said. "He can't do it in a couple of hours. Sit down and pull yourself together."

Fred glared at him.

Enos glared back. "Either sit and slow down a little, or I'm not listening to another word. I'm not going to call Maggie and tell her you've had a heart attack in the middle of my office."

"I'm not going to have a blasted heart attack," Fred snapped. But he knew Enos well enough to know he meant what he said. He lowered himself into a chair, but he made sure Enos knew exactly what he thought of the order.

Enos waited until Fred had settled into place. "All right. I'll give. You think Webb killed Lenore. Why? Give me a motive *and* give me opportunity. He didn't even have his truck last night—Grady took him home from the Copper Penny, remember?"

Fred couldn't hold back an exasperated sigh. "You want a motive? To keep Lenore from putting the kibosh on the gambling petition. And opportunity?" He leaned back in his seat and used a hand to gesture. "You're assuming he didn't leave home after Grady dropped him off?"

Enos opened his mouth to speak.

But Fred held up a hand to stop him. "Did you know that his truck disappeared from the Copper Penny's parking lot some time between one and two this morning?"

This time, Enos didn't try to speak. His face tightened as he stood again and paced a few steps away from his desk. "Did Webb pick it up?"

"Who else?"

"What about Maggie?"

Fred's heart dropped into his stomach. "You're not suggesting Margaret—"

Enos shook his head quickly and his face flushed. "That *she* used Webb's truck to kill Lenore? No. Not in a million years. But are you sure she didn't pick up the truck for Webb?"

Fred waved the suggestion away. "She would have told me when I saw her earlier. She doesn't know anything. She thinks Webb spent the night in the back room at Tito's and that he went to work this morning."

Enos let out a hefty sigh and rubbed his broad face with an open palm.

Fred let a moment or two pass while Enos digested everything. "Webb and Lenore had an argument yesterday afternoon. He threatened Lenore once at his house. In fact, Kent had to drag her away before things got out of hand."

Enos glanced over his shoulder at him, but he didn't say a word.

"They argued again last night at the Copper Penny. Webb threatened her *again,* for hell's sake."

Enos's expression darkened, and he flicked a speck of dust from the top of the filing cabinet. "Sounds to me as if you *want* Webb to be guilty."

"No," Fred said slowly. "But I don't want a murderer living with my daughter and grandchildren, either."

"Are you sure the truck wasn't damaged already?"

Fred struggled to hold onto his rapidly thinning patience. "Tito saw Webb yesterday. He says the truck was fine then."

Uncertainty flashed across Enos's face.

"You think it's a coincidence?" Fred demanded.

"It's possible."

Fred slapped the arm of the chair with his palm. "There's no such thing as coincidence." He didn't care whether Enos liked his tone or not. "I'm telling you, it's Webb's truck you're looking for, and if he gets a chance to work on it, he'll have the damage repaired before you can even see it."

Enos scowled from beneath his eyebrows.

Fred didn't let that bother him. "He's got everything at stake. I told you about the second mortgage he wants. I've told you that he lost his job. If the gambling petition doesn't make it onto the ballot, Margaret and Webb'll be wiped out."

Enos nodded slowly, but he still didn't say anything.

"Lenore Irvine was a threat to the petition—you know that as well as I do."

"She's not the only one," Enos insisted. "The whole damn town's divided."

"But they're not all driving around town in damaged trucks."

Silenced at last, Enos lowered himself into his seat and wiped his face with the palm of his hand again. He sat that way, staring out the window, for a long time. Too long.

"At least look for Webb," Fred urged. "Find the truck before he fixes it. Find out where he was early this morning when Lenore was killed. Check out his story, for hell's sake."

Enos shoved a couple of file folders out of his way. "I know how to do my job."

"Then *do* it. He's not at home. He's not at the Copper Penny. And he's not at Tito's. I'm thinking he's either at Quinn Udy's or at his dad's place."

Enos didn't answer immediately. He propped up his forehead with his thumbs and studied his desktop for a while. "You know what questioning Webb about this'll do to Maggie and the kids," he asked at last.

Fred didn't want to dwell on that. "Of course, I know. I can't think about anything else."

Worry lines creased Enos's face. He heaved a sigh and lowered his head again. "All right," he said at last. "I'll take a look at the truck. If you're right, I'll have a talk with him."

Fred couldn't hide his relief. His shoulders slumped, and his hands relaxed their grip on the chair. "Good."

Pushing to his feet again, Enos paced a few steps away, then wheeled back to face Fred. His eyes were filled with that tender expression that only appeared when he thought about Margaret. "I don't want you to say anything to Maggie. Not yet."

Fred held up both hands. He didn't want Margaret to know, either. Not until everything was certain. "I won't say a word."

Enos crossed to his desk and picked up his flashlight.

Wedging it into the holder on his duty belt, he fished around on the desktop for his keys. But instead of clipping them to his belt, he stared at them as if he didn't know what they were. "On second thought, maybe I ought to have one of the boys talk to Webb first. You know how Webb will react to me. You remember how he acted the last time, don't you? And that time, all I did that time was pull him over."

Of course, Fred remembered. Once, years ago, Enos had stopped Webb for speeding. He hadn't even written a ticket, just issued a verbal warning, but Webb had whined about it to anyone who'd listen for months afterward.

"Maybe you shouldn't go alone," Fred conceded. "But I definitely think you should go. He'll make mincemeat out of Grady and Ivan, and you know it."

Enos made a face and jammed his keys onto his duty belt. "If I send someone else to question Webb, it'll look bad. He'll claim I was afraid to approach him, or that I *knew* I didn't have a case. But if I do it myself, he'll shout harassment." He paced away again. Nervous.

"Take *me* with you."

Enos stopped just before he reached the far wall and shook his head. "Oh, *that* would help."

Fred ignored the sarcasm. "You'll need a witness, so Webb can't claim you said or did anything out of the ordinary–isn't that what you just said?"

Enos glared at him. "That's not exactly what I meant. Besides, if I take anybody, it won't be you."

Fred glared back. "Then what are you going to do?"

"Even if I took someone along, there are a *hundred* people I'd take before I'd let you come," Enos insisted and held up fingers to mark his place while he made his points. "First of all, you're even more emotionally involved in this case than I am. Second, you're a civilian. Third—"

Fred didn't need to hear this tired old argument. "Who are you going to take?" he asked again. "Name one person in this town you can trust to back you in a tight situation and keep their fool mouth shut."

"Grady. Ivan. For that matter, Doc Higgins."

Scarcely able to believe what he'd just heard, Fred stared

at Enos for a second, then snorted a laugh. "Doc? We both know how discreet *he* can be. And if you take either of your deputies, everybody in town will know something's wrong."

Enos rolled his eyes and turned away again.

"Look," Fred said. "We agree you shouldn't go alone. Not right now. Not until you're sure Webb's the one you're looking for. If you start looking for him alone, everybody will speculate about what you're doing. But nobody's going to think twice about you and me going somewhere together—"

Enos snorted in response.

"—and if we just *happen* to pass Quinn Udy's place, or Lamar Templeton's, and you *happen* to see Webb's truck there and notice the damage, even Webb will be hard-pressed to find anything to say about it."

"Webb will find something to say no matter how I handle this." Enos smacked the metal filing cabinet with his palm and paced away again. "To tell you the truth, I don't care what Webb thinks or what he says. It's Maggie I'm worried about." He glanced at Fred and added, "And Jessica. She's not feeling real well. I don't want anybody thinking the wrong thing or talking . . . well, you know."

Fred followed and touched his shoulder. Enos's marriage had never been a good one, and things had been even tougher since Jessica's breast cancer surgery. She'd always been a little paranoid about Enos and Margaret, and illness had only accentuated her insecurities. "Neither do I, son. But you can't let that affect how you do your job. If I'd come in here and said that truck belonged to anyone else, what would you do?"

Enos smiled grimly. "You know what I'd do. But I *wouldn't* take you with me."

"You would if you thought it would help the investigation."

Enos tried to smile, but failed miserably. Fred didn't press. He'd made his point; he didn't need to belabor the issue.

"All right," Enos said at last. "All right. But you have to promise you won't say a word."

Fred struggled not to let his relief show. "You've got it."

"I mean it, Fred. Not a single word."

"I'll keep my mouth shut," Fred assured him. "I'm only going along to make things easier for you." He crossed to the door and pulled it open. "Let's get going before he gets that truck repaired."

Enos reached for his old black cowboy hat and made a face. "I hate it when you do this to me, you know."

Fred knew, but he didn't say so. He just stepped outside and waited for Enos to close the door behind them.

As if by silent agreement, they stood for a minute, staring at the activity on Main Street. Several cars sat in the parking lot at Lacey's, and the double doors of The Good Sport stood wide open, inviting customers inside. Birds still squawked at intruders from the treetops, chipmunks still chattered, and the sun still tried to light up the day as if nothing had happened.

But the world felt different to Fred, and he knew Enos must feel it, too. He only hoped that Webb would be safely behind bars before long and that Margaret would understand why Fred couldn't just sit back and let Webb walk free.

ten

Fred trailed Enos off the boardwalk and down the street to his truck. He started to climb into the truck's cab when a car door closed nearby and someone called to Enos. With one foot on the running board, Fred turned to look.

Kent Irvine stood beside his maroon Park Avenue about four cars away, and Hannah's red head slowly appeared over the top of the car on the passenger's side.

Cupping his mouth with his hands, Kent shouted again. "Sheriff, wait." When he could see that Enos had stopped moving, Kent started away from the car.

Fred slipped out of the truck again and waited beside his open door while Enos waited for Kent and Hannah to reach him.

"Sorry to hold you up," Kent said with a tired smile. He folded his massive arms across his chest and glanced at Hannah. "We wondered whether there's any news about Lenore's killer."

Enos squinted into the sunlight. Crow's-feet lined his eyes, and lines bracketed his mouth. "Nothing definite."

Kent scowled. He obviously didn't like that answer. "What about suspects?"

"We have a few," Enos admitted.

Kent's eyes sparkled with interest. "Good. Who are they?"

"I don't want to name anyone yet," Enos said. "I don't have enough solid information."

Fred leaned against the truck and silently thanked Enos for keeping Webb's name out of the conversation. He'd have felt uncomfortable, at best, standing here in front of the victim's family while they discussed Webb.

"I think we have a right to know," Kent insisted. He unfolded his arms and wrapped one around Hannah's shoulders. "Have you talked to David Newman yet?"

Enos nodded. "Briefly."

"And—?"

"And I'm talking to a few others."

"That's not what I meant," Kent snapped. "What did Newman say?"

The lines around Enos's mouth deepened. "I'm not ready to discuss that yet."

Kent's face reddened. "Oh, come on, Sheriff. You heard what he said at the Copper Penny last night. You saw the way he treated Lenore." He tightened his grip on Hannah. "This is very upsetting for all of us. We drive through town and see people we know, but we have no idea whether we're looking into the face of Lenore's killer."

Enos nodded. "I understand that, but until I have something solid to go on, I'm not going to discuss the case with anyone."

Kent let out a heavy breath and looked down at the top of his daughter's head. "Didn't I tell you? That's the way these small towns are. Everybody's friends. Everybody like everybody else, and they'll protect each other, just you wait and see."

Hannah rested one hand on her father's chest. "Oh, Dad. Please don't start that here."

Fred took a step closer, ready to say something in Enos's defense if necessary.

But Enos didn't seem to need help. He straightened his shoulders and met Kent's gaze steadily. "I hope you're not implying anything about the way my department does its job."

Kent's puffy lips thinned slightly. He used his free hand to push his glasses further up on the bridge of his nose. "I'm implying that something had better be done about my wife's murder."

"Something *is* being done, " Enos assured him, but his voice dropped a note or two and Fred heard a warning there.

Either Kent didn't hear Enos's answer, or he chose to

ignore it. "I deserve to know what that something is. *We* deserve to know."

Hannah's frown deepened. She looked embarrassed. "Dad, don't. Please?"

"Let me handle this, pumpkin." Kent tried to smile at her, but anger outlined every feature and punctuated every gesture. Even the arm on her shoulder looked tensed and ready to swing at anything that moved.

Fred understood that stage of grief only too well. He'd been angry with the world for the first few weeks after Phoebe's death—even with the advance warning cancer provided. He couldn't imagine how he would have reacted if she'd passed on suddenly.

He moved to Enos's side, a silent show of support, but he didn't say a word.

Kent rubbed his forehead with his free hand. "Maybe you don't understand, Sheriff. Someone in this town killed my wife."

"I understand that," Enos said.

Kent went on as if Enos hadn't spoken. "Someone forced her car off the road. One of your friends sent her off the side of a cliff." His hand trembled. He lowered it to his side and balled his hand into a fist. "I drove out there today. I saw how steep the incline was, and I know how terrified she must have been." His eyes misted with unshed tears. "In my imagination, I can hear her screaming. I can't get the sound out of my head."

Hannah ducked her head into his side and let out a soft moan.

Fred held back a groan of his own. Had Webb heard Lenore scream as she plummeted off the cliff? Did the sound haunt him, or had alcohol wiped it from his memory? Fred understood Kent's pain, but he could see how much his words upset Hannah. "Sheriff Asay is doing everything he can."

The girl sent him a tremulous smile, but the sound of his voice seemed to spur Kent to action. Pulling his arm from Hannah's shoulder, he jabbed a finger in front of Fred's face. "What about that damned son-in-law of his?" he demanded of Enos. "Have you talked to *him* yet? Did Fred tell you about what happened at his daughter's house yesterday?"

Enos nodded. "He told me, and I intend to question Webb."

"When?"

Enos kept his answer vague. "As soon as I can."

"And David Newman?" Kent demanded again.

"I'll talk with him as many times as I think is necessary."

Kent huffed a disbelieving laugh. "Yeah. I'll just bet you will. Lenore lived here her whole life. She was one of you people, but the entire time we were married, none of you treated her even halfway decent."

Fred refrained from pointing out why, and he could tell by the way Enos shifted his weight that he had to struggle to keep quiet.

"I know people complained about Lenore," Kent went on, nodding in agreement with himself and shoving his glasses up on his nose again. "But all she ever wanted was to make this town a better place to live. A safer place to raise children for everyone. And what did she get?" Emotion choked him and thickened his voice. He lowered his head and pushed up his glasses so he could rub his eyes. He blinked away the remaining tears before he spoke again. "I heard people say she was closed-minded, and maybe she was. But whoever killed her isn't any better."

Fred couldn't argue with that. He didn't even try.

Hannah touched her father's back with her palm. "Maybe it was an accident." A soft breeze blew in off the lake and lifted her hair into the sunlight. She looked pretty and young and vulnerable, and Fred's heart went out to her.

Kent turned on her. "It wasn't an accident, Hannah, and you know it. Didn't you listen to anything I told you?"

"I listened, but—"

"It *wasn't* an accident," Kent repeated, louder this time. "Someone purposely sent Lenore's car off the road. And why—because they had a difference of opinion?"

Hannah's face crumpled, and Kent's anger seemed to evaporate. "I'm sorry, pumpkin. It's just that I'm so frustrated and helpless. I need to do something."

The girl blinked rapidly and glanced at the boards under her feet. "I just want to go home."

Kent nodded, squeezed her shoulders again, and whispered, "Okay. I'll get you home. You look exhausted." But when he looked at Enos again, the hard edge reappeared. "I want you to keep me updated, Sheriff. I don't want you giving me the runaround. Lenore was my wife. I have the right to know what's going on."

"I'll keep you updated on anything I can," Enos assured him.

"You'd better," Kent warned. "I want whoever killed her to pay for it—with their life."

Fred didn't even want to think about how Margaret would react if she heard Kent say that.

Hannah didn't seem to like it, either. She flicked uneasy glances at Enos and Fred, grabbed the material of Kent's sleeve, and looked up at him. "Don't talk like that, Dad. Please?"

But Kent didn't pay any attention to her. "The Bible says 'an eye for an eye,' doesn't it?"

Nobody answered.

"Well? *Doesn't* it?"

Enos tipped back the brim of his hat. "I believe that's what it says, but the law in this country doesn't always work that way."

"Well, maybe it should," Kent grumbled.

Hannah tugged on Kent's sleeve again. "I don't want to think about this anymore. Take me home—*please?*"

Kent scowled down at her and brushed her hand from his sleeve. "Maybe Lenore was right, after all. Maybe that's exactly what's wrong with our country. Loose morals, no fit punishment for the crime . . . Everybody does whatever they damn well please, and nobody says diddly-squat about it. But it won't happen this time, Sheriff. I can promise you that."

Fred kept his attention riveted on Hannah. She looked pale and waxy, as if she might throw up. She needed time to deal with the tragedy. She did *not* need her father to drag her all over the county on a quest for revenge.

"Don't you think you ought to get her home?" he asked, nodding at Hannah in case Kent had trouble understanding.

Kent glanced down at her as if he really noticed her for the first time. "She's taking this real hard," he said in a near-whisper. "She and Lenore were very close." He urged Hannah toward the car and looked at Enos one last time. "Remember, Sheriff. An eye for an eye."

Lurching slightly as she reached the Park Avenue, Hannah leaned her arm across the car's hood. When she let out a miserable moan and made a couple of soft gagging noises, Kent finally started after her. He waited until she'd pulled herself together, then guided her toward the passenger's side of the car and helped her inside. Crossing behind the car, he climbed behind the wheel. The car dipped and swayed as he lowered his bulk onto the seat. An instant later, he backed onto the street and drove away.

"Poor girl," Enos said softly. "Why in the hell did Kent drag her over here with him? Can't he see how upset she is?"

"He's only thinking of himself right now," Fred said.

Enos grimaced and worked his hat back into place. "Yeah. Well, their causes were always more important to both of them than that poor girl. And finding Lenore's murderer is Kent's latest cause."

His response startled Fred, but he struggled not to look surprised. He followed Enos back to the truck, climbed inside, and settled into the seat. The image of Hannah's pale face floated in front of his eyes. Hannah was only slightly younger than Sarah, the same age as Benjamin, a few years older than Deborah. And he realized they'll all suffer, just as Hannah did, when Enos arrested their father. The thought made him ill.

He sighed heavily and leaned his head against the window. He thought of all the suffering ahead and silently cursed Webb for putting both his family and Lenore's through hell.

In the long run, Lenore's death wouldn't accomplish anything. It wouldn't stop Fred and others from opposing the gambling petition or ensure the petition's success. The murder had been a senseless—and useless—act. In one instant of drunken anger, Webb had destroyed the lives of countless people for nothing.

eleven

Fred leaned forward in the truck's seat and watched the road carefully for some sign of Webb or his truck while Enos drove. But he didn't really expect to see either, and he wasn't surprised when they made it through town and past the Bluebird Café without a trace of his son-in-law.

Enos tried to look as if they were joyriding until they rounded the first curve outside town. Sighing heavily, he accelerated and spoke for the first time since they left his office. "Okay, Fred. Your part in this is done. Whatever happens from here on out, you keep quiet. *I* do all the talking."

Fred had been a model of decorum during the encounter with Kent and Hannah. "For hell's sake," he began.

But Enos cut him off before he could finish the thought. "I mean it, Fred. I don't care who we see—Quinn, Lamar, or Webb himself, you stay in the background and keep your mouth shut."

"Of course I will," Fred assured him. "You know me better than that."

Enos shot him a glance that looked half exasperated, half amused, and signaled the turn onto the road that would eventually take them to Quinn's run-down cabin on the hill above Jefferson's One-Stop. "You're right. I do. Silly of me to suggest anything else."

Fred humphed his response. Enos might be agitated after dealing with the Irvines, but he didn't stop to think how this whole mess affected Fred.

The truck bounced over a rut in the road, forcing Fred to grip the door's handle to steady himself. He watched out the window, as if he might see Webb's truck in the dense forest near his friend's cabin if he looked hard enough.

He honestly didn't know what he'd do if they found Webb. It should be enough for him to see the man behind bars, but with each passing minute his anger grew until it almost matched his fear. Webb's temper had always disturbed Fred, and he'd often worried about Margaret and the kids. But even *he* had never believed Webb would lose control like this.

First and foremost, they had to get Webb safely behind bars. Then Fred could concentrate on helping Margaret rid herself of the bum, once and for all.

He glanced at Enos and thought about voicing some of his thoughts. But Enos didn't look as if he wanted to hear anything. He drove in silence—jaw clenched, eyes narrowed, knuckles almost white where he gripped the wheel.

Half a mile from the highway, the side road narrowed, the pavement ended, and the forest crept closer. Englemann spruce and aspen trees hovered along the shoulder and blocked the sun, throwing the narrow road into shadow. Fred held back a shudder, but he couldn't completely push away the feeling that someone was watching them.

Still without speaking, Enos maneuvered the truck around several more bends in the road. Dust billowed behind them and marked their progress. A flock of birds took flight as they passed a stand of aspen. Enos might as well blow his horn, too. No chance they could sneak up on Webb if he *was* here.

All at once the forest parted and exposed Quinn's dilapidated property in all its glory. Weathered boards clung to the cabin's small frame, almost as if they were afraid of tumbling to the ground. Shutters hung on loose hinges, floorboards on the deck curled up to meet the sun, and an old sofa offered some of its stuffing to the elements.

A collection of rusted metal contraptions lay in piles near the cabin, and several old cars held places of honor in the clearing. A few hardy wildflowers poked their heads out of the tall grass behind the cabin, but even the forest held back, as if it didn't want to touch anything.

Somewhere a dog set up a ruckus, which brought Quinn out the front door to see what all the fuss was about. But Fred could tell, even before they drove through the sagging gate, Webb's truck wasn't here.

Quinn stood in the shadows of his porch for a few seconds. His hair looked as if he'd done nothing more than rake his fingers through it. He obviously hadn't shaved for at least two days, and his clothes looked as if he'd slept in them. Just the sort of friend Webb needed.

Shielding his eyes from the sunlight, he watched Fred and Enos approach. When they drew closer, he ducked under a hummingbird feeder on the edge of the porch and stuffed his hands into his pockets as he stepped off the porch and sauntered across the clearing toward them. His paunch protruded over his jeans and tattooes decorated both arms. "What's going on?" he asked when he drew close enough.

Enos turned off the engine and leaned back in his seat. "Just checking to make sure you made it home okay last night."

Quinn frowned slightly. "Why? You don't usually drive all the way out here to check on me after I've been at the Copper Penny."

If Enos did that, he'd be out here every morning, Fred thought. But he didn't say a word.

"I don't usually have to break up arguments," Enos said with a halfhearted smile.

Quinn made a noise in his throat. "I wasn't involved in that mess, and you know it."

"Oh?" Enos leaned a bit further back. "I got the impression you were. You and Webb seemed pretty worked up when I got there."

Quinn flushed a bit, straightened his posture, and tried to look tough. It didn't work. "Webb might have been worked up, but *I* wasn't."

Enos looked mildly interested. "Is that right?"

"Yeah." Quinn ran a hand over his chin and scratched a spot on his neck. "I'll admit, things did get a little tense last night. But you know how it is—"

Fred certainly knew. A few drinks under their belts and they probably thought they could take on the world.

Enos didn't say anything. He just sat there for several long seconds as if he thought Quinn might say something else, but Quinn didn't oblige.

The silence dragged on for what felt like forever, while Fred battled growing impatience. Obviously, Webb's truck wasn't here, and every second they spent admiring the view gave the dirtbag more time to cover his tracks.

But Enos didn't seem concerned about that. "Now that you're a little calmer," he said to Quinn, "why don't you tell me again about last night."

Quinn tried to look unconcerned. "What do you want to know?"

"How did the argument start?"

"I don't know. How does any argument start?"

Enos scowled at him and sat up straighter. "You were there, weren't you?" He might look relaxed, but his voice left no doubt he wanted serious answers.

Quinn didn't seem to care. He lifted one shoulder in a lifeless shrug. "Yeah, I was there."

"All right, then. Tell me what you saw and heard."

Quinn pretended to think. "I guess it started when that bitch came barging in like she had a right to be there. She started making noise about the gambling petition and trying to tell everyone what to think and how to act. You know . . . her usual crap."

"Are you talking about Lenore Irvine?" Enos asked.

Quinn snorted a laugh. "Who else? You know how she is, don't you? She thinks anybody who has any fun must be the spawn of the devil."

"Did she say that?" Enos asked.

Quinn shrugged again and had the good sense to look slightly sheepish. "Not in so many words," he muttered, then immediately perked up again. "But she practically accused David Newman of being the anti-Christ. Said he was leading the town astray and all that sort of bullshit. I mean, who's it going to hurt if we have a few slot machines in town?"

Fred didn't want to hear about David Newman. He wanted

to know about Webb's part in the argument and where he was right now. He leaned forward ever so slightly, just to get a better look at Quinn's face.

Enos scowled at him and tried to block his view. "How did Webb get involved?"

Quinn's expression sobered. "Same way everybody else got involved, I guess."

"Which was—"

"Hell, I don't know. We were drinking. I don't remember." Quinn held up both hands in a gesture of surrender. "Honestly, I don't. What's going on, anyway? Is the old battle-ax filing a complaint or something?"

"Not exactly," Enos said. Fred expected him to waste more time sidestepping the question. Instead, he pulled in a deep breath and let it out again. "Lenore Irvine was killed this morning."

Quinn's mouth fell open and his eyes rounded. "Killed? How? What happened?"

Enos fished a piece of gum from his shirt pocket and unwrapped it without looking away. "Someone forced her car off the road just past the summit."

Quinn's face lost its color, and he pulled away from the truck. "No kidding? Who?"

"That's what I'm trying to find out," Enos said. "Now, tell me, in as much detail as you can remember, what happened at the Copper Penny last night."

Looking considerably less sure of himself, Quinn raked his hair again with shaky fingers and checked his boots as though they might have the answer. "Okay. Let's see." Giving up on his boots, he scoured the tops of the trees at the back of his property. "She came in, like I said. And she started running around from table to table saying stuff, you know? Hell— We were all just sitting there, minding our own business and drinking a beer. We didn't want any trouble, but she—" He broke off and shook his head. "She wanted to start something with somebody, and I don't think it mattered who."

Fred thought about pointing out how much more she'd gotten than she bargained for, but the look on Enos's face convinced him not to. "You said you were *all* sitting there. Who else was with you?"

Quinn stiffened noticeably and shook his head. "Nobody. Webb and me, that's all. We were sitting a couple of tables away from David Newman. We could tell he was getting upset, but I wanted to stay out of it. I told Webb to ignore her, you know? Not to let her get to him. I mean, arguing with her doesn't—*didn't*—do any good. It was like hitting your head against a brick wall."

"*Did* Webb ignore her?" Fred asked.

Quinn nodded. "Yeah, for a while. David, though— He didn't. He lost it, man. He and Lenore went at each other for a little while, her shouting about loose morals and all the poor people who'd lose their shirts if gambling came to town and him telling her the facts—*trying* to set her straight. I don't know what she said at the very end, but that's when David really lost control. I thought he'd have a fit right there. Started ranting and calling her names and warned her to back off. Said she was an interfering bitch and that she was in over her head this time."

Enos lifted his eyebrows. "What did he mean, *this time*?"

"I don't know." Quinn looked pained. "Because that's when she saw us. It was like she forgot all about David. She came over to our table and started in—" He flicked a glance at Fred and broke off suddenly, as if he'd thought better of what he'd been about to say. "Anyway, it just sort of went from there."

"Why did Webb threaten her?" Enos asked.

"I don't remember. He didn't mean it, anyway. It was just drunk talk, you know? Stupid. He didn't do anything to her, you know."

Enos didn't say a word. Neither did Fred.

Quinn didn't miss the implications. His voice rose a little, and he sounded almost frantic. "Look, she went crazy. Like she wanted to make sure everybody knew what Webb said to her." He shifted position and met Enos's gaze again. "Or more like she wanted to make sure her husband knew what he'd said to her."

Enos looked surprised. "Kent was there at the time?"

"Yeah. He'd been there a while, and then what's-her-name came in, their youngest daughter, you know? And that sort of got everything going, because she's too young to be in the bar. Casey was working, and you know how he is. He went ballistic trying to get her out the door. David was still shouting at Lenore and trying to get everybody worked up about the gambling petition again. And then Webb lost his temper and told Lenore what he thought of her, it was like . . . like everything sort of blew up."

"That's when Casey called us in?"

"Yeah."

Fred let it all settle for a second, but another of Quinn's comments left him confused. "You said David Newman was trying to get everybody worked up about the gambling petition again?"

Quinn nodded.

"If that's the case, what were she and Webb arguing about?" Fred sensed Enos glaring at him, but he kept his attention riveted on Quinn.

The young man's face turned a deep shade of crimson. He pulled away from the truck and shook his head. "I don't know. Just the usual stuff, you know?"

Fred assumed that meant Webb's drinking, but he wanted Quinn to clarify. He waited, hoping that Quinn would decide to fill in the blanks.

But before he could, Enos decided to take charge. "Have you seen Webb this morning?"

Quinn shook his head. "No."

"What about last night after Grady took him home?"

Quinn's lips thinned, and a hood seemed to droop over his eyes. "What about it?"

He was hiding something. Fred could have seen that from a mile away.

Enos didn't seem to notice. "Did you see Webb after Grady took him home? Did you hear from him?"

Quinn's eyes darted back and forth between Enos and Fred for a second. "No."

Definitely hiding something.

Enos still seemed unaware. He looked out over the clearing. "He didn't come here?"

"No."

Fred couldn't help himself. He had to ask. "Do you have any idea where he is now?"

Quinn made a vain attempt to straighten his posture, but he looked shaken and miserable. "I haven't heard from him, and I probably won't. He's not real happy with me right now."

Enos leaned forward and blocked Fred's view again. "Why not?"

Quinn didn't answer immediately. He let several seconds pass. Fred figured he must be thinking hard, because his breathing sounded labored. "He's acting like an idiot," he said at last. "And I told him so. He didn't like what I had to say, that's all."

Fred's opinion of Quinn took a grudging step upward. "About what? Taking out the second mortgage?"

"Yeah." Quinn sounded eager. Or relieved. "He's being a real ass."

Fred flicked another glance at Enos's back. Surely he'd heard the same thing Fred had in Quinn's tone.

Enos didn't say a word.

"But that doesn't mean anything," Quinn went on quickly. "I don't know what happened to Lenore, but I do know Webb didn't have anything to do with it."

"How do you know?" Enos asked.

"Because . . ." Quinn sighed again. "Just because, man. He can be a jerk sometimes, but he's not a killer. He's more just a bunch of hot air, you know? Talks big all the time, but he never really does anything about it. Hell, if he was going to follow through, he'd have—" He broke off again.

"He'd have what?" Fred demanded. He didn't wait for Enos this time.

Enos pulled back to send Fred another intimidating glare, but Fred refused to be intimidated. He could sense Quinn's efforts to hide something, even if Enos couldn't. And he had no intention of leaving without hearing the whole story.

"What would he have done?" he asked again.

Like a little boy caught with his hand in the cookie jar,

Quinn looked from one to the other, then seemed to lose his backbone. "For one thing, he'd have gotten divorced a long time ago. Then he wouldn't be in this mess."

Fred didn't trust himself to speak. And he didn't honestly know what he would have said if he had. He didn't know how long he sat there digesting Quinn's response. He didn't even notice Enos's reaction. Never once, in all the years he'd been watching Margaret's marriage fail, had he thought Webb might be equally unhappy.

"What does his marriage have to do with this?" Enos's voice came out gruff, and Fred knew he'd been stunned by Quinn's answer, too.

Quinn looked surprised. "Hell, man. How's he ever supposed to make Maggie happy? It doesn't matter what Webb does, it's not good enough. She compares him to Fred, here, constantly. Webb doesn't stand a chance. He'll fail at everything because he can't possibly fill Fred's shoes." He waved a hand in the general direction of town. "There's nothing in this place for him, but he can't leave—Maggie won't leave her dad. So, he finally found a way to make his mark. To *do* something, you know? But Fred doesn't approve, so Maggie doesn't approve."

Not true. Not true at all. That was another of the things Fred found so hard to tolerate about Webb—the way he blamed everyone else for his failures. He wanted to protest, but he couldn't manage a word.

Enos shot a worried glance in his direction and started the truck again. "If you see Webb or hear from him, I want you to let me know."

Quinn nodded once and stepped away from the truck. "Sure. But you're looking for the wrong guy. What you ought to do is, find out what David Newman did after he left the bar last night."

Enos muttered something and started to back the truck away, but Fred couldn't leave without knowing the answer to one more question. He rolled down his window and leaned partway out. "If Webb's so miserable, why is he still with Margaret?"

Quinn lifted both shoulders in a gesture of futility. "For the kids, man. Just for the kids."

Enos didn't give either of them a chance to say more. He backed the truck in a wide arc and sped through the gate again. "I'm taking you home."

Fred shook his head. "I'm okay. I don't want to go home. Let's try Lamar's place next."

Enos's jaw tightened. "Absolutely not."

Fred shifted in his seat to face his friend. "I'm all right," he said again.

But Enos didn't even let him finish his thought. "You're not going with me."

"Dammit, Enos— Quit being so bullheaded and listen for a minute."

"No, Fred. *You* listen." Enos dragged his eyes off the road long enough for Fred to see that he meant business. "This isn't going to be an easy investigation. Hell, I've already heard things I don't want to hear, and so have you. And I have a real sick feelings it's only going to get worse."

Fred couldn't deny that.

"I made a mistake letting you come with me in the first place," Enos insisted. "But I don't have to compound it."

"But—"

"No." Enos glared at him. "Even if I wasn't concerned about you—which I am—what in the hell makes you think people will talk to me honestly about Webb with you sitting there?"

"Quinn just did, didn't he?" Fred demanded.

Enos flicked an uneasy glance in his direction.

Fred stared back. *Hadn't* Quinn been honest? He snapped his mouth shut and thought back over their conversation. What had Enos heard that Fred hadn't? "I can't just sit at home and do nothing."

"Well, you're going to have to find something else to do. You aren't coming with me."

They'd been friends too many years for Fred to misread Enos's expression. Any argument he offered now would only make things worse. He sighed and looked out the window at the blur of trees. "You'll go to Lamar's place next?"

"I will."

"You'll let me know—"

"Whatever I can."

Fred leaned his head back against the seat and closed his eyes. And he tried to force himself to be content with what Enos could offer. "Do you think it's true?" he asked after several minutes had passed.

"Do I think what's true?"

"That Webb's only staying with Margaret for the kids?"

"I don't know, Fred. I honestly don't."

No, of course, he didn't. Fred drew in a steadying breath and let it out again slowly. And he wondered how much worse Margaret and Webb would let things get before they finally put an end to their marriage.

On second thought, how much worse *could* things get? Fred opened his eyes and stared at the road through the windshield. He had a horrible feeling he was about to find out.

twelve

Fred walked quickly down the path along the shores of Spirit Lake and tried to find some pleasure in his surroundings. The afternoon sun beat down on his shoulders, the air smelled of rich, damp soil and new leaves, and the sounds of the forest surrounded him.

He usually walked this trail only once a day—early in the mornings for his daily constitutional. But this afternoon, waiting for word of Webb's arrest, he couldn't sit still.

Enos had already been gone over two hours; surely, Fred should have heard *something* by now. He'd spent the first hour sitting in his rocking chair, staring out his front window, and waiting. When he'd grown too nervous to sit any longer, he'd tried tidying up a bit. But he'd finally given up and come outside.

Physical exercise would make him feel better. A quiet walk around the lake would help him clear his mind. It had to. He didn't know how much longer he could wait.

Skirting a drop-off, he ducked beneath the branches of a chokecherry bush and straightened again. He tried to lose himself in nature, but he couldn't stop his mind from replaying the conversations he'd had with Tito, Albán, Kent, and Quinn. And he couldn't stop worrying.

As he rounded a curve in the path, he caught sight of a patch of black moving through the trees ahead. Slowing his step, he watched for a few seconds, then groaned aloud when he realized he was about to run smack-dab into Summer Dey.

Summer was a strange woman, one Fred preferred to avoid

whenever he could. She'd come to Cutler fifteen years earlier to pursue what she referred to as her art. Fred had never seen her wear anything but black—all black. Rumor had it, she dressed that way to keep herself depressed so she could paint. Fred had seen the results of her efforts. Privately, he thought she ought to try a change of wardrobe.

He halted in his tracks and looked around for a place to hide. Maybe she hadn't seen him. Maybe he could turn around and disappear before she realized he was there.

Pivoting on his heel, he took a couple of quick steps back the way he'd come.

"Fred?"

Obviously, he hadn't been quick enough.

"Fred?"

He ignored her and kept walking, but he could hear her footsteps on the path as she scurried after him.

"Fred, wait." She'd drawn too close. He'd have trouble pretending not to hear.

Since he couldn't think of a way to continue ignoring her without being overtly rude, he pasted on a reluctant smile and faced her. "Hello, Summer."

"What are you doing here this time of day?"

"Walking. What are you doing here? Shouldn't you be at the store?"

A couple of years earlier, she'd bought one of the stores along Main Street and renamed it The Cosmic Tradition. Now she used it to sell things that smelled funny, tell fortunes, and indulge in all sorts of other New Age hogwash. And for some reason, she loved to spout her psychic mumbo jumbo at Fred whenever their paths crossed.

Studying his face intently, she closed the remaining distance between them. With her thin blonde hair hanging to the middle of her back, her pale blue eyes and broad, freckled face, she looked like a teenager straight out of the 1960s—until she got closer. "I don't let the clock rule my actions," she said with a delicate smile. "I knew there was a reason I stayed here after lunch, and I knew the universe would eventually tell me what that reason was."

Fred made a noncommittal response and tried stepping

around her. Maybe the universe would tell her to leave him alone.

It didn't. She blocked his path. "You're troubled."

Fred knew his worries were painted on his face. She didn't need to be a fortune-teller to see that. "I have a few things on my mind," he admitted.

She touched his sleeve. "There's been a death."

"Yes."

"Who?" Before he could answer, she rocked back on her heels and lifted one hand to her forehead. "No, don't tell me. It's a woman."

"Yes," Fred said again. But he wasn't impressed. She'd probably already heard rumors. News traveled fast in Cutler.

She closed her eyes and lifted her face to the sun. Fred wondered whether he could sneak away while she wasn't looking, but before he could move, her eyes flew open again. "Lenore Irvine?"

"Word's out, then."

She scowled at him. "You think I'm pretending, don't you? You think I heard about the murder from someone, and I'm trying to trick you now?"

That's exactly what Fred thought, but he didn't want to admit it and leave himself open for the discussion that would follow. "I don't know what I think."

"You're confused," she said. "And frightened, aren't you?"

Now *there* was a trick. "I have a lot on my mind."

Summer smiled gently and folded her arms across her chest. "What is it going to take to make a believer out of you?"

A believer? In her ridiculous notions? Fred snorted a response and took another step away.

Summer obviously had no intention of letting him get away. She caught his sleeve again and tried to look deep into his eyes. A breeze wafted past, lifting a lock of her baby-fine hair to the sunlight, then dropping it again, and her eyes took on a dreamy expression. "You should remove yourself from the trouble this time."

Fred was *trying* to remove himself. She wouldn't let him go.

"You're going to uncover truths you don't want to know about," she warned.

He'd already done that when he uncovered the truth about Webb.

Summer's expression sobered. "There's heartache ahead for you and for Maggie. I can see it clearly." Fred tugged his arm away and backed out of her reach, but she kept herself planted squarely in his path. "You're searching for peace of mind, aren't you?"

Fred didn't even want to waste his time responding to her foolishness. He opened his mouth to say so, but her eyes suddenly popped wide open and she staggered back a step.

"You're looking in the wrong place," she whispered.

Fred snorted again. "I suppose you know where Webb is?"

Her eyes narrowed and her brow creased, as if following him cost a great effort. "I don't think that's what this means. I think you're looking for the wrong person."

Fred snorted again. "Are you trying to tell me you know who the murderer is?"

Summer shook her head quickly. "I don't know. But I *do* know you must be very careful this time."

"Bunch of foolishness," Fred muttered and vowed to be more careful about letting her catch him off guard in the future.

"This isn't *me* talking," she said. "And it's not foolishness. This is advice from my spirit guides. From the universe. You should listen."

But Fred had no intention of listening to anything else Summer had to say. He didn't need to be told about Margaret's heartache. He already knew what she had in store; he just didn't know the best way to help her get through it. And he refused to stand in the middle of the path, flapping Margaret's personal troubles about in front of someone like Summer Day.

Determined not to let her waylay him any longer, he stepped off the path and walked around her as quickly as his old knees would move. "I don't need advice from your spirit guides."

This time, she didn't try to stop him.

Fred breathed a sigh of relief and tried to put distance between them.

"Don't discount the power of the collective consciousness," she called after him. "You can find comfort if you only know where to look."

Fred didn't respond. He just rounded the first bend in the trail and kept moving. Summer thought he could find comfort if he knew where to look, did she? He already knew where to look. He'd find comfort when Enos had Webb safely behind bars. He'd find peace the day Margaret's divorce from the bum became final. He wouldn't find either talking to Summer.

Muttering under his breath the whole way, he made the return trip home in half the time it had taken him to reach Summer's place. But just as his back deck came into view, someone on the path ahead caught his eye.

Allowing himself an annoyed sigh, he looked closer. It was a woman; he could tell that much even at a distance. Less than a breath later he recognized Margaret.

She paced between the water's edge and the old fishing boat Fred hadn't used in years. She looked agitated. Upset. And Fred wasn't the cause this time.

He pulled in a steadying breath and worked up a smile as he drew closer. "This is a surprise," he said, leaning forward to kiss her cheek.

She pulled back and fixed him with a stern look. "What in the hell's going on, Dad?"

Though he'd sensed her uneasiness, the question still caught him a bit off guard. "What do you mean?"

"I want to know why you've been asking questions about Webb all day. Why you and *Enos* have been asking questions about him."

"How in the hell—"

She leaned against one of the spruce trees at the water's edge and smirked at him. "How did I find out you're nosing around again? It doesn't take long for word to get out—you ought to know that."

He did, but he hadn't expected word of his activities to leak out so soon. He gestured toward the bench he'd built for

Phoebe years ago and tried to hide his concern. "Why don't we sit down?"

Margaret straightened her shoulders and pulled away as if he'd tried to touch her. "I don't want to sit down. I want to know what's going on."

"And I'll tell you," Fred said gently. "If you'll sit down with me."

She heaved a disgusted sigh and spent a few seconds thinking about his suggestion. He could see her arguing with herself in every move she made. "All right," she said at last and pushed away from the tree. But she crossed to the bench gingerly and perched on the far edge. "Now, spill it."

Fred brushed dirt and leaves from the exposed seat and tried to come up with a reasonable explanation before he lowered himself onto the bench beside her. "You're right. I've been looking for Webb."

"I know that part. Why?"

"Because Enos has some questions he needs to ask him." So did Fred, but he didn't mention those.

"About Lenore Irvine's murder?" Her eyes glinted with that peculiar golden light, and Fred knew he should tread lightly.

He considered lying to her, but that would only make matters worse between them in the long run. "Yes."

She shot to her feet and paced a few steps away. "I don't believe it," she said, tucking a lock of dark hair behind one ear. "I honestly do not believe this. You really think Webb killed her, don't you?"

Fred didn't answer right away. Strangely his silence seemed to calm her down. Or maybe it worried her.

She took a step back toward him. "Dad—"

Her voice pleaded with him to deny the accusation, but he couldn't. "Yes."

"Because of the dent in his fender?"

"Partly."

"Why don't you just ask him about it?"

"I can't find him."

Margaret ticked her tongue against the roof of her mouth. "He's at work."

Fred dreaded this part. He shook his head slowly and met her gaze. "He's not at Tito's."

"Don't be ridiculous. Of course, he is."

"No, Margaret." He held out a hand to her and beckoned her back toward the bench, but he didn't speak again until she resumed her place on the seat. "The truth is, Webb doesn't work for Tito anymore."

She laughed, but she managed only one harsh note before her smile faded and her eyes grew serious again.

"Tito fired him last week."

"That's ridiculous," she said and started to rise again. "Where did you hear that?"

This time, Fred held her in place. "Tito told me about it this morning. Webb left Lenore Irvine's brake lines loose, and Tito found the mistake." he watched as the realization dawned in her dark eyes. He would have given almost anything to spare her the pain he saw mirrored there.

"It's not true," she said softly. "It can't be." She tried to sound assured, but Fred could hear the doubt in her voice.

"It is true. Tito hasn't said anything because he's trying to keep gossip to a minimum for your sake and for the kids."

"Why didn't he tell *me?*"

Fred resisted the urge to lower his gaze to avoid having to witness her pain. "I don't know, sweetheart."

She sat for a moment, staring at the water. "Enos thinks Webb is guilty of murder?"

"He's checking into it."

"Oh, my God." She did little more than breathe the words, but Fred felt as if she'd stabbed him with them. "It can't be true, Dad. It just can't be." She turned to face him and gripped both of his hands. "I know Webb drinks too much. I know he has a terrible temper, but he isn't a murderer."

Fred didn't respond immediately. He honestly didn't know what to say.

Margaret gripped his hands even tighter. "You've got to help him."

"Help Webb?"

"Yes. You've got to find out who really killed Lenore."

Fred already knew who killed Lenore. He didn't think

Margaret would consider what he knew helpful. "Sweetheart, I—"

"I'm serious, Dad. You're always sticking your nose into Enos's investigations, and I'm always begging you to stop. Well, this time, I'm begging you to *do* it."

"Do you really believe Webb's innocent?"

"Yes!"

"Why?"

"Because I know he didn't do it."

Fred wished it were true. "Margaret, sweetheart, listen to me—"

But she didn't want to listen. She dropped his hands as if they'd suddenly burst into flame and shot to her feet again. "Are you refusing?"

He didn't like to hear it phrased quite like that. "There's just too much evidence against him."

She scowled. "That's never stopped you before."

"Sweetheart—"

She held up both hands to stop him. "I don't believe this. You'll help everybody else, but you won't lift a finger to help your own son-in-law."

"That's not exactly—"

"What about Sarah and Benjamin and Deborah? Are you going to just *sit* here and do nothing while their father is accused of murder?"

"I—"

"You're going to let all of us suffer the gossip, the raised eyebrows, the whispers behind our backs and not lift a finger to help?"

Fred closed his eyes and pulled in a deep breath. He had to say it, no matter how much it hurt her. "Margaret, I don't believe he's innocent."

"Then you won't help him?"

He couldn't do anything but shake his head.

Tears filled her eyes. She dashed them away with the back of her hand and glared at him for a minute. Waves lapped gently against the shore, marking time as he waited for her to say something else. A breeze teased him with the fresh scent of the forest and the lake. If he closed his eyes, he could almost make himself believe everything was fine.

But he kept his eyes open and watched as Margaret turned slowly and walked away without even looking at him again.

Fred forced himself not to go after her. He couldn't do anything for Webb. He couldn't offer Margaret false hope or prove something that wasn't true. But his heart felt heavy, and he couldn't help wondering if he'd just made the biggest mistake of his life.

thirteen

Fred stacked his dinner bowl in the cupboard, dried his hands, and turned to survey the kitchen. He hadn't eaten much. His appetite had definitely been affected by his argument with Margaret. He'd tried one of his favorites—oyster stew sneaked in from its hiding place in the garage, dolloped with butter, and blackened with pepper—but it hadn't held its usual appeal.

He reminded himself once again that he was right—Webb was guilty, and that was that. But he couldn't wipe the image of Margaret's tearful face from his mind.

Well, he wouldn't think about it anymore. He'd finally read the morning paper and watch some television—anything to keep his mind occupied. Snagging his reading glasses from the top of the refrigerator, he flipped off the kitchen light just as the telephone rang into the stillness.

Enos, finally calling to report that he'd arrested Webb.

Fred dropped his glasses to the table and yanked the receiver off the hook before the second ring. "Hello? Enos?"

"Dad?" Joseph's voice boomed through the wire into the silent kitchen.

Fred struggled to keep disappointment from his voice. "Yes?"

"I'm glad I caught you. I tried to call earlier, but you must have been out?"

"I was."

Joseph waited, as if he expected Fred to explain where he'd been.

Fred didn't.

"I see," Joseph said at last. "Listen, Dad. I talked to Doc Huggins today—"

Wonderful. Doc had been flapping his gums again about Fred's health, and Joseph was all set to rehash yesterday's argument. But Fred wasn't in the mood for it.

Joseph didn't give him a chance to say so. "He explained the results of your test to me, and I've got to admit, I feel a lot better."

"That's good."

"He's convinced me you're not in any real danger at the moment."

About time for some good news. Fred relaxed a bit. "Well, I'm glad to hear it."

"So, I thought I'd better call and tell you I've changed my mind about the retirement home."

Even better. Fred smiled. "I'm *real* glad to hear that."

Joseph chuckled softly, and Fred felt himself warming up to his eldest son for the first time in days. "Anyway, Gail and I have been talking about it this afternoon, and we've come up with another solution."

"Solution?" The word wiped the smile off Fred's face. "To what?"

"To the whole issue of you living way out there on your own. We want you to move in here. With us."

Fred froze. He should have known better than to relax around Joseph. He was *not* in the mood for this. Lowering himself into a seat by the table, he spoke clearly and slowly to make sure Joseph understood every word. "I'm not moving anywhere."

"Now, Dad—"

"No discussion, Joseph. I'm not leaving my home."

"I'm serious, Dad. You're getting up there, you know."

Up there? Fred snorted his response and refrained from asking just where *there* was.

"You really shouldn't be alone."

"I do fine on my own."

"But you're *not* on your own," Joseph argued. "Margaret has to check on you every day."

"Margaret doesn't have to check on me, she just does it. Makes her feel better, I suppose."

The response didn't seem to faze Joseph. "Quite honestly, I'm worried about her. I'm just trying to take some of the burden off her shoulders." He made it sound as if having Fred around was like scrubbing the toilet. "She's trying to deal with too much at once."

Joseph had no idea how much Margaret had to deal with, and Fred had no intention of setting him straight. "And you're going to fix it for her." Joseph had long considered it his responsibility to fix everything for his sister and younger brothers. But, as always, he had no clue what they needed.

"I'm afraid having you there—being responsible for you—is putting a strain on her marriage."

Margaret's marriage was strained, all right. But not because of Fred. Fred opened his mouth to respond, but something Quinn Udy said earlier rushed back into his memory. *There's nothing in this place for Webb, but he can't leave—Maggie won't leave her dad.*

His stomach knotted, and the headache he'd been fighting all day revved itself up a notch. He shook his head as if he could stop the memory of Quinn's voice that way, but the words played over and over in his mind and an unwelcome smidgen of self-doubt reared its ugly head.

Maggie won't leave her dad.

"Dad?" Joseph demanded. "Are you there? Are you all right?"

"I'm here."

Joseph breathed a sigh of relief. "Gail and I haven't wanted to say anything before now, but we really think things there have reached a crisis. We honestly believe it'll be the best thing—for you *and* for Margaret—if you come here for a while."

Fred deliberately misunderstood him. "A while? Well, I suppose I could visit for a few weeks. But not right away."

Joseph went on as if he hadn't heard a word. "The case I'm working on right now will be over by the end of the month. I can fly out there in June and help you get the house on the market."

Put his house on the market? Never. Fred's throat tightened painfully. He glanced around the kitchen he'd shared with Phoebe. She'd been gone almost four years now, but she was still in every inch of the house. Living here with her memory was the only thing that kept Fred going some days.

"I'm not leaving here," he said, but to his embarrassment, his voice came out thick with emotion.

"I *know* it will be hard to leave," Joseph said gently. "That's why I'm coming out there. We can have you settled here by summer."

Fred glared at the receiver and wondered how Joseph had ever become so successful in his law practice without the ability to understand simple sentences. "I'm not leaving my home."

"Dad—"

"No."

Joseph let out a heavy sigh. "You're not being rational."

"I'm being completely rational," Fred snapped. "I'm not leaving my home while there's a breath left in my body."

Another sigh. "Be reasonable . . ."

"I am being reasonable," Fred assured him.

"No, you're not. You're not even thinking about Margaret and what this is doing to her. You're not thinking about Gail or me or our kids. You're not thinking about anyone but yourself." Fred hadn't heard Joseph use that tone in many years. He hadn't liked it when Joseph was a boy—he didn't like it now.

"Has Margaret complained?"

"Well— No. Not in so many words. But you know how she is. She suffers in silence."

That was certainly true of her marriage, but Fred resented the implication that he might be responsible for even one second of her unhappiness. "Now listen, Joseph—" he began but broke off again when someone knocked on his back door.

He looked out the window and caught a glimpse of his grandson Benjamin.

Benjamin lifted one hand to wave, then changed his mind and shoved his fingers through his sheaf of blond hair. He looked over his shoulder, back at Fred, and shifted from foot to foot. Something was obviously troubling him.

Fred motioned him inside and turned his attention back to Joseph. "This conversation has gone as far as it's going to go," he said.

Joseph sighed once more, as if dealing with Fred required more patience than he had. It probably did. Patience had never come easily to Joseph. "If you're going to act like this, I'm not going to be responsible—"

That did it. "Nobody asked you to be responsible," Fred shouted. "Nobody *wants* you to be responsible. I'm your father, dammit, not your son. And I'm perfectly capable of taking care of myself."

"See—?" Joseph began.

But Fred cut him off again. "I'm hanging up now. Benjamin's here."

"That's another thing," Joseph shouted. "Have you ever thought that *my* kids might like having you around for a while? They hardly know you."

"Well, now, whose fault is that?" Fred demanded, and for the second time in as many days he slammed the receiver in Joseph's ear.

Benjamin stopped just inside the back door and stared at the telephone, then slowly turned his gaze on Fred. In the months since his sixteenth birthday, he'd finally started to mature. His shoulders had grown broader, his arms and legs a bit thicker, and his voice had dropped an octave. "Who was *that*?"

"Your uncle, the idiot," Fred growled and pointed toward an empty seat at the table.

"Uncle Joe?"

Even Benjamin could see the truth about Joseph. Fred felt better already. He pulled the chair away from the table. "Come on. Sit down and help me forget he called."

Benjamin moved slightly closer, but he looked almost reluctant to get too close.

Fred wiped some of the anger from his expression. "Just ignore all that," he said with a wave of a hand toward the telephone. "What's on your mind?"

Instead of joining him, Benjamin leaned against the wall and shoved his hands into his pockets. "I want to know if it's true you're trying to get my dad arrested."

The question caught Fred by surprise. "Where on earth did you hear that?"

"It's all over town. Everybody's talking about it."

For hell's sake. Fred held back a dismayed groan and patted the table. "I think you'd better sit down. Sounds like we need to talk."

Benjamin shook his head. "I don't want to talk. I just want to know if it's true."

This wasn't like Benjamin. Fred used his most reassuring voice and tacked on a smile for good measure. "I'm not trying to do anything."

"Then why were you looking for him today?"

Fred thought of a couple of weak excuses but discarded them immediately. He didn't want to actually *lie*. "Because when I saw him drive past this morning and I saw the damage to his truck, I got worried. I wanted to give him a chance to explain before somebody else saw it and jumped to conclusions."

Benjamin eyed him warily, and Fred hoped he looked a little less angry. "If that's true, why did you tell Sheriff Asay about it? You know how much he hates my dad."

"Sheriff Asay doesn't hate your dad—"

"Yes, he does, and you know it, Grandpa. Dad says it's because Sheriff Asay's never forgiven him for stealing Mom away."

Good hell. What was Webb thinking to tell the boy a thing like that? "I don't think that's exactly right," Fred said slowly. He'd never discussed Margaret and Enos with any of his grandchildren before, and he had no idea what to say now.

He tried to imagine Phoebe in this situation. She'd have known exactly what to say. She'd been blessed with an instinct for dealing with this sort of thing and a way with words Fred could never hope to match. The only thing he knew for certain was that Phoebe would have been honest.

"If Enos isn't exactly fond of your dad," Fred said, "it's because Enos doesn't think he treats your mom real good."

Benjamin scowled at him. "Yeah? Well, it isn't any of his business, is it?"

"Only as her friend," Fred agreed. "No matter what happened between Enos and your mom, they've always been good friends. He worries about her, that's all."

"He doesn't need to."

Fred sighed softly. "Listen, Benjamin. You're raising issues that maybe I shouldn't talk with you about, but you're not a little boy anymore. You know your parents have trouble sometimes . . ."

Benjamin refused to even look at him.

"Most of those troubles are caused by your dad's drinking." Fred had never voiced that concern aloud to any of Webb's children before, and he felt slightly uncomfortable doing it now.

Benjamin nodded. "Yeah, but—" He broke off suddenly and his shoulders slumped. "Yeah. I guess."

"It hasn't been easy for your mom to live with that, and it hasn't been easy for any of us who love her to watch. Those who love her—" He broke off and amended, "her *friends* are concerned about her. They don't like to see her unhappy."

Benjamin pulled his hands from his pockets, his narrow face reddened, and his eyes flashed with anger. "She's *not* unhappy."

For half a second, Fred thought Benjamin might actually believe that. In the next moment, he saw the look in the boy's eyes. Benjamin knew the truth as well as Fred did, but he thought he could change it out of sheer force of will. Well, wanting a thing had never made it so—especially something like this.

Fred reached a hand toward him. "Benjamin—"

The boy jerked away. "*You're* the one making her unhappy, Grandpa. You and Sheriff Asay. You've decided my dad's a murderer, and you're going around town telling everybody."

"I haven't decided anything," Fred said as calmly as he could. "And I'm certainly not spreading gossip that your dad's responsible for Lenore Irvine's death."

"How do you know my dad's truck's the one the killer used?"

"I don't," Fred admitted. "Not for certain. But it seems too much of a coincidence that it has exactly the kind of damage the murderer's vehicle should have. And nobody seems to remember anything wrong with the truck before today."

"Did you ask my dad about it?" Benjamin demanded.

"I can't find him."

"Then how do you know somebody else didn't wreck it? Maybe somebody backed into him."

"I wish I could believe that."

Benjamin glared at him. "Do you know how this makes me feel? My own grandpa . . ." He threw up his hands in a gesture of futility. "Hell, Grandpa— You might as well just say *I* killed him. It couldn't be any worse."

"But you didn't," Fred said softly. "I'm not manufacturing evidence against him, son. I'm only telling you the truth."

Benjamin's face reddened, and his mouth worked for a second or two as if he intended to offer another argument.

Fred waited, hoping the boy would say something that might help. But in the end, Benjamin wheeled away and tore open the door. "Just leave my dad alone, Grandpa. He didn't do anything."

Without giving Fred a chance to respond, he raced out into the waning sunlight and slammed the door behind him.

fourteen

Fred muttered to himself as he walked up Lake Front Drive in the cool morning air and tried to think of some way to bring up the subject of Lenore Irvine's murder with Enos again. He'd tossed and turned all night, remembering the look on Margaret's face when he refused to help Webb and reliving the moment when Benjamin stormed out of the house.

By the time he'd finished his morning constitutional around the lake shore, he'd decided to go through the motions for Margaret's sake and for Benjamin's. And that meant he had to look for evidence of Webb's innocence, whether he believed in his son-in-law or not. If in the process, he found proof that Webb was guilty, Margaret and Benjamin would have to accept that.

If Enos had any evidence of Webb's guilt, Fred needed to know. But he couldn't just ask. Enos had a tendency to jump to conclusions, and if Fred asked about the murder, Enos would conclude that he was trying to involve himself in the investigation.

No, Fred couldn't ask any direct questions. He'd have to use tact. Finesse. Subtlety.

Pausing on the corner of Main Street, he looked up and down the block, scouring parked vehicles for Enos's truck. The morning sun gilded the trees with the promise of spring, and a soft breeze carried the clean scent of life renewing itself. But to Fred, the beauty of his surroundings felt almost like a cruel joke.

He couldn't see Enos's truck anywhere. Blast. Now what should he do?

He hesitated for a moment and watched the window of the sheriff's office as he pondered his options. One of the deputies should be there, but that didn't mean they would be. Enos didn't like leaving the office unmanned during a workday, but Ivan liked to patrol in his new Bronco too much to stay indoors.

While Fred watched, a shadow crossed in front of the window. Good. Someone was there, and judging from the shadow's height, Fred figured it must be Grady.

Grady should know whether Enos had found Webb and how close they were to an arrest. The boy had a tendency to get a bit testy when he was in the middle of an investigation, but talking to him couldn't be any worse than talking to Enos. Six of one, half dozen of another, Fred supposed.

Besides, Grady *had* driven Webb home from the Copper Penny the night of the murder, and he just might know more about Webb's frame of mind that night than anyone else. It couldn't hurt to ask.

Tucking his hands in his pockets, Fred sauntered across the intersection and onto the boardwalk. He whistled softly, a tune his father had whistled when Fred was a boy, and did his best to look casual when he opened the door.

Grady stood with his back to Fred. He had both hands in the filing cabinet, and his shoulders hunched in concentration. He looked up as Fred entered and marked his place in the drawer with one hand. "What are you doing here, Fred? No. Don't tell me. Let me guess. The Irvine murder, right?"

Very funny. Fred tried not to look annoyed. "As a matter of fact, I just stopped by to say hello."

Grady nodded slowly and frowned slightly. "Yeah. Right." He pulled his hand out of the filing cabinet and pushed the drawer closed. "Okay, what do you want to know? Or did you stop by to tell us you've solved the case already?"

Impudent young whelp. Fred kept his face stoic. "Actually, I was hoping to find Enos here. Have you heard from him?"

"No, and I don't expect to any time soon. Henry Chambers

and Ralph Mikesell are at each others' throats over that property line again."

Fred rolled his eyes. He figured two grown men ought to be able to settle their differences without the sheriff, but Henry and Ralph obviously didn't agree. Crossing the room, he dropped into one of the chairs in front of the battered wooden desk. "Another episode of Mutt verses Jeff? That's all Enos needs. What set them off this time?"

Grady waved an impatient hand. "Henry's been talking about putting a casino on that north section of his, and Ralph's decided he'd rather see Henry dead first."

"Well, that'll keep Enos busy a while." Fred let out a sympathetic sigh, shook his head, and looked around the room as if he didn't have anything specific to talk about. "Do you know if he's had a chance to talk with Webb yet?"

Grady's expression sobered. Positioning himself behind the desk, he squared his shoulders and tried to look authoritative. "I don't know, but even if I did, I wouldn't tell you. This is an official—"

"An official investigation," Fred said with him. "I know. And *you* know that the prime suspect happens to be my son-in-law. You can't blame me for being curious, can you?"

"He's *one* of the suspects," Grady snapped.

Interesting. Fred allowed himself a thin smile. "You're investigating other people, too?"

Grady nodded, but he didn't say anything. He looked suspicious, as if he thought Fred might be trying to put something over on him.

"Well, that's encouraging," Fred said. "Margaret will be glad to hear it. She's convinced Webb's innocent."

"Yeah?" Grady smirked at him. "Well, everybody's innocent unless they're proven guilty, Fred. That's the way our system works."

Fred didn't need Grady to educate him about the legal system, and he almost said so. But he did need Grady to tell him what he wanted to know. So he bit back his frustration and tried to keep his smile in place. "Has Enos had a chance to talk to Lamar Templeton?"

Grady looked wary. Suspicious.

Fred broadened his smile.

"Yes," Grady said at last. "But he claims he hasn't seen Webb for over a week."

Fred didn't believe that, but he knew the lie had come from Lamar, not Grady, so he didn't say a word. "I understand you're the one who drove Webb home after that mess at the Copper Penny the other night."

The young man's expression stiffened. "Yeah, I was."

"I suppose I'd rest a bit easier if I knew what frame of mind he was in when you dropped him off."

Grady didn't rush to set his mind at ease. In fact, he didn't say a word.

Fred tried prodding him. "I've heard all sorts of rumors, of course."

Still nothing.

"Actually," Fred said, stretching in an attempt to look casual and unconcerned, "a number of people seem to think David Newman was more upset that night than Webb was."

Grady cocked an eyebrow at him. "Yeah?"

"Yeah." Fred stretched again and let a moment of silence hang between them. "Believe it or not," he said at last, "I don't have any desire to get involved in this investigation."

Grady let his irritating smirk grow a bit. "I *don't* believe it."

"It's true," Fred assured him. "Every scrap of evidence so far points straight at my son-in-law as the murderer. Can you imagine what it would do to Margaret if I were responsible in any way for putting him behind bars?" He shook his head as if the idea didn't bear thinking about. "She's upset enough just knowing he's a suspect."

Grady considered that for a moment. "Well, cheer up. There were plenty of other people in town who didn't like Lenore. Webb's not the only one with a motive."

Fred looked supremely innocent. "Oh?"

Perching on the edge of the desk, Grady rested one elbow on his sidearm. "You're right about David Newman—he was one of the angriest, but Mrs. Irvine upset a lot of people. And if Hannah hadn't shown up when she did . . ." He shrugged and shook his head. "Who knows what would have happened?"

Fred pretended surprise. "I thought Hannah Irvine was still too young to be in a bar. What was she doing there?"

"I don't know," Grady admitted. "Maybe she was worried about her stepmother. Or about her dad. She's like that, you know."

Fred nodded. After seeing her with her father the day before, he could easily believe that. His grandchildren were exactly the same way. "How old is she now?"

Grady gave his answer some thought. "She's about Benjamin's age, isn't she? Maybe a year older. I think she graduates this year." He laughed softly, but the sound held no humor. "You should have seen the way Mrs. Irvine reacted when she realized Hannah was inside the bar. She was on that committee, you know—PFAAD or whatever it is. And you know how worried she always was about appearances and setting a good example." He allowed himself another soft chuckle. "And there were her own stepdaughters in that bar—" He sent Fred a meaningful look. "That's what got her and Kent arguing, you know."

Fred didn't know. He leaned forward and tried not to appear too eager. "Did you say her own step*daughters*? Plural?"

Grady stiffened, as if he hadn't realized what he'd said. "Yeah," he said slowly. "Paige was there, too."

"Paige? Is she Kent's oldest?"

"Yeah." Grady stepped away from the desk, rubbed the back of his neck, and let out a burst of air. "I thought you knew."

"Knew what?"

"I thought you knew Paige was there."

"Why would I know that? I told you, Grady. I'm not getting involved this time."

"Yeah, yeah. I know that's what you said."

"So—Why would I know anything about Paige Irvine?" Fred mixed righteous indignation with a dash of honest curiosity.

"Because." Grady met his gaze, but he obviously had to

force himself. "She was sitting at Webb's table. That's why Lenore got so upset with him. She started yelling at him and accusing him of . . . all sorts of crap."

Fred's heart settled like a stone in his chest. "What sorts of crap?"

"*You* know."

Fred suspected he knew very well, and he wasn't at all certain he wanted to hear it, but he pressed the issue anyway. "You mean she accused them of having an affair?"

"In so many words."

Fred had to force himself not to leave his chair. This must have been what Quinn had tried so hard not to say. And why Enos had let Quinn's elusive answers slide. Enos must have already heard the rumors before he and Fred paid their visit to Quinn, and he'd purposely avoided telling Fred. Albán must have known and kept silent as well.

"Are they having an affair?" Fred asked around the thickness in his throat.

Grady didn't want to discuss it; Fred could see that in his face.

Fred didn't care. "*Are* they?"

"Nobody knows," Grady said. He sounded miserable. "But Casey tells me they were looking pretty friendly."

Anger burned up Fred's neck and into his cheeks. "I didn't even know Paige Irvine was in town. When did she arrive?"

"I don't know. To tell you the truth, I was surprised when I found out who she was. I'd heard there was some sort of trouble between her and her parents. As far as *I* knew, she never even came to visit them."

"What kind of trouble?"

Grady shrugged. "I don't know, exactly. I don't even remember how I heard about it, unless Hannah said something about it when we were on the Fourth of July committee together last year." He looked down at his boots again. "Look, I shouldn't have told you about Paige and Webb, so just forget I said anything, okay? Enos will kill me if he finds out you know."

Fred wasn't likely to forget, and he didn't like being the victim of a conspiracy of silence. In that moment, he didn't care whether Enos liked him knowing or not. He pushed himself to his feet and started away, then turned back with one more question. "Is Paige still in town?"

Grady's expression grew almost frantic. "You *can't* talk to her, Fred."

"Did I say I was going to talk to her?"

"No," Grady said slowly. "But that doesn't mean you aren't thinking about it. If Enos finds out you've been to see her, he'll know you've found out somehow. And it will only be a matter of time before he figures out I told you."

"He won't hear about it," Fred assured him.

Grady didn't look at all reassured. He stood and tried to use his height to look intimidating. "I'm serious, Fred."

"So am I," Fred said. "Don't worry about it."

"If you talk to her, you'll be interfering with an official investigation," Grady warned, then added softly, "Not that that's ever stopped you before."

Fred didn't find the comment amusing. He crossed to the door and yanked it open. "All I want is for my daughter and grandchildren to be safe and happy. If Webb murdered Lenore Irvine, I want his butt in jail. And if he's cheating on Margaret, I intend to know about it."

Grady started toward the door. "You *can't* say anything to Maggie." He sounded nervous.

Fred glared at him. "Believe me, the last thing I'm going to do is run to Margaret with a rumor like this. She has enough to deal with already." He shut the door behind him and stormed away, but he stopped when he reached the end of the boardwalk to pull himself together.

His stomach rolled, his head throbbed, and his heart pounded a bit too fast for comfort. He gripped a four-by-four post near the steps of the boardwalk and tried to slow his breathing and cool his temper. But he was angrier than he'd been in a long time—with Webb, with Enos for keeping news like this from him, even with Albán.

He supposed he should be glad Enos hadn't found Webb yet. He didn't often feel the urge to hit another human being, but if he'd known where to find Webb at that moment, he'd have kicked the son of a bitch from one end of the county to the other.

Dragging in a steadying breath, he told himself he couldn't accomplish anything this way. This upset, he'd be no good to Margaret or the kids. But nothing cooled his anger.

Maybe, he thought illogically, he should have listened to Summer Dey. After all, she'd warned him to leave well enough alone.

Barking an angry laugh, he let go of the post, straightened his shoulders, and focused on his surroundings. He smiled and waved at Loralee Kirkham as if life were normal, and he put one foot in front of the other and stepped into the warm spring sunshine.

But life wasn't normal. And Fred wondered whether it ever would be again.

fifteen

Fred hurried home along Lake Front Drive, opened the garage, and fired up the Buick. Retracing his route into town, he stopped briefly at the sign on the corner of Main Street and shot across the intersection.

He hoped Grady hadn't noticed him. Everyone knew Fred never drove anywhere he could walk. If Grady saw him in the Buick, he'd know Fred had something in mind.

The warm spring sun had climbed high in the cloudless sky, and it played off the variations of green where the forest scrabbled up the snow-peaked mountains. Rolling down his window, Fred let the fresh air blow through the car, hoping it would help clear his mind and prepare him for what lay ahead.

Half of him wanted to find Webb at his father's house. The other half—Fred's more rational side—knew it would be best for everyone if he didn't see Webb for a while.

But his conversation with Grady had left him with too many questions. And he wanted answers. Now.

He drove across Kilburn's hill, past Spirit Lake, and turned off the highway onto a graded road just past the meadow of budding wildflowers. But as he started up the mountain, doubts began to worm their way into his mind.

Maybe he'd be making a mistake by paying Lamar Templeton a visit. Maybe he'd find Webb there and lose his temper, which would only make matters worse for Margaret and the kids. Trouble was, the rumors about Webb and Paige wouldn't leave him alone, and he knew he wouldn't rest until he learned the truth.

He didn't even know what he hoped to learn from Lamar. Even when they were younger, Fred hadn't been overly fond of him. The mere fact that he'd been responsible for producing Webb earned him a black mark in Fred's book. The way Lamar had encouraged Webb to pursue Margaret, the way he'd helped Webb set up the mortgage in his name alone—along with dozens of other such stunts over the years—hadn't done anything to alter Fred's opinion of the man.

Lamar always sided with Webb in any argument, and Fred didn't expect this time to be any different. If Lamar knew anything about Webb's relationship with Paige Irvine, he wasn't likely to tell Fred about it. But Fred had to ask.

He slowed the Buick and tried to think of the best way to approach Lamar as he drove the remaining three miles up the narrow road. Blunt questions wouldn't get him anywhere, but subtlety would be wasted on Lamar.

The three miles passed too quickly, and before he'd come up with any solid ideas, Fred found himself in front of Lamar's old wood-frame house. When Webb's mother had lived here, the place had been fairly nice to look at. She'd kept flowers planted in beds along the front of the house and managed to get Lamar to cut the lawn on a fairly regular basis.

Since the divorce Lamar had given into his natural instinct and let everything run to seed. The lawn had all but disappeared in the weeds, wild grass had grown up in the flower beds, and plant life of some kind Fred couldn't identify waved in the breeze against the north wall.

He pulled into the gravel drive and cut the engine, but he didn't get out of the car immediately. He couldn't see Webb's truck anywhere, but that didn't mean anything. Lamar had a number of old buildings around the perimeter, several of which would be large enough to conceal Webb's truck.

Pushing aside his mounting apprehension, Fred opened the car door and stepped onto the gravel. The curtain in the living room window twitched, letting him know someone inside was watching.

He stuffed his hands in his pockets and followed the drive to the chipped concrete porch. At the door, he lifted the knocker, but the nails had loosened, and the blasted thing came off in his hand.

Using his knuckles on the peeling wood, he knocked twice and waited. He could hear someone moving about inside, but whoever it was took several minutes to answer.

After what felt like forever, Lamar pulled the door open a crack and scowled out at Fred. "What do you want?"

Still as charming as ever. He hadn't changed a bit. "I'd like to talk to you for a minute," Fred said.

"What for?"

"Why don't you let me inside, and I'll tell you."

Lamar hesitated for a long moment before he opened the door the rest of the way. Even then he looked reluctant to let Fred inside.

Fred handed him the door knocker and stepped through the door. He caught a whiff of something sour. No wonder Lamar wanted to keep him outside. The air reeked of dog urine and something else that might have been rancid food. Fred breathed through his mouth and stole a glance at Lamar.

Lamar didn't seem to notice the stench. He shuffled across the room and stepped over several piles of unidentifiable rubbish. Pushing a jacket and a mud-crusted pair of jeans to the floor, the plopped into a sagging rocking chair and left Fred to fend for himself.

Fred considered remaining on his feet, then thought better of it. If he wanted to learn anything from Lamar, he probably shouldn't appear as disgusted as he felt. He shoved aside a stack of newspapers and perched on the edge of a couch with several bite-sized pieces missing from the upholstery.

Lamar's dog peered into the room from the kitchen, sniffed twice in Fred's direction, and started barking. Fred expected the animal to bound into the room and check out his credentials, but to his surprise the dog didn't move. Obviously, he shared Lamar's lack of ambition.

"Shut up," Lamar snapped without even looking at the dog.

The animal didn't listen. If anything it barked even louder. The sound echoed off the walls and set Fred's ears ringing.

"I said *shut up*," Lamar said, louder this time, and hurled a shoe toward the kitchen door. The shoe bounced off the wall less than two inches from the dog's big head and managed to convince the animal to stop barking. The animal lay in the doorway and propped its head on its front paws, but it didn't take its eyes from Fred.

Fred didn't mind if the dog stayed there. He just didn't want it to get any brilliant ideas about lunch. He did his best to find a comfortable position without touching more of the couch than he absolutely had to.

Lamar watched him readjust, scowled out of his beady eyes, and scratched his side. "So? What do you want?"

Fred gave up trying to get comfortable and propped his arms on his knees. "I'm trying to catch up with Webb. Have you seen him?"

"Why?" Lamar narrowed his eyes until they were little more than slits on either side of his red-veined nose. "What do you want him for?"

"I need to talk to him."

"What about?"

Fred didn't know the best way to answer that. Enos would have told Lamar about the murder, so he didn't waste time pretending to be here on an unrelated mission. He shifted position again but immediately shifted back when something sharp poked his backside. "I wondered whether Webb spent the night here Wednesday."

Lamar leaned back in his chair and slowly scratched his side. "Why? Did Maggie send you to check up on him? Or are you poking around where you shouldn't again?"

"Margaret doesn't know I'm here," Fred admitted.

"So, you're playing ace detective again?" Lamar stopped scratching and focused on Fred with bleary eyes. "I don't have to tell you a damned thing."

"I know you don't. But I'm hoping you're anxious to help Webb."

Lamar's expression grew wary. "You're trying to help Webb? I don't believe it."

"Margaret asked me to help."

"Did she?" Lamar pulled back as if the answer surprised

him. He studied his fingernails for a long moment and flicked something from the ring finger to the floor. "Why?"

"She's convinced he's innocent."

"Is she?" Lamar didn't look as if he believed that, either, but he didn't say so.

"Did Webb spend Wednesday night here with you?" Fred asked again.

Lamar didn't answer immediately. He rocked back in the chair and pondered for a while.

Fred tried to hold on to his quickly evaporating patience. But when several minutes passed and Lamar still didn't speak, he gave up. "Come on, Lamar. Don't play games with me."

Lamar squinted at him. "What if he did stay here Wednesday night? What's it going to help if I tell you?"

"If you can prove he was here, it'll give him an alibi. Was he here?"

Lamar shook his head slowly. "No."

The answer caught Fred off guard. He hadn't expected Lamar to offer the truth so easily. "Did you hear from him that night?"

"No."

"The next morning?"

Lamar shook his head again. "I haven't heard from him since the beginning of the week."

Fred didn't know what to say to that. According to Margaret, Webb came to see his father at least twice a week. "Do you have any idea where he is?"

"Nope. I don't keep tabs on him. He's a grown man."

He certainly didn't act like one. Or, maybe more accurately, he acted just like the one who'd raised him. "He could be in a lot of trouble," Fred warned.

Lamar shook his head. "I know my boy. He didn't do anything wrong."

"I hope you're right," Fred said and caught another whiff of dog urine.

"Course I am." Lamar gave his head one sharp nod for emphasis.

"Do you know anything about Webb's plans to take out a second mortgage and invest in the gambling petition?"

Lamar lifted one shoulder in a lazy shrug. "No. But it sounds like a good idea. It'd get him in on the ground floor. He could end up filthy stinkin' rich."

He *could*, Fred supposed, but he didn't think it likely. He didn't say so to Lamar. No sense starting an argument. "Has Webb ever mentioned Lenore Irvine to you?"

"The cow who wants to put an end to everything but church services?"

"The woman who was murdered."

Lamar snorted a half-laugh and looked at the dog. "Yeah. He's talked about her. She was always trying to start something with Webb. Always complaining. Always blaming him for corrupting kids just because he has a drink now and then."

Webb drank more often than that, but Fred still didn't correct Lamar. He'd been tipping the bottle almost as long as Fred had known him. From his perspective, Webb probably seemed like a social drinker. "What about Paige Irvine? Has Webb ever talked about her?"

"Who's that?" Lamar looked confused, but Fred couldn't tell whether he honestly couldn't place the name or was covering for Webb.

"A young woman who was with Webb the night of the murder. Has he ever mentioned her to you?"

"A young *woman?*" Lamar ran a gnarled hand over his stubbly chin and slanted a glance at Fred. "Well, I guess I'm not surprised. Figured it would come to this one day."

Anger, never far from the surface these days, boiled up again in Fred's chest. "Oh, you did, did you? Why?"

Lamar waved a careless hand. "That daughter of yours isn't exactly warm and loving, now, is she? A woman can only push a man away so long before he'll turn somewhere else to fill his needs."

Of course, Fred thought bitterly. Poor Webb. "If Margaret's pushing Webb away," he argued, "it's only because he's such a lousy husband. He's never home. He's drunk three-quarters of the time. And he hasn't been able to keep a job longer than a year or two their whole married life."

"He's worked steady," Lamar snapped. "Maybe not at the same job, but he's worked. Besides, what's he got to come home to? A bunch of bitching and moaning? Constant complaining? Demands that would drive any man to drink? And when she's not complaining, she's 'daddy-ing' him to death. It's 'dad says this' and 'dad thinks that.'" Lamar's voice rose in spiteful imitation. "What man in his right mind wants to hear that every night? Who can function on the job when just being home is a living hell?"

Fred gripped the arm of the couch to keep himself from doing something he'd regret—like smashing Lamar's red-veined nose down his throat. "What demands?" he snarled. "That he grow up and act like a man for once in his life? That he take a few adult responsibilities? That he treat Margaret with just a little respect and show some concern for his children?"

Lamar bounded to his feet and advanced on Fred from across the room. "My son's a damned good father," he shouted. "He loves those kids. Why, if it weren't for them, he wouldn't be there at all."

Fred stood and met Lamar's hostile glare with a steady one of his own. "What good is that doing the kids? What's he giving them? Nothing but a house full of hostility, an absent father, and a total lack of respect for their mother. He's not doing those kids any favors by staying. He could give them the same thing or more if he *did* leave."

Lamar balled his hands into fists, and for a moment Fred expected they'd come to blows. He didn't back down. Let Lamar take his best punch—considering Fred's mood, it would be his last.

Lamar must have sensed he didn't intimidate Fred. He didn't strike out, but he didn't move away, either. "You're full of shit."

Fred didn't even dignify that with a response. But he knew better than to stick around any longer. He'd said too much already. And though he'd like to say a whole lot more, he didn't want to hear anything else from Lamar. Besides, he and

Lamar couldn't settle this argument. That was up to Margaret and Webb.

He deliberately turned his back on Lamar and picked his way through the trash to the front door, but he kept his senses on full alert in case Lamar decided to do something foolish. "If you hear from Webb," he said as he opened the front door again, "you'd better talk some sense into him."

Lamar yanked the door from Fred's grasp. "You'd better believe I will." He waited only until Fred's feet touched the porch, then slammed the door closed between them.

Keeping his shoulders straight and his eyes straight ahead, Fred marched back to the Buick and slipped inside. He didn't bat an eye as he backed out of Lamar's gravel drive and started down the winding road toward the highway. His heart ached for Margaret, but he refused to let Lamar see him upset.

He wondered if she realized how Webb felt about her and about their marriage. He wondered whether he should say something to her. But he had no idea what he'd say, and he didn't think she'd listen, even if he did.

Times like these were the hardest parts as a parent. He knew what Margaret should do about her marriage, but he couldn't force her to take action. He had no doubt which path she should take, but he couldn't push her toward it or she'd fight him. He couldn't do anything but sit by and watch while she struggled to find the way on her own.

sixteen

Still bristling from his encounter with Lamar, Fred drove slowly. At the junction he turned toward Cutler, but he couldn't stop fuming about the things Lamar had said or his reaction to the news that Webb might be cheating on Margaret.

Two or three cars crept up on Fred's bumper, then whizzed out around him on the two-lane highway. The driver of one even honked as he passed. But Fred ignored them all. He had too much on his mind to take chances on the road. He didn't know why everyone had to be in such a blasted hurry anyway. Life went on at its own pace, no matter how people tried to push it faster.

He smiled and waved at another irritated driver and turned his attention back to important matters. Come hell or high water, he needed to learn the truth about Webb's relationship with Paige. So far he'd heard only rumor. Only two people on earth knew the truth—Webb and Paige. Even if Fred wanted to hear the truth from Webb, he didn't know where to find him. But he did know where to look for Paige.

He turned off Main Street and drove into the foothills, then followed Silver Creek Road through the trees. Recently he'd begun to hate this part of Cutler. With the advent of spring huge new homes had begun springing up, flanking their more modest neighbors and making the whole area unrecognizable.

Fred didn't like the change. He didn't like the heavier traffic in town or the increased demand on services. He resented having to fight for his booth at the Bluebird and waiting in ever longer lines at Silver City Bank. Most of all he worried about the countryside, the lake, and the town he'd called home for every one of his seventy-three years.

If David Newman's gambling petition made it onto the ballot, and if it passed in the election, things would only get worse. New roads would tear through the forest, huge chunks of timber would be felled to make way for parking lots, and casinos would clutter the mountainsides. Common sense should tell people how destructive that would be for Cutler. But lately common sense had been in short supply.

Fred stopped in front of the Irvines' modest ranch-style house and took a moment to pull himself together. He'd need every ounce of concentration he could muster to appear calm and rational while he faced the woman who might be tearing Margaret's marriage apart.

The curtains were drawn on all the windows, and he wondered for a moment if he'd missed them. He craned to look into the garage. The door stood open, and Kent's maroon Park Avenue filled half of the space. The spot beside it, probably the one Lenore had used, was empty. A smaller, sportier car Fred didn't recognize sat in the driveway behind the empty side of the garage.

Praying the sports car belonged to Paige, he climbed out of the Buick, pocketed his keys, and walked up the sidewalk to the front door. He hoped Paige would talk to him, but she probably wouldn't if he asked about Webb immediately. He'd have to work his way up to asking. Gradually. Tactfully.

The door opened almost immediately after he knocked, and he found himself staring into the cool green eyes of a young woman with a small boy of about two perched on one hip. Even if he hadn't been expecting her, he'd have recognized her as Hannah Irvine's sister on sight.

Paige shared her sister's red hair and slightly freckled complexion, but the hair color seemed almost richer on Paige, the freckles less pronounced. Even her facial features seemed better defined. By the world's standards, she would have been considered a beautiful woman, but there was something about her—something in her eyes, maybe—that kept Fred from agreeing.

She wore cutoff jeans and a T-shirt that hugged her torso and revealed more of her figure than Fred found comfortable. Her hair fell in layers around her face and gave the impression of casual abandon, but Fred would have bet anything she spent time each morning cultivating that look. Just the type of woman who would probably appeal to Webb.

She adjusted the child on her hip, a gesture so easy that Fred wondered whether the child might have been hers. But he pushed aside that idea almost immediately. He'd never heard any talk about Kent and Lenore being grandparents.

Paige squinted at him through the screen door and lifted one hand to shield her eyes from the sun. "Can I help you?"

He certainly hoped so. He introduced himself and waited for her reaction.

She didn't even blink. Either his name had no connection with Webb's in her mind, or she was very good at hiding her emotions.

Fred hoped for the former. He wasn't at all sure he wanted her to make any connection just yet. "I just stopped by to offer my condolences. Is your father home?"

She glanced over her shoulder as if she didn't know the answer. When she looked back, something Fred couldn't identify flickered in her eyes. "He is, but he's lying down. I'll let him know you stopped by." Taking a step backward, she started to close the door between them as if she considered their visit over.

But Fred hadn't even gotten started. He pulled open the screen and stepped in front of the door in time to keep it from closing completely. "How are you and Hannah holding up?"

Her expression tightened with annoyance. "We're fine."

"I'm glad to hear it." He used his kindest voice and tried to look sympathetic. "It's a hard thing, losing your mother like that."

"Lenore wasn't my mother," Paige informed him, but she tempered her answer with a gaunt smile. "She was my stepmother."

Fred tried to look slightly embarrassed. "Oh, that's right. Funny, that slipped my mind. Still it's a hard thing, I'm sure." He studied her face for some sign of sorrow or grief.

Her eyes looked clear and bright and hard as nails. "Yes, it is."

"It's a lucky thing you came to visit when you did." Fred said, as if he were making casual observation. "At least you got to see her before she . . . before." He tried to look flustered and to watch for her reaction without giving away any undue interest.

"Yes," she repeated. "It is." But she didn't look as if she cared one way or the other.

Interesting. Grady had been right. Now what?

Fred tried to come up with a clever way to steer the conversation where he wanted it to go, but with Paige so uninterested in chatting he didn't know what to say next.

Before he could speak again, Hannah appeared in the room behind her sister. "Paige? Who is it?" She approached the door almost shyly and peered at Fred over her sister's shoulder. "Oh. Mr. V. What are you doing here?"

Fred repeated his story, offered his condolences, and waited for Hannah to invite him inside.

But she seemed no more eager for company than Paige. "Thanks." She flicked a nervous smile and fiddled with an odd-shaped pendant hanging around her neck. "We'll tell Dad you were here. I'm sure it will mean a lot to him."

Fred didn't know if he believed that, but he pretended to. "I lost my own wife a few years back," he said. "I know what he must be going through."

"Yes." Hannah said, working her way past Paige and gripping the door as if she planned to close it. "I'm sure you do. Like I said, we'll let him know you stopped by."

Frantic, Fred looked straight at Paige and said, "I understand you met my son-in-law at the Copper Penny."

Paige's eyebrows rose. "Oh? Who is your son-in-law?"

"Webb Templeton."

Bull's-eye. She drew back and frowned ever so slightly "Webb Templeton?" She shook her head and pretended to be confused. "I don't know—"

Fred had no intention of letting her play that game. "I've been told you were sitting with him when the argument between David Newman and your mother broke out."

"Stepmother," Paige said again, almost automatically. She tried to smile, but the effort failed. "Lenore and I weren't exactly what you'd call close."

"I see. Well, that's too bad."

As if her sister's attitude embarrassed her, Hannah stepped in with an explanation. "Dad and Lenore hadn't been married that long, you know. And Paige moved out right after they got together."

Fred nodded and looked sympathetic for a second, but he kept his leg planted in the doorway and made certain not to notice the increasingly frustrated looks Paige shot him. "I don't suppose you've seen or heard from Webb since that night?"

The young woman's expression hardened even further. "Me? No."

Fred waited for her to elaborate.

She didn't, but she did start to fidget.

He leaned a little closer and looked from one of Lenore's stepdaughters to the other. "I don't suppose the sheriff has found the person responsible for Lenore's death yet—?"

Paige's mouth thinned, but she didn't respond.

Hannah shook her head. "No."

"It's a horrible thing," Fred mused aloud. "Tragic. I just can't think who might have done such a thing . . ."

This time Hannah looked a little taken aback. She worked the chin on her neck toward her mouth and clamped the pendant between her lips.

But Paige barked a laugh. "Well, *I* can, and I don't know why the sheriff hasn't arrested him yet."

Fred didn't even try to disguise his interest. "Who?"

"David Newman," Paige said. "Who else?"

The answer didn't surprise him. "You honestly think so?"

"Of course, I do," Paige said. "I saw him that night. I saw the way he was with Lenore."

Fred turned to Hannah. "Is that what you think?"

She flushed slightly and took a hasty step backward. "Me? Yes, I guess so. I don't know."

"You *were* there, weren't you?"

"Yes." She dragged the word out as if she were reluctant to let it leave her mouth. "For a minute."

Fred didn't let his face reveal anything. "That's what I heard." To show them both how harmless he was, he chucked the boy on Paige's hip under the chin and made a few grandfatherly noises. "Who's this fine-looking young man?"

Paige lifted her chin and straightened her posture. "This is my son, Trevor." She looked almost defiant, as if she expected him to say something she didn't want to hear.

So, the boy *was* hers. Interesting. Especially because he'd never heard anyone mention him before. "Trevor, eh? How old is he?"

Paige looked down her nose at him—no easy task since she stood several inches shorter than he did. "He's two."

"You know," Fred said. "I didn't think anybody could keep a secret in Cutler, but I didn't even know about this young fella until just now." He worked up an easy chuckle. "Guess that shows what *I* know, doesn't it?"

Paige didn't relax a bit. Even Hannah looked ill at ease.

Fred let a second or two pass, then tried to turn the tables on Paige. "So, have you and Webb been friends long?"

It worked. Her expression grew even more brittle. "I just met him that afternoon."

Fred didn't think he liked her very much. Too sour at such a young age. And he couldn't help wondering what had happened to make her this way. He nodded as if her answer explained everything. "I see."

"Look, Mr. Vickery, we appreciate your concern, but we're all a little upset right now." Paige signaled Hannah with a glance and handed Trevor to her, then gripped the door with both hands. "So, if you don't mind . . ."

Fred reluctantly stepped back. He couldn't think of any way to prolong the visit. Except one. "Do you mind my asking why you're so sure David Newman's the murderer?"

She thought about it for a split second. "Because he told her he'd do *anything* to get the gambling petition on the ballot. And she—thinking she was so clever, I'm sure—said he'd have to do it over her dead body." She gave him the benefit of a bitter smile. "I guess he took her literally."

Before he could react, she closed the door in his face and turned the lock for good measure.

Fred turned back toward the Buick, pondering the latest turn of events. For the first time, he wondered seriously about David Newman as a possible murderer. If you'd asked him a few days ago whether David could have killed someone, he'd have said only if the victim had been killed by boredom. Now, with everyone he'd talked with pointing fingers at the dull young man, Fred wondered whether he'd jumped to the wrong conclusion. According to everyone at the Cooper Penny, David had been angry enough at Lenore to kill her. Of course, that theory left the damage to Webb's truck unexplained, but Fred supposed there might be a reasonable answer, even for that.

Still pondering, he drove back down the hill toward town as quickly as he dared on the winding road. Maybe it was time for him to listen to what everyone around him was saying. Maybe he should pay David a long-overdue visit. Even if David wasn't driving the vehicle that sent Lenore to her death, he might be able to shed some light on the subject.

Fred would have to talk with David—that much had become painfully obvious—but he didn't want to do it with George around. George would monopolize the conversation, jump in with stupid answers, justify his son's behavior, and generally get in the way. Fred needed to find David alone somewhere, and he'd start at the Bluebird Café.

One thing for certain, he thought with a thin smile, if David Newman was the murderer, and if Fred could prove it, he wouldn't have to put up with George's company at the Bluebird Café anymore. George would avoid him like the plague.

The thought made Fred's smile grow. Increasing his speed, he pressed the button to roll down his window and let the fresh spring air blow through the Buick. And he whistled softly to himself as he drove.

seventeen

The instant Fred pushed open the door of the Bluebird Café, the aroma of Lizzie's meat loaf lunch special hit him, and his stomach began to complain. It had been far too long since he'd eaten a decent meal.

Well, there was no place like the Bluebird to remedy that. He pulled in another deep, satisfying breath and waved to Grandpa Jones and Sterling Jeppson as he hurried past the counter and into the dining room. Elvis came to life on the jukebox singing "All Shook Up," and Fred's spirits lifted a little.

Scanning the room, he realized most of the tables were empty. His spirits lifted even further. Sooner or later, David Newman would show up here. In the meantime, Fred could use a few minutes' peace and quiet to gather his thoughts.

He crossed to his favorite booth beneath the *Kissin' Cousins* poster of Elvis in blonde wig, slid onto the seat, and flipped over a coffee cup to signal Lizzie. Before she even noticed him, the bell over the front door tinkled again to signal another new arrival.

He glanced up, half hoping luck would smile on him and deliver David Newman. To his dismay, Doc Huggins stomped inside and closed the door behind him. Fred had a few things to discuss with Doc, but he didn't want to do it now.

Doc chatted with Sterling for a second, and Fred breathed a sigh of relief when he turned toward the empty stool beside Grandpa. But at that moment, Doc glanced into the dining room and noticed Fred. Lifting one hand in a wave, he hurried toward Fred's table.

Fred's smile faded. Doc would have something to say about Fred's lunch order, but Fred had heard all Doc's arguments a thousand times before. He didn't want to hear them today.

Maybe he'd go away if Fred ignored him.

Fred kept his attention riveted on the kitchen door as Doc approached.

It didn't help. Doc ran a palm across his fringe of gray hair and dropped onto the opposite bench with a groan. He was actually a few years younger than Fred, but he sounded like an old man. "Morning, Fred. Or should I say afternoon?"

Fred dragged his gaze from the kitchen door, nodded once, and turned away again. Where in the hell was Lizzie with his coffee?

Doc stared at him. "What's the matter with you?" He'd never been overly bright. If he spent half a second thinking about it, he ought to be able to answer that for himself.

Fred slanted a glance at him. "What are you doing here?"

"I came in for lunch."

"Are you sure you have time? There must be somebody you haven't told about my latest checkup."

Understanding dawned slowly in Doc's blue eyes. "Is that what's bothering you? You're upset with me because I discussed your test results with Maggie and Joseph?"

"Bingo."

Doc rolled his eyes. "Oh, for heaven's sake, Fred. They're concerned about you. Joseph called all the way from New Hampshire. What did you expect me to do?"

Fred lifted one shoulder. "You could tell them to ask me. And you could remind yourself my file is confidential."

"It's not as if they're strangers. They're your children. They have a right to know."

"*I'll* tell them what they need to know."

"*Sure* you will." Doc shook his head and pursed his lips. "How long have you been a patient of mine?"

"Too damned long," Fred snapped.

Doc ignored him and did some mental calculations. "Must

be nearly fifty years by now. And in all that time, I've never known you to volunteer information about your health to anyone—not even Phoebe."

Only because the truth would have worried her. Fred scowled at him. "I tell them what they need to know."

Doc leaned back in his seat and chuckled as if Fred had said something amusing. "Of course you do. If you had *your* way, those kids would believe that heart attack you had three years ago was nothing more than a bad case of heartburn."

"It didn't kill me, did it?"

"What difference does that make? Your children are concerned about you, you stubborn old fool. They care about you, and you ought to be grateful they do. Not everyone is that lucky."

"Lucky?" Fred repeated, loud enough to catch Grandpa Jones's attention at the counter. He forced his voice lower before he went on. "Did Joseph tell you why he wanted to know about my test results?"

Something flickered in Doc's eyes. "No. Why?"

"He's decided I ought to live out the rest of my life in a retirement home in New Hampshire or with him and Gail and the kids."

Doc ducked his head for half a second, then looked back up at Fred. He had the nerve to look amused. "A retirement home?" He tried unsuccessfully to bite back a laugh. "Well, I wouldn't worry about that too much if I were you."

"Wouldn't you?" Fred glared harder. "Why not?"

Doc leaned forward in his seat and propped his forearms on the table. "Because you're so damned bullheaded and ornery, the staff wouldn't want you around for long. They'd kick you out in two days."

"Very funny."

Doc seemed to think so.

"I'd like to see what you'd do if one of *your* kids tried to lock you up in some home," Fred told him.

Doc's laughter faded. "Oh, come on, Fred. Joseph gets worked up about things, you know he does. It'll all blow over in a day or two."

Fred wished he could share Doc's optimism.

Doc laughed softly to himself. He glanced up and smiled at Lizzie, who finally approached with the coffee. "Have you heard the news? Fred's going to be moving away."

Lizzie cocked a glance at Fred. "I doubt that." She filled his cup and raised an eyebrow at Doc in silent question.

Doc shook his head at the coffeepot. "I'll have a glass of iced tea."

She lowered the pot to the table. "You two having lunch?"

"I am," Fred said. "The special with extra gravy."

Just as he'd expected, Doc's expression grew stony. "What are you doing, ordering that just to spite me?"

Fred glared at him. "The special," he said again. "And bring me extra butter for the roll."

Doc glared back. "Bring us two turkey sandwiches with dinner salads. Dressing on the side."

Without a word, Lizzie picked up the coffeepot and headed for the kitchen. Fred figured he had a fifty-fifty chance of getting what he wanted. Lizzie occasionally caved in to Doc's attempts to regulate Fred's diet, but she could also stand up to him when circumstances demanded.

Doc watched her walk away, then leaned back in his seat and spread his arms across the back of it. "You're in a fine mood today. Why don't you tell me what's really bothering you?"

Fred had no intention of discussing the rest of his concerns with Doc. He readjusted his silverware and wiped the table in front of him with a paper napkin.

Doc waited for him to answer. Elvis switched songs.

Fred stared out the window. Doc could wait until hell froze over. Fred didn't like flapping Margaret's personal problems about for everyone to hear.

Doc let out a heavy sigh. "It's the Irvine murder, isn't it?"

Fred slanted a glance at him.

Doc rolled his eyes at the ceiling tiles. "You've decided you need to prove that Webb's not guilty, haven't you?"

Fred didn't say a word.

But Doc nodded as if he had. "You're sticking your nose into Enos's investigation. He's upset with you and threatening to toss you in jail if you don't stop. Maggie's trying to convince you to leave everything alone. And *you're* upset. You're determined to do what you want, no matter what anyone says. Am I right?"

"No."

A look of astonishment crossed Doc's wrinkled face. "No?"

"It's different this time, Doc," Fred admitted slowly. "I don't *want* to get involved. I really don't. I think Webb's guilty, and I want his butt in jail, but I don't want Margaret to hold me responsible for sending him there." He wiped the table again and looked into Doc's wide eyes. "But she's asking me to help him."

Doc looked skeptical.

"I'm serious," Fred insisted. "Not only that, but Benjamin's upset with me for thinking Webb's guilty. And God only knows how Sarah and Deborah feel. Probably the same way Benjamin does."

"Of course, they're upset. He's their father."

"They all expect me to get involved so I can prove he's innocent."

Doc pulled his arms from the bench's back and propped them on the table. "And you're going to do it, aren't you? You're going to get yourself involved."

"I *have* to."

"No, you don't."

"Yes, I do."

Doc leaned closer. "Listen to me, you old fool. If you get involved this time, you'll be making the biggest mistake of your life." Fred started to shake his head, but Doc waved one hand in front of his face to keep him from speaking. "You've got this strange need to fix everything for everybody, but there's no way you can fix this one. Leave it alone. Let Enos do his job."

Fred pushed his silverware away. "I'm not trying to fix anything," he snarled, but he wondered for a second if there was some truth in what Doc said.

"Then let Enos handle it."

"I'm not stopping him."

"You're making it harder for him," Doc said. He glanced

over his shoulder to see if anyone was listening, lowered his voice and went on. "The gossip's already started. There isn't a soul in town over thirty who isn't remembering how Maggie and Enos felt about each other in high school. Half the town's already started speculating they still have feelings for each other." He leaned even closer and lowered his voice to a stage whisper. "Everybody *knows* how you feel about Webb. If you do anything, they're going to start talking conspiracy. You and Enos ganging up against Webb. Is that what you want?"

The scent of Doc's hair tonic mixed with the aroma of sausage and gravy. Fred's stomach knotted and his shoulders tensed. "You know it's not."

"I know you, Fred. The last thing in the world you want is to fuel the gossips in this town. But what do you think they're going to say if you race out there and start asking questions?"

Fred couldn't answer. He settled for a meaningful glance.

It didn't faze Doc a bit. "You know as well as I do what will happen; I can see it in your eyes. How is *that* going to help Maggie? Or Enos?"

"There'll be talk no matter what I do," Fred argued.

Doc nodded. "Yes, there will. But maybe—just maybe—there won't be as much."

Fred wished he could believe that, but he couldn't. Once the talk started, nothing would stop it. He opened his mouth to say so but snapped it shut again when the bell over the door clanged again.

This time Alan Lombard, the town's mayor, burst inside. His round face had turned a deep shade of crimson, and his beady eyes were wider than Fred had ever seen them. He moved his bulky frame to the counter and heaved it onto the stool beside Grandpa Jones. "You're never going to guess what just happened."

Grandpa didn't even try to guess. He dipped a french fry in ketchup.

Alan raised his voice a notch and went on. "I just saw Enos taking Webb Templeton into the sheriff's office."

Hope and fear warred in Fred's heart. He studied his fingers, tried to convince himself everything would work out now, and breathed a prayer of gratitude that he hadn't had to do a thing.

Doc shifted in his seat, flicked a concerned glance in Fred's direction, and turned his attention to Alan. Sterling Jeppson cleared his throat and tried to signal Alan with his head that Fred was sitting in the next room.

Alan didn't notice. "I heard," he said in a tone that might have sounded confidential if it hadn't been so blasted loud, "that Webb's truck is definitely the one that pushed Lenore's car off the road. *And* I heard Fred's the one who turned him in."

Sterling's attempts to get his attention grew a bit more frantic. Grandpa Jones perked up and ran another french fry through the puddle of ketchup on his plate.

Alan readjusted his ample bottom on the tiny stool and took stock of his surroundings for the first time. "You know, I can't help feeling a little sorry for Webb. With Enos *and* Fred against him, he doesn't stand a chance."

Sterling's face went beet red. He cleared his throat and tried once more to signal Alan.

But Alan didn't even look at him. "Even if he's *not* guilty, he'll spend the rest of his life in prison."

Grandpa ate another french fry. Lizzie came out of the kitchen and slipped behind the counter. Sterling nearly passed out trying to get Alan's attention. Doc started to slide off his seat.

"Let's see," Alan said thoughtfully. "Webb's going to prison and Jessica's sick. How long do you think it will be before Maggie and Enos get togeth—?" At that moment his eyes swept the dining room, and he noticed Fred for the first time. He broke off suddenly and swallowed the last part of his sentence.

Grandpa looked disappointed. Lizzie muttered something Fred couldn't hear. Sterling sank back, exhausted.

Doc shifted his gaze back to Fred, and Fred could almost hear the unspoken I-told-you-so.

Fred tried to work up a glare, but even he could tell he failed miserably. "Alan's an idiot," he said around the lump in his throat.

"Maybe so," Doc admitted. "But people will listen to him. You know they will."

Fred wanted to deny it, but he couldn't. People *would* listen. They'd spread the gossip. They'd take great joy in speculating about things that were none of their damned business.

Making a vain attempt to control his temper, he curled his hands into fists on his thighs so tightly the stubs of his fingernails bit into his palms. A hush fell over the Bluebird. Even Elvis stopped singing.

Forcing himself to his feet, he crossed the room and positioned himself at the counter so that even Alan had a hard time ignoring him. "That's the stupidest thing I've ever heard you say, Alan. And I'm warning all of you right now—the next person who says something that idiotic will have me to deal with."

Grandpa soaked another french fry. Sterling kept his eyes riveted on his plate. Alan met Fred's gaze with a steady one of his own. His beady little eyes narrowed, and his thick lips thinned.

Lizzie crossed to Fred's side and spoke softly. "Go on back to your seat. Your lunch is ready."

Fred pushed the suggestion back to her with the wave of a hand and pulled his wallet from his pocket. "Don't bother," he said, tossing a bill onto the counter. "I've lost my appetite."

Pivoting away, he yanked open the door and stepped outside into the sunshine. He hurried back to the Buick, started the ignition, and drove away with his head high. But the minute he rounded the corner onto Pine Street, he pulled to the side of the road and leaned his forehead against the steering wheel.

He'd been wrong. Putting Webb in jail didn't solve anything. Not by a long shot. The real heartache was only beginning.

eighteen

Fred sat at the side of the road for a long time, gathering his thoughts and pondering his options. He'd give anything to be at Enos's office right now so that he could listen to Webb's answers. He'd give anything to be able to go to Margaret and give her the support she needed. But he couldn't do either.

He told himself to go home. To forget about the Irvine murder. To let Enos do his job. To ignore the urgent need building inside him to ask a few more questions—for Margaret's sake, if nothing else.

All the talk about David Newman had left him uncertain. He was no longer totally convinced of Webb's guilt. He couldn't pretend otherwise. He wondered whether Enos had questioned David or whether Fred had thrown him off track by insisting Webb was the murderer.

He studied the tops of the trees and watched the sun slip behind a cloud. Pulling in a steadying breath, he told himself not to worry. Hadn't Grady assured him they were investigating numerous suspects? Enos probably knew more than Fred did. And he wouldn't have brought Webb in unless he was reasonably certain he had the right person. Fred should just drive the Buick home, park it in the garage, and figure out some way to patch things up with Margaret and Benjamin.

Turning the key in the ignition, he put the Buick in gear and pulled away from the side of the road. But the unanswered question still echoed through his mind. Why did everyone he'd talked to insist Webb was innocent? Why had everyone picked David Newman as the most likely suspect?

He drove slowly past the elementary school, past Bill and Janice Lacey's house, and stopped at the sign at the intersection with Aspen. He checked for oncoming traffic and told himself to put his foot on the accelerator and drive through. But he couldn't make himself do it.

He'd bet a month's retirement check that if he turned left and drove two miles down south, he'd find David Newman at his father's house. He hesitated on the corner until Arnold Van Dyke pulled behind him in his brand new Ford Taurus, tooted his horn, and motioned Fred to move on.

Fred waved him past and sat there another few minutes arguing with himself. He shouldn't get involved. He should leave well enough alone and trust Enos to take care of the whole ugly matter. But none of his arguments did any good. In the end, he made the left turn and headed down Aspen Street just as he'd known he would when he pulled up to the intersection. Whether or not it was a wise decision, he couldn't let Margaret down. And since he felt responsible for Webb sitting inside the sheriff's office right now, he needed to set his own mind at ease.

Ten minutes later, he drew up in front of George Newman's old gray house. Sure enough, David's fancy new Chrysler sat in the driveway behind George's Lincoln. Well, good. At least Fred wouldn't have to spend hours tracking David down.

But even after he'd turned off the ignition, he couldn't make himself leave the car right away. How would he explain the reason for his visit? He could count on one hand the number of times he'd been here over the years. Even *he* couldn't pass the visit off as a social call.

He had to come up with a valid reason for being there. Something that would let him guide the conversation to Lenore Irvine's murder. Something that wouldn't immediately put David's guard up and make boring old Grandpa suspicious.

He pondered for another few seconds until someone inside pulled back the living room curtain and peered out at him. Blast. He'd been spotted. He couldn't put off going to the door any longer.

Wearing the most casual expression he could muster, Fred

strode up the walk. Before he could even lift his hand to knock, the door flew open and he found himself face-to-face with George.

"I thought that was you sitting out there by the road," George said. "What are you doing here?"

Fred smiled. "I came to talk to David. Is he here?"

George didn't smile back. "Why?"

"I have a couple of questions—"

"He had nothing to do with that woman's death."

Fred held up both hands to ward off the attack. "I never said he did. Actually, I wanted to ask him about the gambling petition."

"The petition?" George took a step backward. "What about it?"

"Well . . ." Fred said slowly, then plunged in with the only explanation he'd been able to come up with. "I've been thinking maybe I've been too hasty. Maybe I should find out more about David's plans before I make up my mind." He hated lying—even to George.

George narrowed his eyes and studied Fred's face. "You want to know more about the petition?"

Fred nodded and tried to look eager.

"Bull."

"It's true," Fred assured him.

"You've never changed your mind once in all the years I've known you—especially about something like this. What do you really want?"

Fred didn't let his expression give away anything. He struggled to keep his smile in place. "I told you. I want to talk to David."

Footsteps clomped into the room behind George. "Who is it, Dad?"

George planted himself more firmly in the way and spoke without shifting his glance. "Fred Vickery."

David's head appeared over George's shoulder. "Fred? What in the hell are you doing here?"

"Says he came to see you," George said before Fred could answer. "*Says* he's thinking of changin' his mind about the petition."

David's eyes narrowed in an imitation of his father's. "No kidding?" The eyes opened wide again. "Hey, that's great. Come on in. What can I do to convince you?"

Obviously reluctant to give in, George stepped out of Fred's path. "This'd better be on the up and up," he warned.

Fred stifled the urge to ask what he'd do if he discovered it wasn't. "Just a few questions," he said honestly and followed George into the crowded living room.

David dropped into a recliner and waved Fred toward the plastic covered crushed velvet couch. "So, you're beginning to see the light, eh?"

"I'm wondering if I've been too hasty." That part wasn't a lie, even if Fred wasn't referring to the gambling petition when he said it.

"Good. Good." David rubbed his hands together and grinned over at George. "I told you people would come around. We're going to be successful, Dad; I just know it."

Over Fred's dead body, but he didn't say so. He didn't want to tempt fate. He readjusted his smile and tried to find a comfortable position on the couch. The plastic creaked when he moved, and the cushions felt like rocks beneath him. Wonderful.

"So?" David prodded. "What do you want to know?" He crossed his legs and leaned back in his seat.

Fred took a second to phrase his question. He didn't want to lose David now, but he didn't want to listen to him spout off for half an hour about the blasted gambling petition, either. "How do you answer Lenore Irvine's main objections to the idea of legalized gambling in Cutler?"

David lowered his eyes and tried to look sad. "Ah, Lenore. Tragic thing, her dying like that."

George leaned forward in his seat and propped his elbows on his knees. "Is that what you're here for, Fred? To ask about Lenore?"

Fred shook his head quickly. "No. It's just that she was adamant against the idea, and a lot of people listened to her."

"Including you?" George snorted a laugh. "Tell me something I'll believe." He worked his way to his feet and glared down at his son. "Don't talk to him, David. He's trying to trick you."

"I'm not trying to do any such thing," Fred insisted and looked as offended as he could. "She was worried about the effect it would have on the city. So am I. But there are a lot of people who agree with David. I'm just trying to be open-minded about the whole issue."

David shifted in his chair and sent Fred an uneasy smile. "She was worried about people, like Webb, who might not be able to control themselves around the slot machines or the gambling tables. But, really—" He waved one hand in the air as if he could dismiss the whole argument that way. "If a person wants to gamble, they're going to find a way to do it. Same with drinking. If she'd had her way, the consumption of alcohol would have been outlawed in Cutler. She was the kind of person who thought she could regulate other people's behavior. Force everyone to behave by her standards." He leaned forward and held Fred's gaze. "But you can't do that. People will do what they want, regardless of whether it's legal or not."

George moved a step closer. "Watch yourself, David."

David smiled up at George and shook his head. "I'm not afraid to talk about it." He turned back to Fred. "Do you really think Webb would stop drinking just because he couldn't buy liquor in town?"

"No," Fred admitted. He couldn't imagine that, even for a second.

"And if he wants to gamble, don't you think he'll find a way to do it?"

"Yes, but—"

David nodded as if he'd said something infinitely wise. "As for her other arguments," he said with another airy wave of his hand, "Cutler *needs* the economic boost it could get from legalized gambling. We're talking jobs, improvements, increased services, increased business in the stores that exist now— But we've discussed all this before."

They had. And Fred didn't really want to get into it again. "Is this what you and Lenore argued about at the Copper Penny before she was killed?"

"I *knew* it," George shouted. "I knew it. What'd I tell you, David?"

David's smile didn't falter, even for a second. He ignored George and answered Fred. "Yes."

"Don't tell him another thing," George insisted.

Slowly, as if he had to work to drag his gaze away, David faced his father. "I'm not worried about it, Dad. I have nothing to hide."

With George leaping about and shouting like an idiot, Fred decided to dive right in. "I've been told by a number of people that you were very angry with Lenore the night she died."

David nodded for a second before he answered. "I was."

"You were more upset than Webb was, from what I've been told."

David shrugged and tried to look unconcerned, but something flickered in his eyes. "I don't know about that."

George took another step forward and tried to look menacing. It didn't work. "What are you trying to say, Fred? That you think David killed Lenore?"

"I'm not saying anything," Fred assured him. "I'm just trying to figure out what happened that night."

George flapped a hand toward David. "Sure, he was upset with her. And you would'a been, too, if you'd been him. That woman would do anything to get what she wanted."

David seemed to close in on himself. "Dad—"

"What did she want?" Fred asked.

Before George could open his mouth, David rushed to answer. "Nothing. Dad just means that she wanted to make sure the gambling petition didn't make it onto the ballot, that's all."

George paced to David's side. "That woman had it in for David for years," he muttered. "Never could let anything go."

David shot him a dark look. "That's enough, Dad."

But George had never known when to shut up. "After all these years—"

"Dad, stop." David's face flushed a deep red, and his eyes looked almost frantic. "Connie's in the next room, remember?"

That seemed to reach George, but it left Fred more curious than ever.

George stiffened noticeably, flicked a nervous glance at Fred as if he'd just remembered they had company, and backed a step away.

Fred leaned toward David, but he kept his voice low. "You want to tell me what happened between you and Lenore Irvine years ago that she couldn't forget?"

David shook his head, but Fred couldn't tell whether he meant nothing had happened or that he didn't want to discuss it.

Neither answer satisfied Fred. "The argument at the Copper Penny was about that, wasn't it?"

David flushed an even deeper red. He tried shaking his head again, but he couldn't. He gritted his teeth and whispered, "*That* I'm not going to talk about."

"You're going to have to," Fred insisted.

George dropped onto the opposite end of the couch. He looked miserable. "It's none of your business, Fred. Just drop it."

Fred looked from one to the other. They looked like mirror images of each other—both jaws set, both sets of eyes hard, both rigid in their seats. He pressed his palms against his thighs and stood slowly. "All right," he said, as if he accepted that decision. "I'll just pass the information on to Enos and let him ask you about it."

David slumped in his seat. "Good Lord."

"Of course," Fred went on as if it didn't matter to him. "If I was *sure* that whatever it was had nothing to do with Lenore's murder, I wouldn't have to say a thing." He took a couple of steps toward the door.

George muttered something he couldn't make out. David didn't move.

Fred walked slowly to the door. David still didn't cave. Yanking open the door, he stepped outside and glanced back at David one more time. The younger man sat in his chair, shoulders slumped, one hand on his forehead shielding his eyes.

Fred pulled the door closed behind him and started toward

the street, but he took his time. He wanted to give David plenty of time to come after him. Even after he reached the Buick, slid behind the seat and started the engine, he sat for a few seconds, but the door to the Newman house remained closed.

Inching away from the side of the road, Fred pulled into the driveway to turn the car around.

Still nothing. His bluff had failed. David obviously wasn't going to clear up the mystery for him.

He passed the house slowly, willing David or George to come after him.

Neither did.

He drove back into town, replaying the conversation in his mind and trying to make sense of it. Obviously whatever happened between Lenore and David years ago had been a big deal. And it must have happened while David still lived in Cutler.

David might not want to talk about it, but somebody would know what happened. Fred just had to find someone who knew the story and who'd be willing to discuss David Newman's past with him.

nineteen

Fred poured a cup of coffee and settled down at his kitchen table with a pad of paper and a pen. He'd opened the windows to the afternoon's warmth, and the same stiff breeze that whipped tiny waves around the surface of the lake carried the sound of them hitting the shore into the house.

He flexed his fingers and stared at the empty sheet of paper. He supposed Margaret would have been the best source for information about David Newman and Lenore Irvine, but he didn't want to give her false hope. He'd only found one tiny lead; it didn't make Webb innocent.

There had been a large group of kids who'd hung out together all those years ago. Most of them had married and moved away. Enos was still here, of course. And Webb. But Fred couldn't ask either of them.

Sipping carefully, he let his mind wander back thirty years. Margaret had always been well liked, if a little shy. But Fred could remember many evenings when he'd returned home from work to find some friend in the kitchen chatting with Margaret and Phoebe.

Phoebe had loved those visits, and the kids had loved Phoebe—probably because she'd never judged or lectured them, even when they'd done something foolish. She'd asked little of their children but had always expected the best. And she'd usually gotten it.

Treat others with kindness, she'd told them often. And if they found themselves in a situation where they were tempted to do something that would hurt themselves or someone else, think hard before they took action.

An image of Enos as he'd been then flitted through Fred's memory. Enos had been at the house nearly every day back then. He'd been an eager-faced young man with broad shoulders and a husky build, sandy hair, and rugged complexion. His love for Margaret had been painfully obvious to everyone—and hers for him. Not for the first time, Fred wondered what happened between them and spent a few minutes remembering the whirlwind courtship between Webb and Margaret that resulted too soon in marriage and had upset even Phoebe.

As he often did, he wished Phoebe were with him now. He imagined her standing in front of the window, head tilted slightly back as the breeze whisked her dark hair away from her face. He pictured her turning to reach out to him and dreamed of joining her, wrapping his arms around her waist and leaning his chin on her shoulder.

Closing his eyes, he let his mind wander. She'd have covered his hands with her own and held him there. She'd have leaned her soft cheek against his while they watched the lake together. He'd have unburdened himself to her, and she'd have suggested a course of action that would have given him the results he so desperately wanted now.

He caught a whiff of her scent, so soft he knew he'd only imagined it, but it was enough to make him open his eyes and look to see if the past four years without her had been a bad dream.

They hadn't been. He was alone in his kitchen with nothing but a memory.

Pulling himself back to the present, he forced himself to concentrate on the problem at hand. Who else could he ask about David Newman and Lenore Irvine?

Margaret had been friendly with Becky Grimes—or Albright as she'd been then. Even Olivia Locke Simms had made an occasional appearance at the house. He jotted their names on his empty pad as possibilities.

Had David ever been one of the crowd? Fred didn't think so. He'd disliked David enough that he figured he'd remember coming home to find his butt planted in one of his kitchen chairs. Lenore hadn't been around, either. But he'd have bet anything Phoebe'd known about the problem between them. She'd known everything.

He remembered little Natalie Hartvigson—now Preston—and added her name to the list. He thought she lived in Winter Park, or at least somewhere nearby. But before he could think of anyone else, someone's footsteps thundered up his front porch.

Before he could even stand all the way, the visitor pounded on the front door. The knock sounded again before Fred reached the kitchen door. A loud, insistent knock.

Who on earth—?

Fred picked up his pace and crossed the living room. But the visitor hammered again before he could get there.

"All right, all right," he snapped. "I'm coming. Hold your horses." And he yanked open the door before the irritating pounding could start again.

Fred didn't know who he'd expected to find there, but he hadn't expected Webb. Webb's eyes looked wild, his hair probably hadn't been combed all day, and he wore at least two days' growth on his chin. He pushed his way through the front door before Fred could even speak. "I've had just about all I can take from you. You've gone too far this time."

Fred steeled himself. He wouldn't back down. Not this time. "*I've* gone too far?"

For the first time in years, Webb's speech didn't slur. "You've got some nerve, telling Enos I murdered Lenore Irvine."

Fred closed the door behind him and faced Webb squarely. "I told him about the damage on your truck. If you're innocent, you have nothing to worry about."

Webb snorted in disbelief. "*If* I'm innocent?" He paced into the center of the room, jabbed both fists onto his hips and glared at Fred. "You're something else, you know that? *If* I'm innocent. You really think I'm guilty, don't you?"

"Are you?"

For half a heartbeat, Fred wondered if Webb might try to take a punch at him. He balled his hands into fists and adjusted his stance. Thankfully Webb didn't move any closer. "No, I'm not, but I'm sure you won't believe me. You hate me so much you probably *want* me to be guilty."

Fred turned his side to face Webb. He didn't want to give him a straight shot. "You're going to try to make this my fault, aren't you? You've been lying to everybody, you're drinking more than ever since you lost your job, you threatened Lenore twice in the space of twenty-four hours, and you're blaming me for wondering whether you lost your temper and finally went over the edge."

Webb tried to look amused. "You're forgetting one thing, *Dad*. Why would I want to kill her?"

"You're desperate for this gambling petition to bail you out of trouble, and you thought Lenore was going to stand in your way."

Webb forced a brittle laugh. "Sure, I worried about what she'd do. She was a troublemaker. Always has been. It's a wonder somebody didn't kill her before now. But if you think *I* was pissed off at her, you should have seen everybody else that night at the Copper Penny." He slapped his chest with his palm as he talked, then jabbed one finger in Fred's direction. "Anybody else could have killed her—like David Newman. Or Olivia Simms. Hell, even her husband for that matter."

Curiosity got the best of Fred. He took a step closer. "Olivia? Why do you suggest her?"

"What?" Webb tried to look innocently surprised. "Nobody told you about the argument *she* had with Lenore?"

Fred hated to admit it, but he wouldn't lie. "No."

Webb snorted his response, made a complete spin in his tracks, and shook his head in disbelief. "Figures."

"What did they argue about?"

"Hell, I don't know. I just know they were going at it by the ladies' room for a while. You know Olivia— I honestly thought she'd deck Lenore before they got through."

"You didn't overhear anything they said? You didn't hear any talk about it?"

Webb shook his head and shot Fred a sideways glance. "I didn't hear anything."

Fred figured he knew why. He argued silently with himself

for about a half a second about the wisdom of raising the issue, but he had to know the truth. "Is that because you were occupied with Paige Irvine?"

Webb flushed a deep crimson. "I wasn't *occupied* with her. Hell, a guy can't even *talk* to a woman in this town without everybody thinking they're having an affair."

Fred wanted to believe him. He really did. He just didn't know whether he should or not. "You aren't having an affair?"

Webb threw up both hands in futility. "I don't even *know* the woman. I just met her that afternoon, for hell's sake."

Fred looked deep into his eyes for some indication that he was lying. A flicker of an eyeball, maybe. A slight pulling back. But he didn't see anything. "Why was Lenore so upset to find her at your table, then?"

"You got me." Webb must have sensed Fred's growing uncertainty because he relaxed a little. "All I know is, me and Quinn were sitting there having a beer when Paige comes up and sits down with us. I'd run into her outside earlier, so I knew who she was. But I didn't ask her to join us. I didn't even *want* her to. I'm not stupid, you know."

That was open for debate, but Fred didn't argue it now. "What excuse did she give for sitting with you?"

Webb rubbed a palm across his bristly chin. "She wanted to bitch about Lenore. She knew I'd had a couple of run-ins with her, and I guess she thought I'd be sympathetic. You know, a listening ear and all that." He dropped his hand and hooked both thumbs in the pockets of his jeans. "I didn't want to get involved. Quinn didn't want her there, either. He kept whispering to me to get rid of her, but I didn't know how to do it without being rude."

Such a gentleman. Fred took another step closer. "So, you let her stay. And then Lenore found her there."

Webb rolled his eyes at the memory. "God, that woman was a bitch. I'm telling you. Called Paige a slut right to her face. Said she hadn't changed a bit, and was she going to do the same thing all over again."

"What did she mean by that?"

"I have no idea." Webb relaxed enough to take a seat on the couch. "All I know is, she said Paige had brought enough humiliation to the family. That's when Kent realized what was going on and came over."

"What happened then?"

"Then?" Webb took a second to think. "Then he got upset—with Lenore, not with Paige. He told Paige to bring everything over to the house, he wanted her to stay there with them. Lenore said she wouldn't let Paige in the door."

The hairs on the back of Fred's neck prickled. "What else?"

"Kent told Lenore he wasn't going to stand for her crap any longer. He wanted his family back together. And Lenore said over her dead body. And Kent said fine, if that's what it took."

All Fred's senses screamed an alert. "You're sure that's what they said?"

Webb looked righteously indignant. "Positive. That's exactly what I told Enos, too."

Fred crossed to his rocker and lowered himself into the seat. He gripped the chair's arms to still his shaking hands and met Webb's gaze again. "What about your truck? Was the damage there before Lenore's murder?"

This time Webb glanced away. He shook his head, but he looked miserable. "No."

"How do you explain that?"

Webb shot to his feet and paced toward the old oak dining table that held Fred's family pictures. "I can't."

"Do you remember what happened after Grady took you home?"

Webb snorted a laugh. "Do I remember? What? You think I was too drunk?"

Fred did, but he didn't say so.

Webb picked up a picture of his children and studied it for a few seconds, then lowered it gently to the table. "Maggie and I had another fight. You've got her so convinced I'm good for nothing; she won't even give me a chance."

Fred didn't want to get into that right now. He pushed back a surge of resentment and managed to keep his voice calm. "What happened then?"

"I left. On foot. My truck was still at the bar."

"Where did you go?"

"I walked around. I was pissed. Here I've got this great

chance to make something of myself, and Maggie won't even consider it."

Fred forced himself to stay on the subject. "What about the truck?"

"I picked it up the next morning, drove home, and got ready like I was going to work. That's right before you saw me, I guess."

"Did you notice the damage when you picked up the truck?"

Webb shook his head. "No. But I didn't look, either. It was still right in front of the bar where I always park."

Fred leaned back in his seat and pondered Webb's answers for a second or two. "If you left the truck there, and if it was still there the next morning, how do you explain the smashed fender and the broken headlight?"

Webb rubbed his neck and rolled his head to work the kinks out. "I can't."

"They got there somehow—" Fred began.

"No kidding," Webb interrupted. "But I don't know what happened."

"Does anybody else have a key?"

Webb opened his mouth to speak, then clamped it shut again and turned an unbecoming shade of red. "They wouldn't need a key." He dropped back onto the couch, propped his elbows on his knees, and rested his forehead on his fists. "I always leave the key in the ignition when I go into the Copper Penny."

A chill winged up Fred's spine. "You do *what*?"

"I leave the key in the ignition when I'm in the bar," Webb said, a little too loud. "It makes it easier that way. I don't lose my keys."

Fred groaned aloud. "Then you're telling me anybody could have taken your truck, used it to kill Lenore, and parked it back at the Copper Penny without you knowing?"

"That's what I'm telling you," Webb said and lowered his gaze again.

Fred wanted to throttle the boy for being so stupid. He wanted to grab him by the shoulders and shake some sense into his thick head. And, surprisingly, he wanted to give him the benefit of the doubt—just this once.

twenty

Heartened by the warmth of the early morning sunlight, Fred climbed up the Main Street boardwalk and moved quickly toward the furniture store Olivia Sims had inherited after her brother's death. As a business owner, Olivia definitely had a stake in the outcome of David Newman's bid for legalized gambling, but some sixth sense told Fred that Olivia's argument with Lenore had nothing to do with that blasted petition.

He'd been on a wild goose chase for the past two days, tracking down evidence to prove Webb guilty and concentrating the entire time on the issue of legalized gambling. But after listening to David Newman and Webb, instinct warned him he'd been on the wrong track all along.

Lenore had obviously made enemies everywhere she went. Her marriage had been in trouble, and she'd had a bad relationship with her older stepdaughter. There'd been something brewing between her and David Newman for years, and she'd argued with Olivia Simms the night before she died.

Getting Olivia to talk to him wouldn't be easy, but Fred was determined to get to the bottom of this, once and for all. He paused in front of Olivia's to catch his breath and pull his thoughts together, then pushed open the front door and stepped inside.

She sat behind a small wooden desk, working on something that seemed to hold her attention in spite of the buzzer that announced his entrance. When she finally looked up, she smiled as if his visit were a grand surprise. But something wary lurked behind her eyes, and he suspected she'd watched him approach.

Of medium height with a medium build and medium coloring, Olivia wouldn't stand out in a crowd. But once she opened her mouth, you'd never forget her. Even with her newfound financial freedom, she hadn't changed from the days when the lack of money had been her chief concern.

She still wore jeans everywhere, though they no longer looked as if she'd had them for a dozen years. Her tennis shoes looked new. And instead of a ragged T-shirt with some faded slogan, she wore a white T-shirt under a denim blouse.

"Sherlock?" Her voice came out husky, the product of too many cigarettes over the years. "What are you doing here? Looking for a new living room set?"

"Not today," he said and let the door close behind him.

"Damn. And I thought I was about to get a little of your money. So, what's up?"

He crossed to the desk and planted himself directly in front of her. Olivia had never been one to beat about the bush, and Fred knew better than to even try to throw her off guard with small talk. "I hear you had an argument with Lenore Irvine the night before she died."

Alarm flicked across Olivia's face, but she hid it well. "You did, huh? What did we argue about?"

"You tell me."

She shook her head and pursed her lips. "I don't know."

"You deny it?"

She barked a throaty laugh. "Hell, yes, I deny it. Who told you that, anyway?"

Fred had no intention of dropping Webb's name. "Someone at the bar witnessed you arguing with her near the ladies' room."

Olivia pretended to understand suddenly. "Oh, you're talking about at the Copper Penny? Yeah. I guess you could say we had a little argument there." She waved a hand toward the front window. "The gambling thing. You know."

Maybe, but Fred didn't think so. "What else?"

"What else? I don't know what you mean."

"I mean," he said slowly, "what else did you argue about?"

Her eyes narrowed and her expression froze. "Nothing."

"Are you sure?"

"Yes." The word fell like ice between them.

Fred still didn't believe her. "What if I told you someone overheard your argument?"

Her lips curved into a cold smile. "I wouldn't believe you."

So much for that idea. Maybe he should attack from a different angle. He perched on the edge of her desk and tried to look fatherly. "You and Lenore were about the same age, weren't you?"

Olivia nodded, but she looked wary.

"You went to high school together?"

"Yes. Why?"

He shrugged casually. "I was just trying to remember which of you kids hung out together. Were you and Lenore friends?"

Olivia snorted. "Me and *Lenore*? Good hell, Fred. Lenore didn't have any friends, and even if she had, I wouldn't have been one of them."

Fred hadn't thought so. He couldn't imagine two people less likely to be friends than straightforward Olivia and devious Lenore. Hoping to catch her off guard this time, he said, "I've been told it looked like a fairly serious argument between you two that night. In fact, my source says you nearly hit her."

"Your *source*?" Olivia laughed again, but this time she sounded genuinely amused. "I love it when you do that." She leaned back in her chair and met his gaze with her medium brown eyes. "I didn't kill her, if that's what you want to know."

"I didn't ask you that," Fred said, but he didn't bother denying that he'd wanted to.

"What *are* you asking?"

"What did you argue about? And don't tell me it was the gambling petition, because I won't believe you."

She laughed again and held up both hands. "Okay, Sherlock. You've got me. I argued with her just because she was an obnoxious bitch who couldn't keep her nose out of other people's business. She got in my way when I was going into the ladies' room, and I told her about it."

"And that was it?" Fred didn't believe that, either, but he let her think he did. He did his best to look disappointed.

His efforts must have worked because she seemed to relax a bit. "Sorry to disappoint you."

He lifted one shoulder in a casual shrug. "Tell me about this gambling thing. I know you've been backing David Newman's efforts to get it in place."

"I don't know if I've been backing him, exactly. But I can see the value in his idea."

"He ran up against Lenore a time or two, from what I hear. Do you know anything about his arguments with her?"

To his surprise, Olivia grew stiff again and something uneasy flitted across her expression. "David didn't kill her."

Strange reaction. "I didn't say he did," Fred said gently and watched her face closely.

But she'd already pulled herself together. Her face didn't reveal a thing. "You implied it."

"I didn't mean to." He tried to look innocent. "It's just that I heard David and Lenore had problems that go way back."

That struck a nerve. Olivia pushed her seat away from the desk and stood. "Where did you hear that?"

"From David."

Disbelief warred with anger in her eyes, and her mouth tightened into a frown. "I don't believe you."

"It's true. I spoke with him this morning."

She shook her head and turned away for a second. "I don't believe you," she said again.

"You obviously know about it. Why don't you tell me?"

She whirled back to face him, and her voice came out like a growl. "There's nothing to know."

Fred shook his head. "I think there is. What happened?"

"Nothing."

"Dammit, Olivia—"

"Nothing happened," she insisted for the third time.

"I figure it must have been back in high school or shortly after since David left town right after that . . ."

Olivia dropped into her chair and glared up at him. "You're starting to annoy me."

He intended to. "And I figure *somebody* will remember. Somebody remembers everything in a town this size."

"Yeah?" She managed to put on a haughty expression in spite of her obvious nervousness. "Well, good for them."

Fred studied her for a second. She knew something. She probably knew the whole story, but for some reason she didn't want to tell it. The possibilities made his imagination run wild, but he could tell he wouldn't get anything more out of her today.

She worked up a smirk. "It's hopeless, you know."

"What's hopeless?"

"Trying to get Webb off the hook."

Yesterday Fred might have agreed with her. Today he wasn't so certain. "Why do you say that?"

"Because there's a witness. Or haven't you heard?" She looked delighted with herself.

Fred's heart lurched in his chest. "What witness?"

Her smile grew and her eyes danced with mischief. "Thayne O'Neal *saw* Webb driving out of town early that morning. I just heard about it an hour ago."

Without meaning to, Fred glanced out the window at Thayne O'Neal's store, The Good Sport.

Olivia leaned back in her seat as if she were having a good time. "You didn't know about that, did you?"

Fred didn't bother to deny it. "Are you sure he saw Webb? Or was it just Webb's truck?"

Olivia's smile faded a little. "I don't know."

"Did you talk to Thayne? Or is this a rumor?"

"I talked to him myself a little while ago. He's the one who told me Webb was arrested, and he told me what he saw."

For some reason even Fred couldn't explain, he wanted to set the record straight. "Webb wasn't arrested. He was questioned."

She shrugged as if she saw no difference. "Okay, he was questioned. But come on, Sherlock, you have to admit he has a better motive than anyone for shoving Lenore Irvine off the side of a cliff—*and* he had the opportunity."

"I'll admit he has a motive," Fred said. "But I'm not convinced it's a better one than David Newman's. Or Kent's. Or her stepdaughter's." He drew in a deep breath and looked into her eyes. Maybe it was time to shake things up a little. "Or even yours."

She pulled back as if he'd slapped her. "*Mine?* What motive do I have?"

"I don't know yet," Fred admitted. "But I will."

She tried hard to look smug, but she failed. "What about the truck? How do you explain that?"

"That's the funny part," he said with a thin smile. "Webb always leaves his keys in the ignition when he's at the Copper Penny. So, anybody could have used his truck to murder Lenore. It's just a matter of time until Enos finds out who actually did it. And now that there's a witness, my guess is, we won't have to wait long."

Without giving her a chance to respond, he turned on his heel and left the store. Let her worry. He'd just begun to stir the mud on the bottom of the pond. And he had the strong feeling that when it settled, the results might surprise a lot of people.

twenty-one

Determined to talk with Thayne himself, Fred hurried away from Olivia's and crossed the street to The Good Sport. Racks of T-shirts, sweatshirts, jogging outfits, and ski clothes at close-out prices filled the center of the room. Pine shelves and hooks climbing the walls held everything else—tennis balls and rackets, fishing and hunting equipment, skis and accessories, and hiking gear—almost everything a body could think of to use outdoors.

Thayne O'Neal seemed to do a thriving business in Cutler. And no wonder. The town sat in the middle of a narrow mountain valley on the shores of a magnificent lake—if Fred did say so himself. Trailheads spurred off the road into wooded hills, trout swam in the pure mountain streams, and ski areas crawled up the mountains in nearby canyons.

A sportsman's paradise. Fred's paradise.

He let the door swing shut behind him as he scanned the room. No customers. Good. He didn't want to discuss Webb in front of anyone else.

Thayne hunkered down in front of the fishing equipment, stacking something on the lower shelves. He glanced up as Fred crossed the room, tossed the sun-streaked hair of his ponytail over one shoulder, and smiled. "Good. A customer. It's been so slow today, I was beginning to worry."

Many of Cutler's residents had objected to Thayne's hair and earring when he'd moved to Cutler six years before. As time passed, he'd won over nearly everyone, but there were still a few people who refused to look past his outward appearance to the man beneath.

Personally Fred didn't understand why a grown man would want to look that way, but he liked Thayne. He was honest, a caring father to his son, Tyler, and a fair employer for Benjamin.

Thayne gestured toward the boxes on the floor. Fishing reels. Dozens of them. "I don't suppose you're interested? I'm having a great sale."

Fred started to shake his head, then stopped and reconsidered. Why not? He hadn't been fishing since Phoebe's death, and he missed going. He couldn't even have said what made him stop, unless not having her there to refuse to clean the fish took some of the joy out of it for him.

"I don't know," he said. "I'll think about it." He moved a step closer. "I need to ask you a couple of questions. Do you have a minute?"

Thayne nodded without breaking rhythm. "Okay. Shoot."

Fred didn't waste any time. "I just heard that you're a witness in the Lenore Irvine murder."

Thayne stopped working and sat back on his heels. "Yeah, I guess. I didn't see her get murdered, if that's what you're asking."

"No," Fred assured him, leaning one elbow on a shelf. "I heard you saw Webb driving out of town that night."

Thayne's lips tightened into a frown. The question obviously made him uncomfortable. "Yeah, I did."

"Are you sure it was Webb behind the wheel?"

Thayne lowered a reel box to the floor. "Who else would it have been?"

Fred shrugged. "Webb claims it wasn't him. He says he left his keys in the ignition all night. If that's true, it could have been anybody. I need to know whether you actually *saw* Webb or whether you assumed it was him because of the truck."

This time, Thayne looked thoughtful. He stood slowly and brushed his pantlegs with his palms. "I don't know. I guess I just assumed it was him. I waved. He waved back . . ." He let his voice trail off and met Fred's gaze. "*Somebody* waved back, anyway."

"So, you can't swear it was Webb you saw."

"No."

Fred's heart gave a small leap of hope. "Think for a minute. Can you remember anything about the person you saw driving the truck?"

Thayne folded his arms across his chest and closed his eyes for a second or two, then opened them again. "No." He looked almost disappointed by his failure. "I'd had a few drinks at the Copper Penny, and I came back here afterward to pick up some things from the office. I saw Webb—or his truck, anyway—as I was leaving again."

"Where was the truck when you saw it?"

Thayne nodded toward Main Street. "He was driving down Main Street, right outside the store."

Fred shot a glance over his shoulder. "*Here?* Outside The Good Sport?"

"Yeah. Why?"

"Which direction was it traveling?"

Thayne's eyebrows knit in confusion. "West. Like he was going toward your house or something."

That made no sense at all. "Lenore's car went off near the summit," Fred said, almost more to himself than to Thayne, and glanced out the window again. "That's the opposite direction."

Thayne's eyes narrowed. "You're right."

"But the truck was traveling west?"

Thayne nodded. His ponytail fell over his shoulder and landed on his chest again. He flicked it back impatiently. "Yeah, it was."

More confused than ever, Fred paced to the window and looked outside. The Good Sport sat almost directly across from the tiny patch of grass Cutler called its city park. A block west would have taken the driver to the sheriff's office, the volunteer fire department, and the lake, with nowhere else to go. Unless the driver had turned onto Lake Front, south toward Fred's house or north toward the church. But none of those destinations made any sense at all.

He flicked another glance in Thayne's direction. "Did you see where it went from there?"

Thayne shook his head. "I didn't really pay attention. I had a little buzz from the drinks, and I didn't want to drive home. I had a lot to carry, so I didn't want to walk. So, I came into the store, got my stuff, and called Cindy to pick me up."

"Do you know what time it was?"

"Maybe midnight or so. I'm not really sure."

Fred gave that some thought. Most folks were off the streets by midnight—except customers at the Copper Penny.

"How long were you inside?"

"Not long. Fifteen, twenty minutes, maybe."

"And you saw Webb's truck when you came back outside?" Fred asked, hoping something would click into place.

Thayne nodded. "Yeah. So, it was probably twelve-fifteen."

"Was Cindy here when you came out?"

"No. I had to wait for her on the boardwalk."

"You don't know whether she saw the truck on her way here?"

Thayne shook his head. "I don't know. She didn't say. She was upset with Tyler for getting home after his curfew. Again."

And he'd probably been with Benjamin. Another thing Margaret had to deal with. Another reason Fred needed to clear things up for her.

He took another minute to study the view out the window. "Did you see the truck after that—on your way home?"

"No."

It made no sense. If someone took Webb's truck and used it to kill Lenore, what were they doing at *this* end of town where anybody could have seen him or her—and, in fact, someone had? Surely the murderer would have tried to remain inconspicuous. Unless—

Fred's heart beat a little faster as a new idea hit him. He wheeled to face Thayne again. "Is it possible the driver turned right on Lake Front and drove into the foothills?"

Thayne shrugged with his mouth and eyes. "It's possible. But I *told* you, I didn't pay attention."

"Could he have driven toward the Irvines' house?"

"It's possible," Thayne admitted slowly.

Yes, it certainly was. Maybe the murderer had driven out to confront Lenore. Maybe the confrontation had gone badly and the murderer followed her back through town when she left for Denver. That didn't explain why the murderer had taken Webb's truck in the first place, but it opened more possibilities. If the murderer drove to the Irvines' place to see Lenore, someone there—Kent or Paige or Hannah—might have seen or heard something.

"You mentioned that you'd been at the Copper Penny that night," Fred said. "Were you there when the argument broke out?"

"Oh, yes," Thayne said with a nervous laugh. "What a mess."

"Tell me what you heard."

Thayne propped one arm on a revolving rack of T-shirts. "I don't know. It was all a mass of confusion. One minute, David Newman and Lenore were going at it about the gambling petition. The next minute Lenore and Kent were fighting about Kent's daughter—the pretty one."

"Paige?"

"Yeah. I guess so. I was just trying to stay out of the whole thing. I mean, if I've got to take sides about the gambling issue right now, I'd say I'm more in favor of it than against, but I sure didn't want to get into an argument about it."

"Did you hear what David and Lenore said?"

"Most of it. It started out like all the other discussions. David said gambling would be the making of Cutler. Lenore said it would destroy everything. Then David said he couldn't understand why Lenore was so against it, that she lived to destroy things. And *she* said sin was of the devil and must be destroyed at any cost."

"I've been told Lenore said the gambling petition would be passed over her dead body," Fred said. "Did you hear her say that?"

Thayne's eyes rounded. "No." He rubbed his chin thoughtfully. "You don't think *David* killed her because of the petition, do you?"

Fred gave his standard answer. "I don't know what I think."

When Thayne didn't say anything else, he tried a longshot. "Did you see Lenore arguing with Olivia Simms while you were there?"

"No. I didn't even see Olivia."

That disappointed Fred. He'd been hoping for another witness to that argument. "Go on," he urged. "What happened next?

"Well, that's when Lenore saw Paige sitting with Webb. She got really angry then, and I didn't want to stick around—" He broke off and shook his head as if he didn't know what to say next. "Nothing good ever comes from getting involved in family squabbles—you know?"

Fred knew. "But Webb got involved."

"Yeah. But not by choice."

"How much of that did you hear?"

"Not a lot," Thayne admitted. "Lenore had a real problem with Paige, though. I could tell that. Kent just stood there like a lump for the first few minutes while Lenore said some pretty rough stuff to Paige. Webb finally got fed up, but when *he* tried to stick up for Paige, Lenore sort of went crazy. That's when I left. It was getting too ugly for me."

Fred stared at him. "You left before the sheriff's department got there?"

Thayne nodded. "Yeah. I was outta there."

"And you walked back here?" Fred knew he was missing something important. He could feel it. "How long did it take you to get back here?"

"Five minutes, maybe."

Something didn't feel right to Fred. The timing was off. "So, from the time you left the Copper Penny until you saw Webb's truck driving past was what—twenty minutes?"

"About that," Thayne agreed.

That couldn't be right. Enos and his deputies would have needed longer than that to respond to the call from Casey, intervene in the argument, and send everyone home. Webb claimed that when he left the bar, his truck was in the parking lot. But when Albán went outside at two o'clock, he noticed Webb's truck gone. And when Thayne saw Webb's truck drive past, Albán, Webb, David Newman, Lenore and Kent Irvine—even Paige—were all still inside the Copper Penny.

Then who was driving Webb's truck at midnight? And who'd come back to use it later as the murder weapon? It seemed too coincidental to think that two separate people had used Webb's truck that night, but if the same person drove it away at midnight and again when Lenore was murdered, the murderer *couldn't* have been anyone who was at the Copper Penny when the argument broke out. And that let everyone Fred had previously considered a suspect off the hook.

Was it possible that *everyone* who'd been at the Copper Penny was innocent? Maybe. But if so, who murdered Lenore?

He rubbed his forehead and thought furiously, trying to come up with some other explanation, but he couldn't think of anything. Slowly, he became aware of Thayne studying him.

"The whole thing doesn't make sense," Fred said.

Thayne looked as discouraged as Fred felt. "Sorry I couldn't help."

Fred waved his apology away and started for the door. "It's not that. I'm missing something, but I can't for the life of me figure out what it is."

"If I think of anything else, I'll let you know."

Tugging open the door, Fred smiled back at him. "Thanks."

"I could sell you that fishing reel," Thayne said with a grin. "A nice, quiet fishing trip may be just what you need."

In spite of everything, Fred laughed. "Right now, my mind's occupied with the Irvine murder. But I may be back."

Thayne picked up a box from the floor and tucked it under one arm. "I'll set one aside for you."

Fred's smile faded as soon as he stepped outside again. Frustrated and confused, he made the walk home in record time. Somewhere he'd find the answers—he just didn't know where. Maybe he should start over from the beginning. Maybe he ought to strip away all his preconceived notions and look at everything and everyone from a different angle.

In his kitchen, he pulled a carton of almond toffee crunch ice cream from its hiding place beneath the mound of freezer bags full of vegetables Margaret brought him, scooped out a respectable-sized serving, and settled himself at the kitchen table with an empty sheet of paper and a pencil.

He wrote for several minutes as he ate, constructing a timetable. He didn't expect the answers to suddenly become clear, but he hoped looking at the sequence of events would help. When he finished, he spooned a bite of ice cream and let it melt slowly in his mouth while he studied the list.

Sometime before midnight on Friday, the twelfth of May, Lenore Irvine and a few friends stormed the Copper Penny to protest Cutler's drinking laws and the gambling petition. Lenore and David Newman argued about the petition until Lenore spotted Webb and Paige sitting together at a table. An argument erupted between Webb and Lenore about Paige, which led to an argument between Lenore and Kent. Around that time, Casey Daniels called the sheriff's department. They arrived, broke up the argument, and sent or delivered everyone home. Grady drove Webb home, but Webb argued with Margaret and left again. Kent took Lenore home, but they'd argued and Lenore left for Denver to recruit backup for her anti-gambling crusade. Someone driving Webb's truck followed her and sent her car off the side of the road.

Fred's initial reaction put him right back where he'd always been—with Webb behind the wheel of his truck at the time of the murder. Webb couldn't account for his whereabouts—at least, he hadn't bothered to account to Fred. But Webb wasn't the only one with a motive to kill.

Frustrated, Fred scratched his chin and pushed the paper away. If the killer wasn't at the Copper Penny Lounge, why had he or she killed Lenore that particular night in that way?

Maybe Fred's first step should be to find out who drove Webb's truck down Main Street at midnight. But he didn't have a clue as to how to do that. If the driver was the murderer, he or she wouldn't run around town talking about that midnight drive; nor would he confess if Fred asked about it.

He supposed there was only one logical place to start looking—the Copper Penny Lounge. Maybe someone there noticed something as they came or went through the parking lot. Maybe someone saw the murderer making off with Webb's truck. Fred didn't think it likely, or they would have already come forward, but it couldn't hurt to ask.

Spooning up his last bite, he smiled softly. Making a decision helped him feel a little better. He'd go back to the bar, but this time, he'd go in the evening—when most of the regulars would be off work and in their usual places.

At least he'd be doing *something*.

And this time he'd dig until he learned something new.

twenty-two

Walking slowly, Fred approached the front door of Lacey's General Store. He hoped against hope that he'd find Bill Lacey alone in the store—without his wife, Janice. Her love of gossip was exceeded only by her ability to spread it, and Fred didn't have the energy to deal with her today.

He tried one last time to convince himself he could get by for a few days on what little food he had left in his kitchen, and he might have succeeded if he hadn't been almost out of coffee. No way around it, he had to go inside.

Stiffening his shoulders in anticipation, he opened the door and peered into the store. Bill Lacey stood behind the pharmacy counter in his white smock, arguing softly with Hettie Jeppson. A few customers browsed the aisles, and Janice stood in the place of honor—behind the check-out stand.

Fred bit back a sigh of resignation and pasted on a friendly smile as he stepped inside.

Janice noticed him immediately, of course. Not much slipped past her nose. "Good morning, Fred." She looked tired. Her gray curls lay nearly flat on her head, her eyes lacked their usual spark, and her nose didn't even twitch when she saw him.

He lifted a basket from the stack near the door, waved a hand over his head, and turned down the canned food aisle.

Not surprisingly, Janice trailed after him. "Fred, I'm so glad to see you. I'm worried about Maggie. How's she holding up?" A generous amount of stomach protruded above the waistband of her pants. The T-shirt she'd chosen to disguise her figure stretched tight across her ample middle and only seemed to emphasize the problem.

Fred tried not to look. "Margaret's fine," he said and kept moving until he reached the soup display.

Janice pressed one hand to her substantial bosom and let out a sigh. "Oh, I'm glad to hear it. She was in here a little while ago. She looked terrible, and I couldn't help thinking how rough this must be on her."

Janice certainly wasn't wasting any time. She never did. Fred cocked an eyebrow at her and pretended not to understand. "*This?*"

"*You* know." Janice lowered her voice to a near whisper. "Everything that's happening with Webb. And Lenore Irvine's murder on top of that." She widened her eyes a bit with each word, as if eye contact would enlighten him.

Fred made a noise low in his throat and turned his attention to the cans on the shelf.

Not surprisingly, Janice took that as a signal to continue. "You know how much I care about Maggie. We've been such good friends for so long . . ."

Fred had never noticed a bond between Margaret and Janice, but he didn't say a word.

"I'll tell you," Janice said, resting one hand on the edge of a shelf, "that man puts her through more than any woman should have to tolerate."

Fred couldn't deny that. He didn't even try. "She's holding up."

Janice opened her mouth to say something else, but snapped it shut again when Donnelle Freckleton wheeled a cart around the corner and started toward them. Odd. Janice didn't usually worry about whether anyone overheard her conversations. In fact, she usually staged them so she *would* be overheard.

Fred struggled not to stare at her. He picked up a can of oyster stew and dropped it into his basket.

Janice flashed a thin smile at Donnelle, but she didn't speak again until the younger woman reached the end of the aisle and turned the corner. Then, she stepped closer and stage-whispered, "Is it true Webb's out of work again?"

Fred didn't know why the question surprised him—he should have expected the news to fly. But how should he answer? If he confirmed the gossip to Janice, the entire county would know about it before he reached home again.

"Where did you hear that?"

She waved one hand vaguely toward the front of the store. "I don't remember. Someone mentioned it."

"Someone ought to keep their mouth shut," he grumbled and pulled another can from the shelf.

She fixed him with a steely gaze. "I'm not asking out of morbid curiosity, Fred. I'm concerned about Maggie *and* about Webb. I'd like to help."

Fred didn't even try to disguise his shock. "Help? How?"

"Any way I can." She leaned closer. He could smell garlic on her breath. "I don't for one minute believe Webb killed Lenore."

Fred couldn't help himself. He had to ask. "Then who did?"

Janice managed to look affronted. "Well, I'm sure *I* don't know."

"You haven't heard any rumors? Nobody's talking?"

"Everybody's *talking*," Janice snapped. "I'm just not listening."

Fred found that hard to believe, but he pulled two more cans from the shelf and settled them in his basket while he tried to decide how to respond.

Janice didn't seem to care whether or not he spoke. That, at least, was typical behavior. "You don't know how difficult this is for me. One of my dearest friends was murdered, and another is the prime suspect."

Fred knew Janice and Lenore had been friends, but he wondered whether she'd considered Webb such a dear friend *before* the murder. He didn't think so.

"It's as if all my childhood friends are involved," Janice said with a sniff. "If people don't suspect Webb, they think David killed her. And then there's poor Maggie, suffering like she is. And Enos—" She broke off and looked down at her feet. "Can you *imagine* how hard this whole thing is for him?"

"It's rough," Fred admitted.

She looked back up at him with sad eyes. "Do you know what Emma Brumbaugh had the *nerve* to say to me today?"

Fred didn't think he wanted to know.

"She said the only reason Enos took Webb in for questioning in the first place was because of how Enos feels about Maggie."

Fred's next breath caught. He stared into Janice's eyes, expecting to see some sign that she was enjoying herself.

But she looked honestly outraged. "I nipped *that* in the bud, of course. Gave her a piece of my mind. And I told her that if I hear anyone else say something so *stupid*, I'd hold her personally responsible."

"Good. Glad to hear it." Fred didn't know what else to say, or even what to think. This woman looked like Janice, but she didn't sound like Janice. Did she really like Margaret and Enos enough to leap to their defense? Had she cared so much about Lenore?

To his relief, someone else opened the front door and came inside. He allowed himself a flicker of hope that maybe now Janice would leave him alone.

She whipped her head around to check on the newcomer, then looked back again with eyes wider than ever. "It's *Paige Irvine*." She sounded more like herself now. Her voice cracked with disapproval.

Fred craned his neck to see. Sure enough, Paige crossed in front of the checkout stand to the magazine rack, holding her son on her hip. She wore a pair of jeans every bit as tight as the slacks Janice had on, but where Janice's ill fit was an accident of nature, Paige's was by design. A loose-fitting shirt skimmed her shoulders and upper torso but ended below her chest, leaving a fair expanse of tanned stomach exposed.

Little Trevor clutched a piece of fabric at Paige's shoulder in one hand and used the other to play with his mother's hair.

Janice stole another peek, then slanted a glance at Fred. There was purpose in her expression. "*Someone* needs to have a talk with that girl."

Fred planned to talk with her, but not the kind of talk Janice meant. "Why?"

Rolling her eyes in exasperation, Janice lifted one hand to cup her mouth. "*Look* at her," she whispered and stepped in front of him to follow her own advice. "She was such a disappointment to Lenore." She shook her head as if it was all too much to bear.

"Really?" Fred tried to peer around her, but he couldn't see Paige very well. "I hadn't heard."

"Oh, my, yes." Janice patted the back of her hair again and sighed heavily. "You know that little boy was born out of wedlock."

Fred hadn't known that for certain, but he'd suspected.

Janice lowered her voice and moved even closer. "Lenore was beside herself. After *everything* she did for that girl after her real mother died—"

Knowing Lenore, she'd kept track—kindnesses performed tallied against Paige's conduct. Paige had obviously come up lacking. The scent of old garlic mixed with Janice's stale perfume wafted into Fred's nostrils. He took a step back. "She hasn't been around much."

"Well, no." Janice sounded as if Paige's absence were the most natural thing in the world, but he could tell she was dying to fill him in.

As if Paige felt them watching her, she chose that moment to look up.

Embarrassed that he'd been caught staring, Fred worked up a friendly smile. Janice managed a stiff nod.

Paige's face clouded. She clutched Trevor a little tighter and turned back to the magazine rack.

"Why she didn't take Lenore and Kent up on their offer, I'll never know," Janice muttered.

Fred hated to encourage her, but he had to ask. "What offer?"

"You didn't *know*?"

Fred tried to tamp down a flare of irritation. She knew darned well he didn't know, and she was enjoying every minute of this. "I haven't heard a thing."

"Well . . ." Eyes glittering, nostrils flared, voice hushed, she moved in for the kill. As always, a juicy bit of gossip brought her to life. "Like I said, Paige was never married to that poor little boy's father. Nobody even knows who the man was."

Fred would have bet Paige knew, but he didn't blame her for not sharing the information with Lenore.

Janice plowed on. "Lenore told me—and she was heart-broken about this—that the guy deserted Paige the second he found out she was expecting."

Unfortunately that sort of thing happened. Always had. Fred thought that experience alone had probably been enough to cause the girl's animosity. Still, for Paige to raise the child alone was probably better than to marry someone who didn't love her or want the responsibility of a family. Marriage between two people who truly loved each other could be difficult enough.

"Naturally," Janice rushed on, "Kent and Lenore wanted to do everything they could to help."

Naturally.

"Having an illegitimate child doesn't carry the same stigma it used to," Janice said, as if everyone knew it should. "But it still isn't good for the child. They offered to adopt that poor little boy so they could give him a decent upbringing in a good Christian home. But Paige *refused*."

"She did?" In spite of Lenore? Fred tried to steal a glance at the girl. Good for her. She obviously had some steel in her backbone.

Janice bobbed her head and glanced over her shoulder to make sure Paige hadn't moved any closer. "There's no question it would have been the best thing for the boy."

Fred didn't know whether he believed that. He'd known more than one instance where very good things came out of less than ideal circumstances. Judging from what little he'd seen of Paige and her son, he thought they were probably doing very well together.

"What kind of life can a girl like that give a child?" Janice demanded with a bob of her gray head for emphasis. "Oh, she works . . . as a waitress. But she can't make much money at it, and Lenore was always concerned about the hours she had to put in."

"She seems to love him," Fred said quietly.

Janice glanced over her shoulder again as if she hadn't noticed. "Well, I'm sure she does. But love isn't always enough."

"Neither is money."

"Lenore would have learned to love that boy if Paige had been reasonable about it," Janice argued.

Learned to love? Interesting choice of words. "So that's why Paige hasn't been around much?"

"Oh, she would have been around if Lenore had let her," Janice said with a sniff. "And she'd probably have drained her poor father's bank balance in the process. Lenore gave her a very sensible offer—they wanted to adopt the boy. They would have let Paige visit whenever she wanted, but Paige wouldn't even consider it. Lenore had no choice but to put her foot down. She told Paige they wouldn't give her any help—financial or otherwise."

"I see," Fred said. He was beginning to, anyway.

"Naturally, Lenore was concerned about Hannah, as well." Janice folded her arms high on her bosom and studied Paige for a second or two in silence. "You know how easily led Hannah is. A follower, not a leader like my Denise was." She fell silent for a moment, no doubt paying silent homage to her eldest daughter.

"Lenore was worried about Paige seeing Hannah?"

Janice looked shocked. "Of *course* she was. She had to protect Hannah, didn't she?"

She probably thought she did.

"She had to tell Paige that unless she agreed to turn her life around, she wasn't welcome in their home." Janice's eyes narrowed dangerously. "And do you know, that ungrateful girl got angry with Lenore. She accused her of interfering, of trying to ruin her life." Her head bobbed again in agreement with herself. "She said some *horrible* things to Lenore. But the truth is that Lenore was the only reason those girls turned out even *half* decent . . . at least, Hannah did. *That* one—" She broke off and used her head to point toward the front of the store. "I'll tell you what she's like. She gave up all contact with her father and her sister—and with Lenore—rather than take any steps at all to get herself on track. They haven't seen or heard from her for two years—until this very weekend."

"Is that right?" Fred took a step away from Janice so that he could see Paige better. No wonder she hadn't grieved over Lenore's death. No wonder she seemed bitter. Lenore had certainly been an influence on Kent and his daughters, but she hadn't been a positive one.

New possibilities raced through his mind, followed by even more questions. The door he'd been searching for had finally opened, and he didn't intend to walk past.

He flashed a thin smile at Janice and stepped around her. "Given a choice like that, I guess I'd have made the same decision Paige did."

Janice's mouth dropped open, but she clapped it shut again and glared at him. "You *wouldn't* have."

He adjusted his grip on the basket and met her gaze steadily. "Yes, Janice. I would have," he said and walked away, leaving her staring after him.

twenty-three

As Fred neared the front of the store, he watched Paige rub a hand along Trevor's back and kiss his cheek. She might have been a disappointment to Lenore, but she loved her son. Just now, smiling at Trevor that way, she looked young and vulnerable. And Fred found himself hoping she hadn't murdered her stepmother.

She looked up as he approached. Her smile faded, and the wary expression that seemed such a permanent part of her crept back into her eyes before she glanced away.

Fred tried to look nonthreatening. He nodded a greeting, but she didn't relax.

He smiled at Trevor. "What are you doing, young man? Helping your mom find something good to read?"

The boy stared at him with huge eyes, but he didn't make a sound. Paige readjusted her grip on the boy, but she kept her attention riveted on an entertainment magazine.

"I thought maybe I'd pick up a magazine while I'm here," Fred said to no one in particular.

Paige still didn't look at him, but Trevor ducked his head into her shoulder.

"Fishing," Fred said. "I think maybe I'll take it up again this year."

No response.

He picked up an issue of *Field & Stream* and flicked through the pages in silence. From the corner of his eye he could see Janice reach the front of the store, sling a scornful look in their direction, and slip behind the check-out stand again. And he could tell by the way Paige's shoulders stiffened, she'd seen it, too.

He smiled at her again. "Finding anything interesting?"

Paige hesitated for several seconds, then shrugged. "Not really."

"Not a very good selection, is it?"

She slanted a curious glance at him. "Not really," she said again.

He could feel Janice watching them, wondering about their conversation, storing everything away. On second thought, maybe he didn't want to talk to Paige in here.

He replaced the magazine on the rack. "Tell me something. Do you know anything about reincarnation and fortune-telling . . . that sort of thing?"

An expression he couldn't read stole through her eyes, but it disappeared almost immediately. "A little."

"Have you ever been to The Cosmic Tradition at the other end of town?"

She shook her head, but she still looked curious, as if she suspected him of something underhanded. One hand moved across Trevor's back in a jerky motion. "No."

Janice pulled a dustrag from beneath the cash register and started dusting the counter. She took a couple of steps closer and pretended to be engrossed in her cleaning.

Fred glanced at her, then back at Paige. "It's a pretty good place if you're interested in that sort of thing. Not my cup of tea, but you might like it."

Paige's eyes darted from Fred to Janice and back again. Nervous as a cat. And no wonder. "Maybe."

He lowered his voice and sent another meaningful glance in Janice's direction. "It can't hurt to look in."

"No," Paige said slowly. "I guess not."

He shifted his basket to the other hand. "In fact, I'd be glad to show you where it is if you'd like."

Paige took a step back. "No, thanks."

"Well, it's up to you," he said softly. "But I thought you might be more comfortable there than you are here."

This time, Paige seemed to understand. She glanced once more at Janice, who'd reached the end of the counter and sidled another step closer, and for half a beat Paige looked young and vulnerable again. "Okay."

"Good." He shifted his basket again, glanced down at the four cans inside. He didn't want to buy them now, and he figured he could borrow enough coffee from someone to get him through tomorrow. He didn't want to spend one more minute listening to Janice or risk exposing Paige and Trevor to her malicious tongue.

Lifting one finger to tell Paige he needed a moment, he plopped the basket on the counter in front of Janice and smiled broadly. "Changed my mind." Without waiting for her response, he motioned Paige to walk in front of him and followed her out the door.

Once outside, Paige seemed to relax slightly. She turned her face to the sun and pulled in a steadying breath, then opened one eye and fixed him with her gaze. "Why did you do that?"

"That woman gets on my nerves," he said thoughtfully and started walking slowly toward The Cosmic Tradition.

Paige fell into step beside him. "You looked pretty friendly with her when I walked in."

He barked a laugh. "Friendly? With Janice? It must have been a self-defense tactic."

She almost smiled. "It looked as if you were having an interesting conversation."

"She was telling me all about you."

To his surprise the admission made her smile. "You don't beat around the bush, do you?"

"Not if I don't have to."

Paige tightened her grip on Trevor, brushed another kiss to his cheek, and used her free hand to push some of her hair from her eyes. "So, you found out everything you wanted to know about me."

"She told me a few things," he admitted. "But I'm sure there are one or two things even Janice doesn't know." He glanced at her. "If it makes you feel any better, I wasn't asking."

This time, she laughed. "Okay, so what's the scoop? What did she tell you?"

Fred shrugged and stepped from the boardwalk onto the street. "She told me Lenore and your dad wanted to adopt Trevor when he was born, but that you refused."

Paige's mouth tightened, and her face might have been made of ice. She followed him into the intersection. "That's true."

"I thought it might be."

"Did she tell you the whole story? Did she tell you what a horrible sinner I am? How I'm going to taint Trevor with my evil ways?"

"She mentioned something like that."

Paige pushed out a scornful laugh. "Lenore certainly didn't waste any time spreading that around, did she?" She pushed the hair from her eyes again and stared off into the distance. "She was a horrible woman, Mr. Vickery. I'm not sorry she's dead."

"I never thought you were."

Her bitter smile softened, and she flicked a glance at him.

But Fred waited to speak again until they'd stepped onto the boardwalk on the other side of the street. "Why did you come to Cutler?"

For a few seconds he thought she wouldn't answer him. At long last, she sighed in resignation. Her free hand started its jerky movements on Trevor's back again. "To see my dad."

That sounded reasonable. "Did he know you were coming?"

She nodded and glanced at him again. "Yes. He asked me to come."

"Did he? Why?"

"*Why?* Didn't Mrs. Lacey tell you?"

"I don't think she knew, or she would have."

Paige seemed to accept that. "He's my father."

"I was under the impression he and Lenore told you to stay away until you decided to turn your life around."

"Lenore told me to stay away. Dad just didn't fight her." The admission made her look sad. She slowed her step. "He was finally starting to see the truth about her. It was the whole deal with Hannah's school, I guess. Anyway, he'd decided he wasn't going to let her keep us apart any longer. He told me he was going to tell her how wrong she'd been, and how wrong *he'd* been to let her push him into something he didn't agree with. So, I came." She looked into his eyes. "I miss my family, Mr. Vickery."

He imagined she did. "What happened with Hannah that made your father change his mind?"

Her lips curved into a crooked smile. "I didn't know there were any secrets in this place."

"There are a few."

She let out another soft sigh and studied the window of RaeGene's Knit Shop. "Have you ever heard Hannah play the piano?" she asked at last.

Fred shook his head. "I didn't know she could play."

"She's wonderful. Talented. She has a God-given gift for music." She looked at him again and managed a thin laugh. "What's the matter, didn't you think I believed in God?"

He smiled. "I never said that." But he couldn't help thinking Paige's God was probably a bit different than the one Lenore had believed in.

Her expression sobered again. "Anyway, Hannah won a scholarship at a performing arts school in New York. You know how quiet she is—never pushes herself, never stands up for herself. I used to always tell her she had to get some backbone. I guess she finally did. Applied for the scholarship without telling Dad or Lenore. And she *got* it."

"She must be thrilled."

"She was," Paige admitted. "Until Lenore found out." Bitterness and something else—hatred, maybe—filled her eyes again. "Lenore refused to let her go."

"Why?"

"Sin, Mr. Vickery." Paige's hand slowed on Trevor's back. Her lips thinned and everything about her seemed to harden. "Same reason she wouldn't let Hannah have anything to do with me. She didn't want Hannah *tainted*."

Fred tried to keep his expression steady, but he knew he must have looked stunned. "When did you find out about the scholarship?"

"A while ago. Actually I've known ever since it was awarded to her."

"Then you had contact with someone here?"

Paige nodded. "Hannah and I kept in touch through Felicia Arnesson—she's a friend of Hannah's. Felicia let me send letters to her house, and Hannah picked them up there. Once in a while, when Felicia's mother was working or something, Hannah would use their phone and a long-distance card to call me."

"Did Lenore ever find out?"

Paige shook her head quickly. "No. She would have killed Hannah if she had. And since Dad wouldn't stand up to her, we couldn't tell him, either."

For half a second he wondered how Lenore had justified breaking the family apart that way. But finding excuses for her behavior had never been Lenore's problem. "How did your dad find you?"

"Hannah told him. I guess he and Lenore had a huge fight one night. He talked to Hannah afterward about how bad he felt and she told him everything."

"So he called and asked you to come."

"Yes. Felicia agreed to sit with Trevor while I met Dad at the Copper Penny." She cocked a half-smile at him. "We figured it was the one place Lenore would never go."

"But she chose that night for her protest, and she found you there."

"Yes."

"You were sitting with my son-in-law."

Paige stopped walking entirely and faced him, but she tightened her grip on Trevor. The boy looked mildly uncomfortable. "Yes, but it wasn't what you think."

"What was it?"

"Like I told you at the house, I met Webb that afternoon. He came in upset and talking about Lenore. Naturally I was curious to know what she'd done."

"Naturally."

Trevor made a tiny noise and squirmed in her arms. Paige loosened her grip and murmured an apology against his forehead. "We had something in common—we both hated my stepmother—and we just sort of hit if off. He was easy to talk to and he understood what I was feeling. Talking to him made me feel better."

In his wildest dreams Fred couldn't imagine Webb as a sympathetic listener. He'd had some other reason for talking to Paige, but Fred didn't like thinking what that reason might have been.

Did Webb feel anything for Margaret? Or was he staying with her because of the kids, as Quinn and Lamar had both suggested? Had he been susceptible to Paige's face and figure, or had he indulged himself for some other reason entirely?

Paige started walking again. "I feel bad, you know."

Fred stilled his thoughts and matched her gait. "About what?"

She looked straight at him. Her eyes had turned a deep shade of green, and she looked solemn. "About Webb."

Fred almost didn't want to ask. "Why?"

"Because . . ." Conflicting emotions darted across her face for a second. She flicked a nervous glance at him. "Because he's in a lot of trouble, but he didn't kill Lenore."

"There's a lot of evidence that says he did," Fred reminded her.

"I know, but he didn't kill her, Mr. Vickery. You've got to believe me."

"Why? How do you know he didn't?"

There it was again, that look of indecision. Almost as if she were arguing with herself. She took a step away and spoke over her shoulder. "This is going to make you mad, I just know it will."

"Try me."

She pulled in a deep breath and watched a car pass on the street.

Fred waited. Overhead a chipmunk chattered and a bird answered. A burst of laughter erupted from one of the nearby stores.

Too slowly, she faced him once more, but this time she looked utterly miserable. "Because he was with me when she died."

twenty-four

Fred's world grew still as he took in Paige's meaning. The sounds of nature faded, the laughter muted, and the street seemed to tilt on an invisible axis.

"Webb was *with* you?"

Paige flushed and lifted her free hand to ward off the implications. "Not *that* way. I just meant we were together. Talking."

"Where?" The word came out hoarse. Gruff. But Fred didn't care. All the anger he'd been working to keep at bay boiled to the surface.

Paige reddened and used her head to point back in the direction they'd come. "In the park." The little gazebo on the other side of the block. We were there until the sun came up."

Fred didn't trust himself to speak. He sucked air and tried to calm himself, but it didn't work.

"You're angry with me," Paige whispered. "I knew you would be."

"Did you know he was married when you agreed to meet him?"

She shook her head. "He didn't mention it." She averted her eyes and sighed heavily. "So now he's in trouble. But he's not going to tell anyone where he was because he doesn't want to make me look bad."

Fred doubted that. If Webb was keeping his rendezvous with Paige secret, he had purely selfish motives.

"I'm only telling you because . . . because I don't want him to pay for something he didn't do."

Fred tipped his face to the sky and tried once more to push back the anger that threatened to choke him.

"Mr. Vickery?" Paige sounded frightened, but he couldn't reassure her. He didn't trust himself to speak. "I didn't know he was married until you came to the house. When you told me he was your son-in-law, I felt horrible."

Fred rubbed his forehead and tried to see what hid behind her eyes. She sounded sincere, but he didn't know whether to believe her or not.

"Mr. Vickery? I don't want your daughter to think—"

"I don't want Margaret to know anything about this," he interrupted. "Not yet." He might have said more, but the sound of quick, heavy footsteps caught his attention.

Enos. Fred would recognize his step anywhere.

Paige froze, then darted a nervous glance over her shoulder. She looked back up at Fred with wide, frightened eyes. "Oh God. It's the sheriff."

Her reaction surprised him. Why should she be frightened of Enos? Unless she had something to hide. "Why don't you tell him what you just told me?"

She shook her head hard enough to make the hair fall back into her eyes. "I can't. Webb made me promise not to tell anyone."

"Why?" Fred asked, but even as the word left his mouth, he knew the answer. Webb had to know how quickly the word would spread through town. He knew how angry Fred would be and how upset Enos would get if he even suspected Webb of cheating on Margaret.

Casting another anxious glance down the boardwalk at Enos, Paige pivoted on her heel and started away. "I've got to go. I shouldn't have said anything."

"But you did," Fred pointed out. "And you need to tell the sheriff."

"No," she said, stepping around Fred. "I can't."

Fred tried to catch her arm, hoping to keep her there until Enos could reach them, but she darted away from him and almost ran toward the corner.

She rounded the corner just as Enos drew abreast of Fred.

Enos watched her disappear and pushed back his hat. "Who were you talking to? Paige Irvine?"

"Yes."

Enos lifted one sandy eyebrow. "What are you doing, Fred? Sticking your nose into another of my investigations?"

"Rescuing her from Janice Lacey," Fred said. He didn't know whether to tell Enos this latest piece of news or not. If it were true, Webb just might be innocent. On the other hand, it seemed odd that Paige would tell *him* something like this but ask him to keep it secret.

Did she expect him to tell Enos anyway? Was her protest only a token one? Or was there some reason she didn't want Webb to know she'd provided him with an alibi?

Maybe she'd made it up. Maybe Webb hadn't really been with her. She'd *seemed* genuine, but Fred knew only too well that people and things weren't always what they seemed. And he couldn't ignore the fact that, in providing Webb with an alibi, she'd also established one for herself.

Enos propped one elbow on the butt of his gun and stared out into the street. His eyes tilted down at the corners, and his mouth formed a thin line.

"You look tired," Fred told him.

He managed a weak smile. "I am." He pushed back his hat and scratched the top of his thinning hair. "I've got to admit, this investigation has me baffled."

"Then you don't think Webb's guilty?"

Enos looked out over the street as he readjusted his hat. "I just don't know. That's the trouble." He slanted a glance at Fred. "So, what were you and Paige talking about?"

Fred lifted both shoulders. He still didn't know how much he should say to Enos, but he didn't like holding out on him, either. "This and that."

Enos lowered his gaze and wagged his finger. "Don't start with me, Fred. I know you've been asking around, in spite of the fact that I asked you not to. I know you've got information that could be pertinent to an ongoing investigation. And the mood I'm in lately, I won't hesitate to arrest you for withholding that information from me."

He looked serious.

Fred worked up a thin smile. "How much do you know about Paige's relationship with Kent and Lenore?"

"I know there were bad feelings, and that there had been since Paige's son was born."

"Do you know why?"

Enos nodded. "Yeah. Do you?"

"I do."

"Is that what you were talking to her about?"

"Partly," Fred admitted. He hesitated another second, then decided to just get it over with and tell Enos everything. The story would come out sooner or later anyway. "She was also telling me that Webb was with her the night Lenore was killed."

Just saying the words aloud made the heat rise in his neck and face again and the anger start to churn.

Everything on Enos's face froze except his eyes. "That son of a bitch."

"She claims they didn't do anything," Fred added quickly. "That she didn't even know Webb was married until I told her after Lenore died."

Enos didn't respond to that. He clenched and unclenched his fists and worked a muscle in his jaw.

"I don't know whether I believe her or not," Fred admitted.

"About which part?" Enos's voice came out clipped and harsh. "That Webb was with her or that they didn't do anything?"

"Either. Both. It gives *her* an alibi too, you know."

Enos nodded and tried to smile over at him, but it came out looking more like a grimace. "Yeah. It does. I guess I'm going to have to talk to both of them again." He rubbed his face with one of his hands. "I really don't want to talk to Webb again—especially now that I know this. He's cocky and belligerent and pushy, almost as if he *wants* me to arrest him. Sitting across from him, asking him questions and looking into his face was the hardest thing I've done in a long time. I'll be honest with you. If it turns out he *is* cheating on Maggie . . ." He squared his shoulders as if he were preparing for battle, then sent Fred another miserable glance. "Hell, there isn't anything I *can* do."

Fred put a hand on Enos's arm. "I'm hoping it won't come to that."

"So am I," Enos said slowly. "But why would Paige lie about it? And why tell *you* of all people? She's got to know you'll confront Webb."

Fred had no answer for that.

But Enos didn't seem to want one. "My gut instinct tells me she's telling the truth."

So did Fred's. "I guess you've talked to Thayne O'Neal about seeing Webb's truck."

Enos looked surprised by the switch, but he nodded.

"How do you account for the timing?"

Enos's eyes narrowed as if he didn't fully understand the question.

"Thayne saw the truck just after midnight," Fred explained. "Webb, Kent, Lenore, Paige, David, and Olivia were all still at the Copper Penny at that time. The truck was back in the parking lot when Grady took Webb home and gone again when Albán left for the night."

"You've been busy."

"You bet your life, I have. Margaret asked me to help clear Webb."

"Maggie asked you to help Webb?" Enos pondered for a moment, rubbed his face again, and let out a heavy breath. He shook his head in resignation. "Are you trying to tell me Thayne didn't see the murderer?"

"Maybe. Or the murderer wasn't at the Copper Penny that night." Fred leaned one hip on the rail of the boardwalk. "It doesn't make sense, though. If the murderer wasn't at the Copper Penny, why did he or she choose that night and Webb's truck to murder Lenore?"

"The murder *has* to be connected to what happened at the Copper Penny," Enos insisted.

"I think so, too," Fred admitted. "But I just can't explain why Webb's truck was heading down Main Street—in the *opposite* direction of the murder scene."

"I don't suppose Maggie—" Enos began, then broke off with a shake of his head. "She had no reason to take Webb's truck. Did she?"

"I can't imagine why she would. She has her own car."

Enos gripped the handrail and focused on something across the street. "Does she know about Webb and Paige?"

"No. At least, I don't think she does."

"If Paige's alibi is valid, Maggie will find out, you know."

Fred would give almost anything to prevent that. On the other hand, maybe it would be the straw that finally broke the camel's back for her. Maybe it would finally galvanize her to action and force her to end her miserable marriage.

As if he could read Fred's thoughts, Enos looked down at his feet. He scuffed the toes of his boots against the boardwalk and asked, "What do you think she'll do?"

"When she finds out about Webb and Paige?" Fred shook his head slowly. "I know what I'd like her to do. I know what she *should* do."

Enos let out another heavy breath. "All these years, I've tried so hard to put her behind me. I've tried not to care what happens between her and Webb. But it's been hell, knowing she's miserable and watching that louse treat her like crap. I just don't want to see her hurt anymore."

His honestly took Fred by surprise. They'd all stepped around the subject so many times over the years, they'd grown almost comfortable with the pretense, and Fred had all but given up wondering what had happened between Enos and Margaret. "I haven't asked you this for many years," he said, facing Enos squarely. "But I'm asking you now. Why did you and Margaret break up?"

Enos looked down again and watched his boot for another few seconds before he answered. "She wanted more than she thought I could give her, I guess. She used to talk about moving away, living somewhere like Los Angeles or San Francisco or Phoenix. Hell, even Denver."

Fred could only stare at him. He'd never once heard Margaret talk of leaving Cutler.

With a shrug and a thin laugh, Enos went on. "Then Webb came along with all his big talk and fancy plans. He swept her off her feet. He told her what she wanted to hear. And she believed him. She came to see me one night before they got married." He turned to Fred then, and the look in his eyes nearly broke Fred's heart. "She said she loved me, but she didn't want to be stuck in Cutler all her life, and she asked me to reconsider my plans. But I knew I'd be miserable trying to be something I wasn't." He laughed again, a short, choking sound. "How was I supposed to know I'd be even more miserable knowing that the one woman I've ever truly loved belonged to someone else?"

He pushed away from the railing and adjusted his hat. "Aw, hell," he said, trying to sound gruff. "What good does it do to think about it? She made her choice."

"She made the wrong one," Fred said gently.

Enos blinked rapidly and looked up the street toward the sheriff's office. "Maybe. I don't know. She's stayed with him all this time."

"She might not have if you'd still been free."

Enos managed a thin laugh. "Yeah." He didn't sound convinced.

"She still cares about you, Enos. She always has." He hated admitting the next part aloud, but he had to. "It's obvious to everyone. Even Webb."

"Yeah," Enos said again. He drew in a deep breath and scowled at Fred. "Look, Fred, Jessica wanted me. Maggie didn't. That's the whole story right there."

"That's why you married her? Because she wanted you? What about you? Did you love her?"

"Yes." The word snapped from Enos's mouth like a gunshot. "I loved her enough. And I sure as hell wasn't going to go through the rest of my life alone."

Fred's heart felt like a stone in his chest. His own marriage to Phoebe had been the most important thing in his world. His haven from the storms of life. The one truly safe place he'd ever known. Even after forty-seven years together, the mere sight of her had made his heart beat faster; the gentle touch of her hand on his leg had filled him with warmth. He couldn't imagine what his life would have been like without her in it. Even worse, what it would have been if he'd had to watch her sail through life on another man's arm.

For the first time in days, he thought about moving to New Hampshire. He remembered the suggestions that he'd been responsible for keeping Margaret in Cutler. He didn't want to believe them, but he couldn't ignore the niggling doubts any longer.

"What are you thinking about?" Enos asked. "You've gotten quiet all of a sudden."

Fred slanted a glance at him and lifted one shoulder. "Nothing important. You want to get a cup of coffee at the Bluebird?"

Enos smiled with relief. "You bet. I could use one." He started walking, as if he couldn't get away from this spot fast enough.

Fred fell into step beside him and tried to concentrate on the sounds of nature, the warm spring sunshine, and the companionship of a good friend. But he couldn't still the questions racing through his mind.

He'd had a good life. He'd done almost everything he'd wanted to do. He'd known love and security. But maybe he'd been too stubborn and self-centered to realize he was robbing his daughter of the chance to have the same for herself.

twenty-five

Fred took a bracing sip of coffee and leaned back in his seat to let its warmth wash through him. They'd missed the lunch rush at the Bluebird, so they had the place nearly to themselves. Just the way Fred liked it.

Across the table, Enos stirred two spoonfuls of sugar into his cup and leaned back with a pleasurable groan. "This was a good idea. Maybe the coffee'll help clear my head so I can think again."

The jukebox clicked on and the beginning strains of an old Patsy Cline tune filled the room. Fred didn't even have to look up to know Randall Grimes had arrived—he chose that song every time.

Immeasurable sadness followed the trail of the coffee's soothing warmth, and Fred wondered again whether he could survive leaving this place. Heaven only knew he didn't want to leave, but self-doubt and concern for Margaret seemed to grow with every passing minute.

Scowling, Enos leaned forward and studied Fred's face. "What?"

Fred's expression must have given him away. He waved away the question with one hand and struggled to keep his face impassive. "Nothing."

Enos obviously knew him too well. "Don't tell me 'nothing.' Something's bothering you."

"I've got a lot on my mind, that's all."

Enos lifted his cup, but he didn't take his eyes from Fred's face. "If you're thinking about the Irvine murder, you might as well stop right there. I've turned a blind eye on you long enough."

Frowning slightly, Fred shook his head. "That's not it."

Enos added another half spoonful of sugar to his coffee and stirred so hard the spoon clinked against the stoneware, and the coffee made a tiny whirlpool in his cup. "Then you must be thinking about Webb and Paige."

Fred shook his head again. "No. Not directly, anyway."

Enos's brows knit. "Then something I said out there upset you."

Fred didn't want to discuss it. Not just now. He needed more time to figure out how he felt. Without confirming or denying, he took another sip of coffee.

But Enos didn't want to let the matter drop. "What did I say? Did I offend you?"

"No." Fred picked up the dessert menu from behind the salt shaker and studied it for a few seconds, but he could feel Enos's eyes on him the entire time.

Genuine concern darkened the younger man's eyes and pulled his mouth into a tight scowl. "This isn't fair, you know. *I* was honest with you out there."

Yes, he had been. And if Fred could trust anyone with his problem, he could trust Enos. Maybe he needed a cooler head to help him think things through. Someone more objective to help him put things in the proper perspective.

Lowering the sheet of paper, he met Enos's anxious gaze. "What you said out there—about Margaret wanting to leave Cutler all those years ago—I never knew. She never said a word to me."

"I know."

"Why?"

Enos lifted one shoulder in a shrug. "You're her dad."

"That's supposed to explain it?"

Enos managed a sheepish laugh. "We were young and foolish, Fred. Dreamers— Hell, we were kids. You don't think your parents will understand your dreams when you're that age." He lifted one shoulder in a casual shrug. "Sometimes Maggie would try to talk me into taking a map of the United

States, closing our eyes and pointing to a spot, and then moving there—wherever it was."

"That's what she wanted?"

Enos shrugged again. "Yeah, I guess so. I don't know. I'm not sure *she* even knew."

Fred let out a weary sigh. "Instead she got stuck here." He fiddled with the handle of his cup. Patsy Cline stopped singing, and the beginning notes of Elvis's "Moody Blue" blared from the jukebox speakers. "You heard what Quinn Udy said the other day . . . About it being my fault Webb and Margaret never left Cutler."

Enos nodded warily. "I heard. But you know that's not true."

Fred didn't know anything of the sort.

"Margaret and Webb made their choice to stay," Enos said. "You had nothing to do with it."

Fred tried to believe him. He *wanted* to believe, but he couldn't. "Margaret thinks she has to stay here to take care of me, doesn't she?"

"Maybe she does now, but she didn't when she was twenty and you were still in your prime. Hell, Fred, if she'd really wanted to leave, she would have done it. Obviously she doesn't want to go anywhere, so maybe you're just a convenient excuse."

Fred lowered his gaze again and stared at his fingers. Once, his hands had been large and capable. Now he had the fingers of an old man—skin sagged at the knuckles and his joints were large and misshapen. The hands of a stranger. "What do you think Margaret would do if I left?"

"If you *left?*" Enos's brows shot up in surprise. "What in the hell are you talking about?"

Fred didn't say anything.

"You're not seriously thinking of moving to New Hampshire, are you?"

"I don't know. I might."

"That's ridiculous. You'd be miserable." Enos wagged his head slowly and rubbed his face with one hand. "I can't believe you're even considering it."

"Maybe it would be the best thing all the way around."

Fred knew he sounded sorry for himself, but he couldn't seem to shake the overwhelming self-pity. "You know I don't want to leave, but I can't help wondering if maybe I'm being selfish."

"You're being *ridiculous*," Enos said, raising his voice a notch or two. "You're letting a few stupid remarks made by a few idiotic people goad you into a decision you'll regret for the rest of your life."

"Maybe." Fred shrugged and looked out the window. "And maybe I'll regret it more if I stay and make Margaret miserable."

"You're not making Margaret miserable," Enos insisted. "Besides her kids, you're the only positive thing in her life right now, and you know it."

A tiny spark of hope flickered in Fred's chest, but he couldn't allow himself to believe Enos. "I'm wondering if I'm a burden to her. Joseph seems to think I am."

Enos glared at him. "Joseph's an idiot."

That warmed Fred's heart. He almost smiled.

"I don't *believe* this," Enos said, but his words came out sounding almost like a growl. "What the hell's wrong with you? That sounds like something Doc would say."

Fred glowered at him. "I do *not* sound like Doc."

Enos leaned across the table and held his gaze. "You sound exactly like he did when Sharon was in trouble. Remember? He was going to give up his practice and retire?"

Fred remembered.

"Well, you're doing exactly the same thing. What is it with you guys and your daughters?"

Fred didn't answer.

Enos let out a hefty sigh. "This is because of Webb's involvement in the Irvine murder, isn't it?"

"It might be," Fred admitted.

"Well, then, give me a few days to solve the case before you start making decisions. If Webb *is* guilty, Margaret's going to need you. If he's having an affair with Paige Irvine . . ." Enos let his voice trail off and left the thought unfinished, but a muscle in his cheek jumped. Pulling in a deep breath, he forced himself to go on. "If I can get everything cleared up, the crisis will be over and you'll be able to think clearly again."

Fred had to admit that made some sense. But he didn't want to say so.

"Whatever you do, *don't* tell Joseph you're even considering moving to New Hampshire, or he'll start packing your bags." Enos broke off with a shake of his head and muttered something under his breath Fred couldn't quite make out. But he caught the gist of it.

Maybe it wouldn't hurt Fred to wait before making his decision. Maybe he could give Enos a few days to clear up all the confusion. Maybe Fred *was* being a touch hasty.

"All right," he said at last. "I'll wait."

"Good. Thank God you're at least still listening to reason." Enos shook his head again and looked at Fred as if he'd never seen anyone so foolish. "Whatever you do, *don't* say anything to Maggie. Can you imagine how she'd feel if she knew you were about ready to sacrifice yourself for her?"

She'd be riddled with guilt—even Fred knew that. "Fine. I'll wait. But just until you solve the Irvine case. I'm not going to make Margaret suffer anymore for my own selfishness."

To his surprise Enos snorted a laugh. "Good billy hell, Fred." He shook his head from side to side and wiped his face again. "You don't make a good martyr. You know that, don't you?"

"I'm not trying to be a martyr, you blasted fool. I'm trying to do the best thing for my daughter and my grandchildren. I'm trying to be just the teeniest bit unselfish."

Enos pushed his cup away. "Yeah. That's obvious." He leaned both elbows in the table and stared straight into Fred's eyes. "I have your promise?"

Fred stared back. "Yes."

"Good. Then, I'll get cracking on the case. And you'll keep out of it—right?"

Fred kept staring.

"No more conversations with David Newman," Enos insisted. "No more visits to Olivia's. You won't pay any more condolence calls on the Irvines."

Fred didn't look away.

"No more trips to the Copper Penny—"

If Enos was going to get ridiculous, Fred had a few conditions of his own to throw into the works. "You'll figure out who was driving Webb's truck down Main Street at midnight?"

"Of course I will."

"And you'll find out why David and Lenore hated each other so much?"

Enos's face froze. "What makes you think they hated each other?"

"Oh, come on, Enos. You know as well as I do, something happened between them when you kids were in high school. They still hated each other all these years later. Are you going to find out what it was?" Sudden realization hit him, making the last few words came out slower than the rest. "Or do you already know?"

Enos tried to look innocent. He failed. "Know what?"

"You *do* know, don't you? What was it?"

Enos pushed out a hefty sigh, and for a second Fred thought he'd try to worm his way out of telling. Instead, he leaned back in his seat and propped one arm on the table. "If I tell you, you'll let it drop there—right?"

Fred bobbed his head once, enough to look as if he were agreeing.

Enos seemed satisfied. "David has hated Lenore for years. He blames her for making Olivia break up with him. Are you sure you didn't know about that?"

Fred could only blink in surprise. "Breaking up? David and Olivia?"

"They went together for almost three years," Enos said. "In face, they were planning to get married."

"David and *Olivia?*" Fred tried to imagine them as a couple, but the picture wouldn't form—not even when he remembered them as they'd been thirty years before. "Are you sure?"

Enos's lips curved into a ghost of a smile. "Oh, yes. I'm sure. They were as hot an item as Maggie and I were."

Why hadn't Fred known that? Surely he would have seen

them around school together. Or Margaret would have mentioned something about them. "I don't remember ever seeing them together."

"That's probably because Olivia's dad didn't like David. He refused to let her go out with him, but you know what that does."

Fred nodded slowly. If he'd forbidden his kids something, they'd have moved heaven and earth to do it—even if they didn't really want to. Stubborn. Like their mother.

"So, what did Lenore do?" he asked.

Enos's smile faded. "She seduced him."

Fred's mouth fell open. "Lenore?"

"I don't think they actually had sex," Enos said quickly. "But Lenore didn't think David was right for Olivia, and she decided to prove it." He lifted his cup and stared into it for a second or two. "It happened at a party about a week before we all graduated. Lenore got David into a bedroom with her. None of us ever knew how—David has always refused to talk about it. Anyway, Janice was 'helping' Olivia look for him—you know Janice. She and Lenore planned the whole thing. She led Olivia straight to the bedroom and opened the door. David and Olivia were on the bed, fully clothed—" he said with a tight smile. "But they were kissing and . . . things. It broke Olivia's heart. She refused to see him again. And, of course, Lenore and Janice excused what they did by saying the end justified the means. They'd proved to Olivia how untrustworthy David was."

"And David's hated Lenore ever since."

"You got that right."

Fred let the idea stew in his brain while he took a sip of coffee. "I guess that explains why Olivia hated Lenore, too, doesn't it?"

"I'd say so." Enos readjusted his position in the seat. "Anyway, David left town right after that, and the next thing we knew, Olivia was married to Bill Simms."

"Is that why David hasn't been back in so many years?"

"Probably." Enos pulled his cup a little closer and sloshed the coffee around for a few seconds. "He was head over heels in love with Olivia."

"You knew Olivia and Lenore got into quite an argument that night at the Copper Penny, didn't you?"

Something that might have been surprised flicked across Enos's face, but he recovered quickly. "Of course, I did."

Fred didn't think he'd known, but he didn't say a word. He knew now. That was enough. "Do you think David could have killed Lenore because of what happened back then?"

"I don't know. I guess so. He refuses to talk about that night. Always has."

"And with Lenore dead, you let him refuse?"

"Look, Fred." Enos's voice deepened and took on its no-nonsense tone. "Just because I know a piece of information exists, that doesn't mean I can force someone to tell me about it. David can lie or withhold any information he wants."

"Get a subpoena. Have Judge White hold David in contempt if he doesn't tell you."

Enos slanted a glance at him. "What good would that do? If David doesn't want to talk about it, he won't."

"You could get it out of him . . ." At least, Fred knew *he* could if he could get David alone.

"How? Put him in stocks? Tie him to the rack? Last time I checked, those things were still illegal."

Fred couldn't have missed the sarcasm if he'd tried. "So, what are you going to do?" he demanded a little louder than might have been absolutely necessary. "What if David killed Lenore? What if this whole gambling thing just brought the old hatred back up again?"

Enos shot a glance over his shoulder, then glared back at Fred. "Good billy hell, Fred. Would you keep your voice down?"

Fred was too frustrated to care who heard him, but he lowered his voice anyway. "Well—?"

"If what happened back then has anything to do with Lenore's murder, I'll find out. And I'll deal with it."

"How?"

Enos's mouth thinned and his eyes narrowed. "I'll do whatever I need to. You don't need to worry about it."

Fred couldn't help but worry. "Every day that goes by—" he began.

"Brings me and the boys closer to the murderer," Enos finished for him. He glanced at his watch and made a face. "I've got to go. I've been here too long, anyway. I want to get home early tonight if I can. Jessica hasn't been feeling well the past couple of days." He pushed halfway to his feet and snagged his flashlight from the table.

"Anything serious?"

"I hope not."

Fred watched him work the flashlight back into place on his duty belt. "What are you going to do now?"

"I'm going to have a talk with Olivia. *You* are not."

"I wasn't even going to ask." Fred might be an old man, but he still knew how to calculate odds, and he knew he didn't stand a snowball's chance in hell of going anywhere with Enos this time.

"Good." Enos dropped his battered cowboy hat over his thinning hair and gave his duty belt another twitch. "Are you going home?"

Fred shrugged without answering.

"Let me rephrase that. You're going home now. Right?"

"Don't worry," Fred grumbled. "I'm not planning to follow you to Olivia's."

That earned a tight smile, but it disappeared almost immediately. "And you're not planning to ask any questions about the Irvine murder. Anywhere."

Fred met his gaze squarely. "I'm not planning to ask any questions about the Irvine murder. But if I happen to get in a conversation with someone, and they start talking about the murder, I won't walk away."

Enos stared at him for what felt like an eternity. At long last, he muttered, "One of these days, Fred . . ." Giving his duty belt one last hitch, he pivoted away.

Fred watched him cross the dining room, yank open the front door, and step outside. He waited until the door closed again, then leaned his head against the seat back and closed his eyes. The last few days had taken their toll on him. He hadn't eaten or slept well, and he could feel in his bones every moment he'd spent worrying.

Maybe he'd be wise to follow Enos's advice—to simply

go home and put his feet up and leave everything in Enos's capable hands. He couldn't do much of anything right now, anyway. He couldn't stop by Olivia's, it was still too early to visit the Copper Penny, and George would never let him through his door again. But Fred knew himself too well—he wouldn't rest as long as he had unanswered questions. It would be useless to even try.

Pushing to his feet, he tossed a couple of bills onto the table and followed Enos outside. Sure enough, he'd made a beeline across the street and was headed for Olivia's.

Well, good. Fred didn't care who talked to Olivia, as long as someone sorted through the whole story. He stuffed his hands into his pockets and started walking slowly toward home. He kept his eyes carefully averted as he passed Olivia's, just to prove his good intentions in case Enos noticed him passing.

And he thought. He listed suspects and motives and mentally ticked each off on his list. But no matter how many different combinations he tried, nobody emerged as a clear suspect.

As he stepped off the boardwalk to cross the intersection, the sound of tires squealing on the pavement drew him up sharply and pulled him back to the present. He glanced up just as Margaret's Chevy jolted to a stop in front of him.

Leaning across the seat, she rolled down the passengers' side window. Her eyes snapped with the golden light of anger, and her mouth formed a thin slash across her face. "Get in the car, Dad."

"What's wrong?"

She glared up at him. "Just get in the car." The words dropped between them like stones.

Fred didn't bother with any more questions—he could already tell he wouldn't get an answer. Tugging open the car door, he slid into the seat, but before he could close the door tight, she stepped on the accelerator and sped away.

She didn't speak. He didn't press. But he couldn't help wondering what on earth he'd done now.

twenty-six

Fred clutched the edge of his seat as Margaret drove. She whipped around several corners, made a pretense of stopping at a couple of stop signs, and zipped past Fred's house into the forest. Near the southern tip of the lake, she pulled to the side of the road and shoved the gearshift into park.

She shifted in her seat to face him. "How long have you known about Webb and that woman?"

Fred's heart dropped and his stomach knotted. "How did you hear about that?"

"How did I—?" She barked a bitter laugh. "In *this* town? Come on, Dad. How long have you known, and why didn't you tell me?"

He thought quickly, wondered if there were some way he could deny knowing, then abandoned that idea as a lost cause. "A couple of days," he admitted. "But I didn't tell you because it's only a rumor. In fact, the both deny—"

"They both deny it?" she interrupted. Her voice sounded like acid. "Oh. Well, then. I feel so much better now." She flicked an angry glance at him. "Do you have any idea how it feels to pick up on a piece of gossip like that? At *Lacey's*, of all places?"

No, but he could imagine. "Sweetheart, I'm—"

"And then, to find out *you* knew all along. That you'd been asking questions . . ."

"Margaret, I—" This time, he cut himself off. He had no excuse to offer. "I'm sorry. I thought I was doing the right thing. I didn't see any reason to upset you—especially if it turned out to be untrue."

She shook her head. "It doesn't matter whether it's true or not. It was like being in hell, standing there in the middle of the store and listening to Janice and Emma talk about my husband and that girl."

"Did they know you were there?"

She looked at him as if she couldn't believe he'd asked such a stupid question. "Of course, they did."

Yes. Of course. "Sweetheart . . ." He began tentatively. When she didn't cut him off, he got a little braver. "I know you're hurt, but there's no proof that Webb and Paige were seeing each other. Both claim they met just that afternoon and spent some time commiserating over Lenore's shenanigans, but that's as far as it went."

"I'm not hurt." She spoke so softly at first, Fred almost didn't hear her. "I'm angry. No— I'm pissed off as hell." Her voice grew louder with every word.

"Well, I know. But—"

She slanted a sideways glance at him and let out a lengthy sigh. "Oh, Dad. You know better than anyone how bad things have been between Webb and me. They've been that way for a long time."

Her honesty caught him off guard, but he tried not to show it. "Yes, I know."

"I thought about getting a divorce once about five years ago, but Webb convinced me we needed to stay together."

Fred could only blink in response. He'd had no idea she'd thought about divorce. Apparently, there were a good many things he didn't know about this daughter of his.

She didn't seem to notice his reaction. "Webb hated the fact that his parents were divorced. He believes kids should have the stability that comes with a home and two parents, and he convinced me our responsibility to the kids was more important than anything each of us might need or want. So, I stayed."

"And you've been miserable ever since."

She nodded and glanced at him almost shyly. "We both have been, really. Why do you think he drinks so much? Why do you think he stays at the Copper Penny until all hours of the night? We have nothing in common anymore. We don't enjoy each other's company, and I haven't wanted him to touch me in a long time." She sent another glance at him. "It's funny, in a way—all this about Paige Irvine. I'm really not hurt. I'm angry. Angry that he made me stay and then pulled a stunt like this. As if all of a sudden, when some young thing with thin thighs comes along, the kids don't matter anymore."

Fred couldn't even process everything she said fast enough to get a word out.

She laughed again—one sharp note without humor—and gripped the steering wheel with both hands. "The thing is, I'm not sure we did the right thing to begin with. Sarah left home the minute she graduated, and she rarely comes homes anymore. She doesn't like to listen to us argue. Benjamin is *never* around, and even Deborah is starting to spend more time at her friends' houses than she does at home. It's like I sacrificed everything for something they didn't even want."

"Well," he said when several long moments of silence had dragged past. "Maybe you did."

She looked up at him then, and her eyes were filled with anticipation. As if she thought he might have something wise and wonderful to say.

Nothing would have pleased him more. He would have given anything to set her mind at ease, but nothing brilliant popped into his head.

She flicked a glance at him and her lips curved into a soft smile. "You're not going to make me feel better, are you?"

"Not if it means lying to you."

That earned a genuine laugh from her.

"Look, sweetheart," he said. "I don't think there's anything more valuable in this world than a good marriage—the kind of marriage your mother and I had. You know that. And if you and Webb honestly loved each other, I'd urge you to work through your problems and stay together. But if there's no love there—if all you're doing is tolerating each other—maybe you ought to reconsider."

"What about the kids?"

"What about them?"

She looked at him for a moment, then glanced away again. "Divorce would be hard on them. They need stability—"

"What kind of stability is there in a home where the parents don't love each other?"

She didn't answer.

"What are you teaching them about love? About marriage and family? How are *they* going to have happy marriages if all they've seen is a lot of bickering, their father running off every night to avoid being home, and their mother moping around the house being miserable?"

"I don't *mope*," she protested.

"Some days you mope," he said, but he followed it with a smile to take away some of the sting.

She glared at him and fell silent.

Fred let the stillness ring between them for a few minutes before he spoke again. "Why didn't you ever tell your mother and me that you wanted to leave Cutler when you were younger?"

Her eyes widened and she drew back against the car door. "Who told you that?"

Fred didn't want to name names.

She waited for a few seconds, then let her shoulders slump and turned her gaze out the windshield as if something on the street fascinated her. "Mom knew."

The simple admission found its mark in Fred's heart, but he supposed he shouldn't have been surprised. "But you couldn't tell me."

"I was young, Dad. I knew how much you loved this place, and I watched you when Joseph and Jeffrey left . . . and then Douglas, too." She let her voice trail away and lifted her shoulders in a halfhearted shrug. "I didn't think you'd understand."

"Is that why you stayed? Because I was disappointed when your brothers moved away?"

Slowly, she let her gaze meet his again. "No. Not really. I thought I wanted to live somewhere else when I was younger, but Webb . . ." She stopped, gave her head another quick shake, and flashed him a trembling smile. "I can't blame this on Webb. I think he really wanted to move away, but by the time he started actually looking for a job somewhere else, I'd realized I couldn't leave."

"Why couldn't you? Because of your mother and me?"

"No." She stared at him for a long moment, then allowed herself a halfhearted smile. "I'm too much like you, I guess. I love it here."

Fred wanted to believe her. He just didn't know if he could.

She studied his face and her smile grew a little stronger. "Really, Dad. Can *you* imagine living anywhere else?"

She knew him too well. He sighed and turned away. "You know Joseph wants me to move to New Hampshire with him."

"I know. It's the stupidest idea he's come up with yet." He could feel her watching him. "You're not considering it, are you?" When he didn't immediately respond, her voice rose a notch and she leaned forward, trying to see his eyes. "You're *not*, are you?"

He shrugged.

"Who's moping now?" she demanded with a brittle laugh. When he didn't laugh with her, she flopped back against the seat. "Okay, spill it. Why are you even thinking about doing something so ridiculous?"

How could he explain without making her feel guilty? He cast about for an answer, but he didn't find one soon enough.

"Because of me?" she demanded.

He tried to look shocked at the suggestion, but even he could feel how far short of the mark he came.

"Oh, Dad." She lowered her head and stared at her lap for a long time. "What did Joseph tell you?"

"It's not just what Joseph said," Fred admitted, but he still couldn't meet her gaze.

She waited for him to go on. He couldn't.

Leaning forward again, she placed one hand on his. "I don't know what's going on inside your head, Dad. But that's nothing new. I never do."

He managed a weak smile.

Obviously encouraged, she went on. "But I'll tell you right now, I don't know what I'd do without you here. Honestly.

Oh, I'll admit you're as stubborn as a mule half the time. And you *are* ornery—"

"*Ornery?*" He flicked a glance at her and snorted his reaction to that.

She laughed. The sound ran up the scales of delight and warmed his aching heart. "Yes, ornery—in a charming sort of way, of course." She grinned and pulled an answering smile from him.

"I've been told I'm a burden on you."

"A *burden*?" She laughed again. "You're not a burden. You keep me on my toes. You keep life interesting."

He couldn't deny he liked hearing her say that, but he offered one last token protest. "Maybe if you didn't think you had to check on me all the time—"

She looked at him with narrowed eyes. "You know I worry about you, but I'm grateful you live close enough for me to see you every day. Imagine how much I'd worry if you were across the country. Besides"—she slanted a sly look at him—"without you and your tricks, what would I have to look forward to?"

He worked up an outraged expression. "*Tricks?*"

She waved a hand toward the windshield. "Yes, tricks. You know—running around town, getting yourself into trouble, sticking your nose where it doesn't belong, getting Enos upset with you, arguing with Doc, eating what you shouldn't. Tricks."

In spite of himself, Fred smiled. He patted her knee and felt himself relax for the first time in days. He couldn't have said whether every word was true, but he liked thinking so. "You really don't mind having your old dad around?"

"Mind?" This time, her eyes misted. "I don't know what I'd do without you, and that's the truth. You've seen me through every crisis I've ever had."

"And caused half of them," he said, only half joking.

"Well . . ." She bit back a grin. "Maybe not quite half. Let's say one-third."

This time he laughed aloud. But a second later he sobered again. "I love you, Margaret."

"I love you, too, Dad." She sighed softly and leaned her

head against the seat back. "You know, it's funny. Mom always said I was a lot like you, but I never could see it when I was younger. But here we are—you think I stayed in Cutler because of you, and you're thinking of leaving because of me. Maybe we are a lot alike."

"Maybe." He certainly liked thinking so.

She flicked a glance at him. "So, tell me . . . what do you think I should do?"

"About what?"

"About Webb. About my marriage. About my life."

Half a dozen suggestions welled up in his throat, but he held back all of them. He'd already said far more than he should have. He'd have to tread carefully from here on. "I think you should try not to jump to conclusions about Webb and Paige Irvine. Wait and see if there's any truth to the rumor."

She rolled her eyes toward the car's roof. "It's not just that. Our marriage is dead. And there's his drinking. He's getting worse. And the job. He lost his job, but he never told me about it. You did. I had to *ask* him. I'm just not sure I can live that way anymore."

"Whether you do or don't, that's a decision you'll have to make. I can't tell you what to do."

"You could," she said. "But you won't."

"That's right."

She rubbed her hands along her knees for a few seconds and watched her fingers as if she'd never seen them before. "You think I should divorce him, don't you?"

"I think it's a decision you need to make on your own. There's no way I'm going to tell you what to do and have you come back on me in a few months when things get difficult."

"Now you sound like Mom."

"Thanks. Now I know I said the right thing."

She let another few seconds pass before she spoke again. "Do you think it's true—about Webb and that girl?"

"I don't know."

She looked away from her hands and let out a sad sigh. "I guess the biggest question I have is not whether anything actually happened, but whether he *wanted* it to."

"I don't know the answer to that, either."

"Maybe I should talk to her."

"To Paige?" Fred pulled back a little. "I don't know, sweetheart—"

"Why not? He's my husband. I think I have the right to know what happened that night and whether anything has happened since."

"Well, yes. But—" He squared his shoulders and firmed up his voice. "I don't think it's a good idea."

"Why not?"

"I just don't. I think you'd be setting yourself up for a very uncomfortable confrontation."

"And you think I should avoid it just because it would be uncomfortable?"

"I think," he said carefully, "you should avoid it because Janice Lacey and her friends would have a heyday with something like that. And until you know whether it's true or not, you'd be wise not to stir up anything else."

He could tell she didn't like hearing that, but she shrugged as if she'd give it some consideration. "You think she'll say things I don't want to hear?"

Fred shook his head. "No. At least, that's not the whole reason. Actually, I'm not convinced she's telling the truth. Her story may give Webb an alibi, but it also gives her one. And she got pretty upset by the idea that I'd ask him about it."

Margaret looked interested in that. "Did you ask him?"

"Not yet."

"Are you going to?"

"I haven't decided," Fred admitted. "Does he know you've heard about it?"

"I haven't told him, but he'll find out soon enough. Benjamin heard about it at school."

Fred's heart sank. He didn't want the kids to know. "How did he react?"

"He's upset—naturally. He came bursting in the front door after I got home from Lacey's, shouting all sorts of things about his dad . . . and about me, and then he left again. I have no idea where he is or what he's doing—not that *that's* anything new." She picked at something on the steering wheel with a fingernail. "Actually, I guess that's what made me come to find you—knowing that Benjamin knew. It would have been so much easier to deal with this if we'd had some advance warning."

"Maybe I should have told you."

She shrugged. "Maybe. Probably. Just don't ever keep anything like that from me again, okay?"

He couldn't promise that. He dipped his head and let her draw her own conclusions as to his meaning.

She reached for the keys and started the ignition. "So? What now?"

"Now you can take me home. I've been gone all day, and I'm tired."

Her eyes narrowed. "You're not going to let me go with you, are you?"

"Go with me? Where?"

"To see Paige Irvine?"

He could only stare at her. "What makes you think I'm going to do that?"

She lifted one shoulder and pulled the gearshift into drive. "It's what I'd do. I'd go talk to her again. Pin her down about that night. Find out whether she and Webb were really together or whether she's using him to give herself an alibi."

"Would you?"

"I would," she said, as she checked over her shoulder for oncoming traffic and started maneuvering the car through a three-point turn that would face them in the right direction. "Or I'd talk to Webb."

Fred had to admit both ideas made sense. But he didn't want Margaret anywhere around if he followed through on either. "I've been given strict orders not to talk to anyone."

She smiled at him. "And you're going to follow orders? Why start now?"

He purposely kept his answer vague. The less said, the better. "I don't want to upset Enos."

"No, of course not." She didn't sound as if she believed him.

"This is a very complicated case."

"I know it is." In fact, she sounded almost sarcastic.

He leaned back in his seat and watched the lake through the trees while she drove. Its surface, clear and endlessly blue, sparkled in the sunlight, beckoning him. He'd solved many a problem walking the path around that lake. The clear mountain air had always helped him think more clearly.

He sat up a little straighter. "Margaret. Sweetheart. Would you mind stopping the car?"

"Why? Is something wrong?"

"No. But I think I'll get out here and walk home."

"Then you're really *not* going to the Irvines?"

"I'm really not."

Without another word she veered to the side of the road and brought the car to a halt. But when he started to open the door, she put a restraining hand on his arm. "Dad?"

"What, sweetheart?"

"I meant what I said about needing you here."

He leaned across the seat and kissed her cheek. "Thank you."

"Promise you won't give in to Joseph?"

He smiled—couldn't help himself. It was the first promise anyone had asked for all day he knew he could keep. "I promise."

Climbing out of the car, he closed the door between them and crossed the road. He stood there on the shoulder and watched her drive away. His heart ached for her, but he felt better than he had in a long time. She'd been honest with him, and no matter how hard some of the things had been to hear, he liked knowing her head was on straight—or almost, anyway.

When she'd disappeared around the bend, he tipped his face to the sky and soaked up the sun's soothing rays. He stood that way for a long time, listening to the birds squawking and the chipmunks chattering, to the sounds of the gentle waves washing up on the lake's shore.

If there were answers to be found, he'd find them here.

twenty-seven

Fred stepped around an aspen tree and rounded a curve in the path. He pulled in a deep breath of clear mountain air and let it out again slowly. He'd been right to get out of Margaret's car and walk. He hadn't had any brilliant flashes of insight yet, but if he were going to have any, he'd have them here.

He glanced at the lake, pulled in another deep breath, and tried to clear his mind. The muddy shoreline stretched away in either direction, disappearing into the trees a few feet to his left, leading to an outcropping of rocks several hundred feet away on his right.

Fred had spent many hours fishing from that spot. He thought about walking onto the rocks now, but someone else already stood there, and Fred didn't want to waste time on conversation. Not today. He had important things on his mind.

He started to turn away, but something about the lone figure drew his attention one more time. This time, he recognized Benjamin's lanky frame, narrow shoulders and chest, and his sheaf of blonde hair. So this was where he'd run off to.

Giving up on solitude for the moment, Fred shifted direction and picked his way through the muddy soil toward where Benjamin stood. He stuffed his hands into his pockets and tried to look and sound casual as he approached. "You'll catch more fish if you use a pole."

Benjamin looked over his shoulder and stiffened when he saw Fred standing there. "I'm not fishing."

"You look pretty serious," Fred said, taking a couple of steps closer. "You must have a lot on your mind."

"Yeah." Benjamin stared out at the lake.

"Do you want to talk about it?"

"Nope."

Fred moved closer. "You're still upset with me."

This time Benjamin didn't even bother to answer.

"I see." Fred closed the remaining distance and rocked back on his heels. "I just spoke to your mom a few minutes ago. In fact, she dropped me off here so I could walk home."

The boy didn't say a word.

"Do you want to walk with me?"

"Nope."

"So, you're going to stand there all day being mad at me?"

Benjamin shot him a hostile glance. "Maybe."

"I see," Fred said again and tried not to sound impatient. But this wasn't getting them anywhere. He decided to take the bull by the horns and say what was on both their minds. "Your mom tells me you're upset about some rumors you heard at school."

That got the boy's attention. "I don't want to talk about that. It's *disgusting*."

"It's just rumor at this point, you know."

Benjamin glowered at him and turned away again.

"Have you asked your dad about it?"

"No, and I'm not going to, either. I don't want to hear his excuses."

Fred considered that for a moment. "What makes you think he won't tell you the truth?"

"*My* dad?" Benjamin snorted his opinion. "He wouldn't know the truth if it hit him in the face."

Interesting. Especially coming from a boy who'd been so eager to leap to his dad's defense just two days ago. Fred looked out over the lake and tried to decide what to say next. He didn't want to close the channels of communication again.

Water lapped gently against the rocks. Overhead, a bird chattered an intruder warning. "You don't want to give your dad the benefit of the doubt on this one? At least until you find out whether it's even true?"

Another snort, then silence.

Fred took that to mean no. He stooped to pick up a pebble and skipped it across the water. Buying time. Searching for the best thing to say next.

The silence seemed to reach Benjamin as nothing else had. He lowered himself to the rocks and buried his face in his hands. "I hate him, Grandpa."

Fred didn't like hearing Benjamin talk like that, but he didn't argue. He'd learned long ago not to even try to deprive someone of a strong emotion. Better to let the boy work through his pain and anger.

Forcing his stiff knees to bend, he joined Benjamin on the ground. The chill from the rock seeped through the fabric of his trousers and sent a shiver racing along his spine. He'd have a hell of a time getting up from here, but he didn't want to carry on the rest of this conversation from even a short distance.

He reached a tentative hand toward Benjamin and touched his shoulder lightly. "I'm sorry you had to hear the gossip, son."

"Mom says you knew about it." The boy's voice came through his hands slightly muffled.

"I'd heard talk," Fred admitted. "I didn't tell any of you because I didn't know if it was true. Do you want to know what your dad says about it?"

Benjamin lifted half of his face from his hands and fixed Fred with one unwavering eye. "No."

Fred looked out over the lake again. "Well, I think I'm going to tell you anyway. I think you need to know."

He half expected Benjamin to lurch to his feet and try to leave, but the boy just stared at him with that one cold eyeball.

"He says he met Paige that afternoon at the Copper Penny and that they talked for a while about Paige's stepmother. You know how upset your dad was with Mrs. Irvine—"

Benjamin bobbed his head once. "Yeah, I know."

"Well, Paige was angry with her, too. Family problems. So

your dad and Paige talked for a while and shared a few horror stories." He turned his gaze back to Benjamin. "He says nothing else happened."

With an exaggerated roll of the eye, Benjamin turned away again. "Yeah. I'm sure."

"It might be true," Fred suggested.

"Yeah," Benjamin snarled. "And it might be another one of his lies. What does he need with her, anyway?"

Fred didn't even want to speculate.

Benjamin ran the fingers of one hand along the neck of his T-shirt. A medallion of some kind dangled from the end of the chain. It looked familiar to Fred, but he couldn't place where he'd seen it before. "She's *way* too young for him. She's closer to *my* age than his."

Fred couldn't deny that. Webb could easily have had a daughter Paige's age if he'd started his family a year or two earlier. "When you get older, you'll find that age differences don't mean so much. A year or two can be a huge gap when you're seventeen, but twenty years is nothing at my age."

The boy didn't look impressed.

Fred let another few seconds of silence lapse. "I've been asking around, you know. Just like you and your mother wanted. I've been trying to find out if anybody knows anything that will help your dad."

"Yeah? Well, don't bother."

Fred didn't let Benjamin pessimism stop him. "You know what has me most baffled right now?"

No response.

"Thayne O'Neal saw your dad's truck heading down Main Street a little after midnight. Now, what I don't understand is, who was driving that truck? Because everyone else who might be a suspect in Mrs. Irvine's murder, including your dad, was still inside the Copper Penny at that time."

Benjamin flicked a curious glance at Fred.

"I'll tell you what's even stranger. The truck was *back* in the parking lot less than an hour later when the sheriff's department got to the bar."

A muscle in Benjamin's jaw twitched.

"And it was gone again when Albán locked up at two

o'clock." Fred propped his elbows on his knees. "Now, don't you think that's odd?"

Benjamin lifted his shoulders in a casual shrug. "I don't know."

"What I need to find out is whether anybody saw anything as they were coming or going from the Copper Penny that night."

"Like what?" Benjamin looked interested. At last.

"Maybe somebody standing near the truck. Somebody walking through the parking lot. Anything at all."

Benjamin sighed heavily and dropped his head into his hands again.

Such an odd reaction, goosebumps pricked the back of Fred's neck, and the rock beneath him seemed to grow colder. "I don't suppose you were out that night?"

Benjamin didn't react for several long seconds, then he sighed again and slowly lifted his head. "I might have been."

"Surely you remember whether you were or not."

"Okay." Benjamin reared back and glared at him. "Yeah, I remember. I was out."

"Anywhere near the Copper Penny?"

"Yeah. For a few minutes."

"Did you see anybody near your dad's truck?"

Another pause, this one even longer than the last, as if he had to consider his answer. "No." He met Fred's gaze steadily. Too steadily.

"Do you know anything about who took the truck?"

Benjamin indulged in another telltale pause before he lurched to his feet and bolted away a few steps. "Okay, I'll confess. Is that what you want? I took my dad's truck, all right?" He waved his arms around and thumped himself in the chest hard enough to make the medallion jump. "*I* took it."

Dread settled like a stone in the pit of Fred's stomach. "When?"

"Around midnight, I think."

"Why?"

The boy shoved his fingers through his hair and paced another few steps. "Just helping a friend."

"What friend?"

"Just a *friend*, all right? I can't tell you."

Fred took a few seconds to work back to his own feet and closed the distance between them. Benjamin's medallion reflected the light into his eyes, and he remembered where he'd seen its mate. But the answer didn't make him feel any better. "I think you'd better tell me everything."

"I can't."

"Why not?"

"Because . . ." Benjamin waved his arms again in a gesture of helplessness. "Because, I just *can't*."

Fred stood more squarely in front of him. "Who are you trying to protect?"

"Nobody."

It was a lie. Fred knew it, and Benjamin knew he did. He used his sternest voice when he spoke this time. "Now you listen to me, son. We're not playing games here. We're talking about a murder. Your dad's truck was involved. You were in that truck a couple of hours before the murder. I think you'd better start telling me the truth."

Benjamin's face grew stony. He clamped his lips shut and threw up his arms in frustration.

"All right. Fine," Fred said. "We'll go see Sheriff Asay, and you can tell him."

When he reached for Benjamin's elbow, the boy jerked away. "I'm not going to tell him anything, either."

"You're going to have to." This time Fred managed to snag the boy's upper arm. He started toward the path again with Benjamin in tow, well aware that Benjamin had grown strong enough to get away if he really wanted.

"I *can't*, Grandpa."

Fred halted in his tracks and faced the boy. "You'd better tell me. Right now. And if it's something Enos needs to know, you'll have to tell him, too."

"It isn't. I swear." Benjamin hung his head and tried to look pathetic.

"Out with it."

"Okay, but let go of my arm."

Fred shook his head and firmed his grip. "After you're through talking." He wasn't about to let Benjamin make a run for it. He couldn't even hope to keep up with the boy on the uneven trail.

"It's this girl I've been seeing. She was having some trouble at home, and she needed me to come and get her."

Fred's stomach knotted. He already knew, but he forced himself to ask. "What girl?"

"Grandpa—"

"What girl?" Fred could hear the ice in his words. He didn't care.

"She's just this girl."

Fred started walking again. Fast enough this time to make following a little difficult for Benjamin, off-kilter as he was.

"Okay, okay. Jeez, Grandpa, what's the matter with you?"

Fred halted again. "Tell me the girl's name."

Benjamin shifted position and tried again to tug his arm away.

He almost broke Fred's grip, but Fred managed to hold on. "It's Hannah Irvine, isn't it?"

Benjamin studied his face for a long moment. He tried to look tough, even intimidating, for a second, but his efforts failed. His bravado evaporated, and his face fell. "You've got to promise you won't say anything to anybody."

"I can't make a promise like that."

"All right. It was Hannah. She needed a ride to the Copper Penny because she found out her stepmom was on the way over there with her group from PFAAD. Hannah knew Paige was meeting her dad there, and she wanted to warn them to leave before Lenore caught them."

"And she called you for a ride?"

Benjamin shook his head quickly. "No, she called to see if I knew anybody who could get a car. Tyler O'Neal was at the house with me, so we took my dad's truck and picked her up. I knew I could because Dad always leaves his keys in the truck."

Fred's pulse skipped a beat. "Did you tell *her* that?"

Benjamin nodded miserably.

"What happened then?"

"Ty and I took her to the Copper Penny, and then I drove Ty home. I wanted to stay with Hannah, but she didn't want me to. She said she'd ride home with her dad, and Ty was already late getting home."

Fred had trouble taking it all in. "How long have you and Hannah been dating?"

"We're not dating, exactly. Her stepmom wouldn't let her see me because of the way my dad drinks and everything. So, we met whenever we could and talked on the phone whenever Mrs. Irvine wasn't around." The boy's face reddened and his chin almost quivered. "Now there isn't anybody to keep us from seeing each other, but she's leaving."

"Leaving?"

"She has a scholarship to a music school back east. And the worst part is, her dad's decided he doesn't want to stay in the house here, so he's selling it. They're moving away, so even when Hannah comes home, she won't be coming here."

"Did your dad know you were friends? Or that Mrs. Irvine wouldn't let you see each other?"

Benjamin looked at him as if he'd never heard such a ridiculous suggestion. "Hell, no. Can you imagine what Dad would have done if he'd known Mrs. Irvine did that?" The words dropped between them and hung there in the silence. "I didn't mean *that*," Benjamin said quickly.

Fred added this new piece to the puzzle and let it slide into place. Benjamin had just told him something important, but he still didn't know exactly how it fit into the puzzle.

Hannah had known about Webb's keys. She'd had access to his truck. She'd certainly had ample reason to resent her stepmother—the scholarship, Benjamin, driving her sister and nephew away. But had she hated Lenore enough to kill her? Or had she inadvertently planted an idea with Kent or Paige—both of whom had equally strong motives for murder—when she explained how she got to the Copper Penny that night? Or had Webb killed her, and was he now taking advantage of the confusion to hide his guilt?

Fred didn't have all the answers, but he had more than he'd had ten minutes before. For the first time in days, the puzzle pieces were starting to shift into place.

twenty-eight

Fred met Benjamin's gaze and held it. "You have to tell Enos about this."

Benjamin shook his head. Stubborn young buck. "Grandpa, I can't get her into trouble."

"Don't argue with me, son. If you don't tell Enos, I will. Hannah may be in more serious trouble than you even imagine."

Benjamin's eyes widened. "You don't think *she* did it? Grandpa, she's not like that."

"Listen, son." Fred tried to keep his voice from rising, to remove any trace of impatience or anger, but even he could tell he hadn't been successful. "Maybe you know what's been going on in that family. Maybe you don't. I'm not even sure *I* know everything. But Lenore caused a lot of hostility. A lot of anger. Any one of them might have killed her."

"Not Hannah."

"We'll let Enos figure that out," Fred assured him. "We'll call him from my house."

Benjamin puffed out his chest as if he intended to argue. But Fred didn't stop to listen. He tugged the boy's arm and led him along the path. The breeze that had seemed so warm a few minutes earlier suddenly took on a chill, and the sun passed behind a cloud. Benjamin lapsed into a sullen silence, and Fred did nothing to break it. At least the boy wasn't putting up a fight.

When they reached Fred's back deck, he pulled his keys from his pocket and spent a few seconds trying to fit the key into the lock with one hand. He didn't release Benjamin until they were inside with the door shut behind them.

While Fred snagged the receiver from the wall and punched in the numbers for the sheriff's office, Benjamin dropped into a chair by the kitchen table and propped his chin in both hands. He looked sullen. Fred didn't care.

He waited eight rings without an answer, muttered a frustrated curse, and disconnected. Where on earth—?

Olivia's. Enos had been on his way there last time Fred saw him. Maybe he was still there.

Fred pulled the telephone book from under a stack of mail, located the store's number, and punched another set of numbers.

This time, he was rewarded almost immediately by Olivia's husky voice on the other end.

"Olivia's."

"Olivia? It's Fred."

"What do you want, Sherlock?" She didn't sound overly friendly.

He resisted the urge to ask her about David Newman and concentrated on the issues at hand. "I'm looking for Enos. Is he still there?"

"No."

Very helpful. "How long ago did he leave?"

"Not long enough."

Obviously, Olivia hadn't enjoyed their conversation. "Do you have any idea where he went?"

"You're the ace detective," she snapped. "*You* figure it out." And without giving him a chance to ask anything else, she hung up on him.

Fred dialed George Newman's number next.

George answered on the second ring. "Yeah?"

"George? It's Fred. I'm looking for Enos—"

"Why? So you can tell him more lies about my David?"

Fred held back a sigh of impatience. "This is important, George."

"Well, he isn't here," George grumbled and followed with a distinct click as he disconnected.

Fred stared at the receiver for a few seconds, trying to think of somewhere else to look. He tried Enos's house. No answer. He called the Bluebird, but nobody there had seen Enos since he'd walked out after coffee with Fred.

Pacing to the window, Fred stared out over the lake. He could feel Benjamin watching him.

"What's the matter?" Benjamin asked. "Can't you find him?"

"No." Fred pulled in a deep breath and thought. Enos might still be on his way to George's place. Or he could be somewhere else entirely. But where? He turned back to face Benjamin and opened his mouth to say something else, then snapped it shut again when he realized one other place Enos might have gone. "I think I know where he is."

"Where?"

"He must have gone to talk to the Irvines again. I'm going to have to run over there and let him know what you've told me when he comes outside."

Benjamin started to stand. "I'm going with you."

"No." He'd inadvertently put Benjamin in danger once before, several months ago. He couldn't let anything like that happen again. He crossed to the boy in two strides and pressed him into his seat. "I'm not taking any chances this time. You go home."

Benjamin's face took on that stubborn look he wore more and more as he grew older. "If Hannah's going to be in trouble, I want to be there for her."

"All I'm going to do is drive up to the house and see if Enos is there. If he is, I'll ask to speak to him outside. If not, I'll drive off again. Even if I let you come, which I won't, you wouldn't see Hannah."

Benjamin tried again to stand. "Grandpa—"

Fred pushed him back into his seat. "The best way for you to help Hannah is to go home and keep trying to reach Enos in case I'm wrong. And don't think you're going to follow me somehow. It won't work."

Benjamin still looked as if he wanted to argue, but he didn't struggle too much against Fred's hand.

"I mean it," Fred warned. "If you want to help Hannah, do what I tell you."

The boy glared at him. "I'm not a baby, Grandpa."

"I never said you were. But Kent and Paige will probably both be there—"

"Paige?" Benjamin grimaced as if he'd tasted something bitter. "I don't want to see *her.*"

"Then go home. I'll let you know what happens."

Benjamin gave a reluctant nod and dropped his chin back into his hands. He still didn't look happy, but Fred knew he'd won this round.

He snagged his keys from the hook near the telephone and started for the back door. He didn't want to waste time on foot. "If you reach Enos, tell him where I've gone."

Benjamin answered without looking at him. "I will."

A few minutes later, Fred pulled the Buick onto Lake Front Drive. He drove as quickly as he dared into town and looked for Enos's truck as he crossed Main Street, but Enos's parking space stood empty.

He tried to remain calm as he turned off Main Street and maneuvered through the neighborhood toward the Irvine house. But he couldn't stop thinking that someone there had killed Lenore and that he held the key that might help unlock the mystery.

If Fred had been a betting man, he'd have put his money on Paige as the murderer. Love for a child could drive a person to strange and desperate measures. He couldn't even imagine what Phoebe would have done if someone had threatened to take away one of her children.

He reached the Irvine house in less than five minutes. But to his dismay, Enos's truck wasn't there, either. He slowed the Buick and crept past the house. Nothing. Two houses down, he pulled into a driveway and turned the Buick around. If Enos wasn't here, where in the hell *was* he?

He started to drive away, when a movement on the front porch of the Irvine house caught his eye. Red hair, loose-fitting jeans, and a long plaid shirt that fell past her hips. Hannah.

She closed the door behind her and started across the lawn toward the street. Fred watched her, smiling softly to himself.

Well, well, well. He couldn't have found a more perfect setup if he'd asked for one.

He supposed he really should drive on by—Enos would have something to say if he stopped. On the other hand, if he talked to Hannah first, if he found out who she told about Webb's truck key, he'd have something more than speculation to pass on when he finally found Enos.

Hesitating only a second, he waited until she'd almost reached the street, then urged the Buick slowly forward.

When she heard him approaching, she jerked her head up like a deer caught in the wild by a hunter. Her eyes rounded, her mouth formed an O, and she froze in her tracks. She relaxed slightly when she recognized his car, but she still looked like a trapped animal. The past few days had definitely taken their toll.

Stopping the car in front of her, Fred pressed the automatic window button and leaned across the street. "How are you, young lady?"

She forced a nervous smile. "I'm okay."

"Are you going somewhere? Can I give you a lift?"

"No. I'm taking a walk. I need to think." She managed another weak smile. "But thanks, anyway."

Fred spoke quickly, before she could walk away. "I just left Benjamin at my house."

Her gaze shot to his face again. She tried to look confused, as if she couldn't imagine why he'd mention Benjamin to her. But he could see the stark interest in her eyes.

"I think you and I need to talk for a few minutes." Fred tried to keep his voice gentle. Nonthreatening.

But she recoiled as if he'd slapped her. "Why?"

"Do you want to get in the car? Or should I join you out there?"

She sent a frightened glance toward the house. "I can't."

"We need to talk, Hannah. Either in the car or out there, I don't care which."

She tried to stare him down, but he didn't move a muscle. At long last, resignation washed over her. It almost replaced the fear on her face. "Drive down to the corner," she said almost too softly for Fred to hear. "I'll meet you there."

He didn't like the idea of leaving her free to bolt back inside, but he had no choice. Rolling up the window, he drove away. But he kept one eye on his rearview mirror and held his breath until she wrapped her arms around herself and started walking in his direction.

When he was certain he couldn't be seen from the house, he pulled to one side of the road and stopped the car again. Hannah walked slowly, head down, shoulders hunched. She looked tired and weak. Frightened.

Again, Fred realized she must have been under a terrible strain the past few days. She must have suspected her father or her sister, but that was too much for a girl that age to handle alone. And he suspected Paige and Kent were too caught up in their own turmoil or guilt to offer much consolation.

After what felt like forever, she reached the car, tugged open the door, and slid onto the seat beside him. Trying to look tough, she met his gaze, but she couldn't maintain the bravado. Her face crumpled. "What?"

"I just had a long talk with Benjamin," Fred said again. "He told me he drove you to the Copper Penny the night your mother died."

Something flashed through her eyes too quickly for Fred to identify it. "She wasn't my *mother*. My mother died when I was five. Lenore was my stepmother."

"Okay," Fred conceded. "Benjamin picked you up in his dad's truck and drove you to the Copper Penny the night your *step*mother died."

She nodded without meeting his gaze again.

"Is that why you called him? Because you knew he could take his dad's truck?"

She pulled away from him and pressed her back against the door. "No. Ben's my friend. I called because I needed to get to the Copper Penny before Lenore did. She was going to pick up a couple of people, and I thought I'd have time to warn Dad and Paige she was on her way. Ben said he could come and get me because his dad always left his keys in the truck."

At least their stories matched. "Benjamin left me with the impression the two of you were a little more than friends."

Another expression flashed across her face, but this time Fred thought he recognized it. Panic. "We're *friends*."

"You weren't seeing him against Lenore's will?"

She lifted a shoulder. "Sort of."

Sort of. He couldn't see any *sort of* about it, but he let it pass. "How did you feel about Lenore telling you not to see Benjamin?"

"I don't know."

"Did it upset you?"

"Sort of."

Fred took that as a yes and moved on. "Paige tells me you've been awarded a scholarship to a performing arts school."

She answered with a wary nod.

"I understand Lenore didn't want you to go."

"She didn't."

The girl wasn't exactly a font of information. Fred held back a sigh and tried again. "Did you resent that?"

"Yeah. I guess. A little." She accompanied her answer with another lifeless shrug, but her eyes darted to his face and back to her hands. He'd hit a nerve.

"Maybe more than a little?"

"Yeah. I guess."

Well, that was helpful. On to the next motive. "What did you know about Lenore's plan to take Trevor away from Paige?"

Her fingers tightened, her shoulders stiffened, and her face froze. Bingo. "A little. Why?"

"You did know about it, then?"

"Yes." A splotch of color crept into each cheek.

"How did Paige feel about it?"

She looked at him as if he'd just landed from another planet. "How do you *think* she felt?"

"I don't imagine she was very happy with the idea. What about your dad?"

"He was supposed to stop Lenore. He promised Paige he'd stop her. That's why Paige agreed to come up here in the first place. Because Dad *promised*." She clamped her lips shut as the last word left her mouth, as if she'd just realized she'd said too much.

Fred's pulse picked up a notch. "But he didn't follow through?"

Hannah shook her head, slowly this time. She looked wary.

"Then, he was going to help Lenore take Trevor from Paige?"

"No." She rubbed her forehead and pushed some of her red hair from her face. "No. He wouldn't have done that."

"Did Paige know he was going to break his promise?"

She unraveled her fingers and picked at something Fred couldn't see on the leg of her jeans. "Yes."

"And she was angry."

Hannah nodded. "Wouldn't *you* be?"

"Yes, I would." Fred shifted in his seat to face her better. "Did you tell Paige how you got to the Copper Penny that night?"

She stiffened again and stopped working on her pantleg. "What do you mean?"

"Did you tell Paige that Benjamin picked you up in his dad's truck?"

Her eyes darted around the car again. "I don't remember."

Fred pretended to believe her. "So you don't remember telling Paige that Webb always left his keys in his truck?"

Her mouth puckered into a tight frown. "No, I don't remember. Why?"

He decided to take a chance and answer honestly. "I'm trying to figure out who knew about those keys."

"Why?" Her voice rose a notch.

"Someone besides Benjamin drove Webb's truck that night. Someone used the truck to push your stepmother's car off the highway. I'm just trying to figure out who knew about them."

All the color left her face. In contrast to the milky paleness, her freckles became even more pronounced. "Paige didn't kill her."

"Are you sure?"

"Yes, I'm sure."

"How do you know?"

"Because I *know*." She reached for the door handle as if she intended to get out.

But Fred wasn't through with her yet. He put a restraining hand on her arm. "Was she with you at the time of death?"

"No."

"Then, you're not sure."

"Yes, I am," she insisted. "Paige didn't kill Lenore. I swear."

Fred used his free hand to rub his chin. He tried to look perplexed. "If she wasn't with you, how can you be sure?"

"I just *am*, okay?"

"What about your dad?"

"My dad didn't kill her, either." She tried to tug her arm away from him.

But Fred refused to loosen his hold. "Hannah—"

With a shrill cry she jerked her arm again. "Let go of me. I don't want to talk to you anymore." She flailed against his grip, and tears filled her eyes.

He tried to soften his tone a little. He didn't need a hysterical young girl bolting from his car and causing any new gossip. "I'll let go of your arm if you'll calm down a little. Okay? Can you do that?"

She didn't acknowledge his question but tried once more to wrench her arm from his grip. "Leave me *alone*."

"Listen, Hannah." He worked to keep his voice level. "I'm not accusing your dad of anything. Or Paige. But there are some questions I'd like to clear up, and I think you can help me."

"I don't want to help you," she shouted, but her efforts to pull away slowed a bit. "You think Paige killed Lenore, don't you?"

"*Someone* did."

"Not Paige. And not my dad, either."

"Can you prove that?"

She glared at him, and the color rushed back into her face. "My dad was home, and Paige didn't even know Lenore was going to Denver to hire the lawyer. She didn't know anything about it until the next morning."

Fred could only stare at her. Lenore was going to Denver for an attorney? Not to find support for her anti-gambling campaign? With effort, he pulled himself together and tried not to look as if his heart was racing far too fast. "A lawyer for the custody battle?"

In spite of his efforts, Hannah seemed to realize she'd given something away. Her eyes widened, and she began to tremble.

"That's why Lenore left home that night, isn't it? To get a lawyer to help her take Trevor away from Paige."

Hannah didn't voluntarily move a muscle, but her entire body quivered.

"You and your dad were the only ones who knew, weren't you?"

Still no answer.

"Did your dad know about Webb's keys?"

The tears came back full force. They filled her big green eyes and spilled onto her cheeks. Within seconds, huge, racking sobs shook her slender frame.

Fred couldn't help but feel sorry for her. So young. So frightened. So worried about her father. He loosened his grip on her arm and used his most grandfatherly voice. "Why don't you tell me about it?"

For a second or two, he thought she would refuse. He half expected her to bolt from the car and run away. But she lowered her face into her hands and began to sob in earnest. She muttered something, too softly for Fred to hear.

He leaned a little closer. "Tell me, Hannah."

After a long moment she raised her eyes to meet his again. "I can't."

"Whatever it is," Fred said, "it's eating you up inside." He could see it in her eyes, the set of her face, the slump of her shoulders. He could hear it in every shuddering breath. "Tell me what happened after you came home from the Copper Penny that night."

She sat there for a long time, crying softly and rocking back and forth in her seat.

"Hannah, you're going to have to tell me. Sheriff Asay is going to find out the truth anyway. He always does."

She shook her head. "I can't."

"Your dad and Lenore got into an argument about Trevor," Fred prompted. "Lenore left for Denver to get an attorney. Am I right so far?"

She nodded weakly.

"Your dad followed her—"

"No!" She jerked her head up and met his gaze with red-rimmed eyes. "No, he didn't."

"He knew he could use Webb's truck because you'd told him, without thinking, that Webb left his keys in the ignition . . ."

"No!" The word tore from her throat.

But Fred didn't let up. "Your dad went to the Copper Penny, borrowed Webb's truck, and followed your mother out of town."

She shook her head again. Her eyes looked wild, her face contorted. "Lenore said she'd take Trevor away." Her voice pleaded with him to understand.

Fred did understand, perhaps better than he wanted to.

"She said she'd been calling around, and she knew an attorney who'd get the job done," Hannah said.

"And your dad wanted to stop her."

"Dad said he wouldn't give her a penny to pay for it, but she just laughed at him. She said she'd been saving money for a long time—since before Trevor was born—so she didn't need his money." The memory sent a shiver through her slight frame. She wiped her nose with the back of her hand, then wrapped her arms around herself and held on.

Without a word Fred reached into the back seat for the box of tissues he kept there and placed it beside her on the seat.

She pulled a couple of tissues from the box and mopped her face. "She said it was Dad's fault. Dad's fault and my mom's. She said my dad was a rutting pig, and Paige was just like him." Tears poured from her eyes unchecked. "She said my dad was cheating on my mom and that Mom was *leaving* him when she got into the accident and died. But it wasn't true. It *wasn't*."

Fred didn't know about that. The Irvines hadn't lived here

then, and if there'd been talk when they moved in, he hadn't paid attention.

"She said it was her duty to save my dad's soul—and Paige's. And *mine*."

Fred didn't doubt that for a minute.

"Dad warned her. He told her he'd stop her, but when she left the house, he just *stood* there. He didn't do anything. I watched him from my bedroom door—just *standing* there and letting her leave."

Warning chills of a new kind zinged up Fred's spine.

"I couldn't let her do it, Mr. V. I couldn't. But I didn't mean for her to die. I only wanted to stop her."

twenty-nine

Fred's pulse drummed steadily in his ears. His heart gave a sickening lurch, and his stomach clenched. He didn't want to believe what he'd just heard, but he could see the truth in Hannah's wide green eyes and pale freckled face.

He forced himself to speak. "Does your dad know?"

She shook her head and cried so hard Fred thought she might throw up on his car seat.

"You went back to the Copper Penny and took Webb's truck so you could follow Lenore?"

Hannah managed a shaky nod and took a couple of shallow breaths. "Dad came outside and started fighting with her again, but I knew she'd win. She always won." Her body shuddered with a leftover sob, but when she spoke again, her voice sounded a little stronger. "I caught up with her leaving town, and I tried to pull in front of her to block the road, but she wouldn't let me pass. I was so mad, Mr. V. I *hated* her. She always talked about what a good Christian woman she was, but she was mean. She never said anything nice about anybody—except maybe Mrs. Lacey. And she hurt people—on purpose."

Hannah looked at him, as if she expected him to say something. Fred knew every word was true, but he hesitated to agree aloud. He muttered something noncommittal and waited for her to calm down a little.

"Paige is a good mother," she whispered so softly he almost didn't hear her.

"I know she is."

"I'm going to prison, aren't I? Or worse. Like Dad says, an eye for an eye."

"I don't know what will happen," Fred admitted. He wondered if her age would play a factor in the court's decision or if she'd get a lighter sentence because Lenore's death was an accident, but he didn't want to offer false hope.

"Yes, I will," she said. "I'll go to prison for murder. Or they'll kill me."

"If you tell Sheriff Asay the truth—right away—the county attorney will probably take that into consideration."

That only set off a fresh burst of tears.

He reached for the gearshift. "I'll drive you there now."

"No!" She recoiled as if he'd hit her, but she sucked in a few more deep breaths and pulled herself together. "No. I have to tell my dad first. You don't know how bad he'd be hurt if he found out from somebody else."

He probably would be, but Fred had a sneaking suspicion Enos wouldn't grant Kent's hurt feelings the same priority Hannah obviously did. "Maybe we should tell your dad now."

A tiny ridge formed between her eyes. "He's not home."

"Is he at work? We could call him, or I could take you to see him."

"No." The ridge deepened. "I don't know where he is. I'll talk to him when he comes home."

Fred didn't like the idea of driving away and leaving Hannah here, but he certainly couldn't force her to go with him. And he didn't want to do anything that might put the case in jeopardy for Enos. He made one last suggestion. "I could stay here with you until he gets back."

She shook her head again. "No. He'd kill me if he came home and found someone there he wasn't expecting." Opening the car door, she stepped onto the shoulder of the road. "I'll be okay. Honest."

Fred didn't worry about that. He just didn't want her to change her mind.

As if she could hear his thoughts, she leaned to look in the car again. "I'll tell, Mr. V. Don't worry." Her expression grew haunted. "I've been miserable the past few days. It's all I can think about. I've been worried about Ben's dad. About *my* dad and Paige. I can't live like that anymore."

Fred had no choice but to accept her word—or at least appear to. But he'd tell Enos about her confession and let him take it from there—just as soon as he could find him.

He watched in the rearview mirror until she reached her front lawn again and disappeared from view. Slowly he put the Buick into gear and pulled onto the road.

He thought about Benjamin and what this news would do to him. He wished he could prepare Benjamin for the news before Hannah went to Enos, but he knew he couldn't say a word.

The boy would be crushed—and probably angry. The way Fred's luck had been running, Benjamin would probably accuse him of torturing Hannah until she confessed.

Fred shook his head sadly and retraced his route back to Main Street. He wanted this investigation to be over and for life to get back to normal. Quite honestly, he didn't know how much more of this he could stand.

Fred replaced the receiver on the telephone and glanced at the clock on the kitchen wall. Already after ten o'clock and still no answer at Enos's house or at the sheriff's office.

Just after dinner he'd phoned the Bluebird hoping to find Grady visiting his mother. Lizzie'd told him Grady had the day off, and Enos had rushed Jessica to her doctor in Denver. Which left Ivan Neeley on duty. Ivan had been called out to Henry Chambers's place after Ralph Mikesell showed up with a shotgun, which explained why Fred couldn't raise anyone on the telephone.

Frustrated, he padded down the hall to his bedroom, kicked off his slippers, and climbed beneath the covers. Had Hannah already told Kent about her role in Lenore's death? Had they tried to call Enos? He wanted answers—some resolution before he went to sleep, but he wouldn't get them. Not tonight.

He flipped off the bedside lamp and lay in the dark. He closed his eyes and listened to the house creaking—the same sounds he'd been listening to forever, but tonight they didn't offer their usual comfort. He didn't know how long he lay there, unable to sleep, watching the moon-painted patterns on his ceiling from the trees outside, before the first strange sound caught his attention and brought him fully alert. He couldn't have even said what he'd heard—a click that shouldn't have been there? A creak on the floorboards? Something didn't sound right.

He froze in place and paid attention. For several seconds he heard nothing but a tree branch against the outside wall and his alarm clock ticking too loud in the night.

All at once, the refrigerator hummed to life. Startled, he jerked, then let out his breath and tried again to relax. He was nervous as a cat. Jumpy. The events of the past few days had worn on him.

He closed his eyes and pulled in a soothing breath. But another creak on the floorboards outside his bedroom brought his eyes wide open again. No doubt about it, someone was out there.

His heart raced, too fast for comfort. Nothing to worry about, he told himself. It was Margaret. Or his youngest son, Douglas, arriving unannounced again. But he knew he was deluding himself. None of his children would have crept down the hallway in near silence. They made the floorboards sing, even when they tried to be quiet.

Slowly, as silently as he could, Fred slipped off the mattress and crouched at the side of the bed. His knees protested the sudden movement, and he could only hope they'd let him stand again if the need suddenly arose.

Almost without drawing breath, he watched the door. His heart thumped a bit more steady now and so loud he wondered whether the intruder could hear it. It kept time with the only word running through his mind. *Hannah. Hannah. Hannah.*

He should have known better than to leave her alone after her confession. He shouldn't have trusted her, but she'd fooled him with her youth and act of innocence. He took slight comfort in knowing that, if she were out there, he could overpower her easily—as long as she didn't have a weapon of some kind.

He took a mental inventory of the darkened room, hoping to think of something he could use to defend himself. The bedside table held his alarm clock, a reading lamp, the latest Deloy Barnes western novel, and an assortment of herbal remedies Margaret had brought home from Denver one weekend for him to try. Nothing particularly useful there.

He kept his hunting rifle and shells in the garage—impossible to reach without going down the hall, which would put him right in the intruder's path. His boots, heavy leather and thick-soled, sat in front of the closet across the room. But they wouldn't be much use unless he threw them at her.

What else was there? Phoebe's silver-handled brush sat on the dresser. Useless—unless he broke the glass in the mirror. He'd never anticipated a break-in, never taken precautions, never thought about protection in his own home.

The intruder didn't move for what felt like forever but was probably no more than a few seconds. He imagined Hannah listening at the door to make sure he wasn't awake. Maybe even arguing with herself—trying to talk herself out of this. Fred hoped her more rational side won.

He forced himself to take shallow, silent breaths. But his legs were losing feeling and his right knee growing weak under the strain of holding him there so long. He tried to redistribute his weight, but his knee refused to bend the way it should have.

He lost his balance and started to fall backward. Suppressing a cry, he pressed his hands to the floor to catch himself. He managed to remain on his feet, but his back brushed against the nightstand, and the handle of the drawer dug into the muscles below his shoulder.

He forced himself upright again, cursing the slight noise he'd made when he hit the drawer and hoping he hadn't given himself away. Sharp pain in his back gave way to a dull throb just as the door across the room began to inch open.

Fred concentrated on the doorway and forced his breathing to remain steady and quiet. In. Out. In. Out.

Inch by agonizing inch, the door opened until he could make out someone's outline—nothing more than an inky black shadow against the dusky gray of the night. It stood there for a long time, watching. And any faint hope Fred might have had that his visitor was friendly disappeared as the seconds ticked past.

He'd have sold his right knee in that moment for a weapon of some kind. Anything. Preferably something with bullets, something sharp, or something heavy he could use as a club.

The instant that thought formed, he realized what he *did* have—right behind him in the drawer of his nightstand. A flashlight. But he couldn't get it now. The intruder would notice any movement he made.

He breathed and watched, alert to every sound, every shift in the shadows, every change in the light from the moon, until at long last, the intruder stepped away from the corner and into the doorway. The shadow grew larger than Fred had expected—a trick of the light, no doubt.

It moved into the room, one cautious step at a time. Closer. Close enough to see the empty bed. All movement stopped for one long agonizing moment before the shadow drew back into a spill of moonlight coming through the open curtain.

Fred managed not to gasp aloud when he realized why the intruder looked so much larger than he'd expected. Instead of Hannah, he found himself looking straight into the broad face of her father.

Forcing himself to remain calm, Fred stared into Kent Irvine's wild eyes until the other man moved out of the moonlight and became a shadow once more. Fred stood a chance against Hannah, but Kent outweighed him by at least sixty pounds. The only thing Fred had more of than Kent was age–twenty years, at least. No advantage there.

Maybe Kent would give up now that he saw the bed empty. Maybe he'd turn around and leave. And Fred could call . . . nobody. Grady was probably still out on the town. No doubt Ivan was still dealing with Henry and Ralph, and Enos wouldn't have time to drive back from Denver before another hour or more passed.

Kent hesitated so long that Fred thought his lungs would stop working. His knees began to tremble, and he had to clutch the bedclothes to keep himself in position. The top quilt slid a few inches toward him. He let go as soon as he realized the danger, but not soon enough.

Kent saw the movement and bolted toward him. His footsteps echoed on the floorboards, and his breath came in heavy gasps.

Fred waited until Kent rounded the foot of the bed, then shoved off with his legs and caught Kent's thighs with his shoulder.

Kent took two stumbling steps backward, caught his balance, and lunged at Fred. He caught Fred's shoulders with both hands and dragged him to his feet.

Fred steeled himself for the blow he expected to come next. Surprisingly, Kent didn't take a swing. Instead, he shoved Fred backward onto the bed and fastened both hands around his neck.

Struggling to catch his breath, Fred tore at Kent's hands. He tried to roll onto his side to break away, but Kent held him fast. He tried to roll to the other side, then back again. No good. Kent planted a knee on his stomach to hold him still.

Desperate for oxygen, near retching, almost blind from the pain, Fred dug at Kent's hands again. He caught one of Kent's thumbs with his fingers and wrenched it toward his chin. Blessedly, Kent's grip loosened just enough to allow a shallow breath into Fred's burning throat and lungs.

He gulped air and managed to tear Kent's other hand from his throat the same way. Without wasting even a heartbeat, he locked his hands together and struck Kent in the throat with every ounce of strength he had left. Fred pummeled Kent again and again, striking away his hands, connecting with his throat when he could, his back, his side, his stomach—anything he could reach until, at long last, Kent's knee slipped off his stomach.

Mustering strength he didn't know he had, Fred shoved the larger man sideways and rolled with him. He struggled to stand and fought to pull air into his lungs, but he didn't let up. He couldn't. Nobody expected Kent to come after him. Nobody would even check on him until morning.

Kent lurched off the bed and hit Fred in the jaw with a fist.

Fred's face exploded in pain. He swung back, using a right then a left, but his blows didn't do much.

Kent lunged at him again, using his arm to catch Fred in the throat this time. Fred stumbled backward, ran into the bed, and fell heavily on the mattress. Before he could stand, Kent threw himself on top of Fred and pressed a pillow over his face.

Fred gulped air again and immediately regretted doing so. He'd use what little oxygen he had too quickly if he did that again. He tried to hit Kent, but he didn't have enough strength left to do any damage.

Kent pressed harder, robbing him of even the tiny bit of air he'd been able to breathe. His lungs ached, his head spun, and red spots danced in front of his eyes. Frantic, he struck at Kent again and again but it did no good. He drew back his hand to swing once more and brushed the bedside table with his knuckles.

Hope flickered. He hadn't realized he was so near the table. He had to get the flashlight. It was his only chance of staying alive.

While Fred kicked and twisted and used his entire body in the fight for his life, he inched his hand along the table, found the drawer, and ripped it open.

Thank God the flashlight was there in the front of the drawer. Fred gripped it, pulled it out of the drawer, and aimed blindly where he hoped Kent's head would be. He heard a satisfying thunk and a groan, and the pressure on the pillow weakened for a heartbeat.

That was all he needed. He swung again, connected again, and tore the pillow from his face with his left hand. Something warm and wet dripped onto his face.

Blood.

Blinking rapidly to let his eyes adjust to the dim moonlight, he took aim and hit Kent once more. This time, Kent's eyes rolled, his body went limp, and he lost consciousness.

But he fell flat on top of Fred.

Aching everywhere, Fred tried to shove the heavier man off of him. No good. Kent might be heavy awake and fighting—unconscious, he felt like a boulder.

Gulping air, Fred used both arms to lift one of Kent's shoulders far enough to slide out from beneath him. Inch by inch, praying Kent wouldn't come to before he could get away, Fred worked his way out from beneath the dead weight.

Finally, he managed to slide from the bed to the floor. He landed with a thunk on his backside, but his knee twisted as he went down and fresh pain shot up his leg.

He did his best to ignore the pain. He couldn't risk staying here for even a few minutes. Using the nightstand, he pulled himself to his feet, glanced at Kent long enough to make sure he was still breathing, and hobbled down the hallway toward the back door as quickly as he could.

He passed the kitchen phone, but he didn't bother stopping. He could call for help after he had Kent secure. He worked his way into the garage, forced his aching knees to climb the ladder, and retrieved his hunting rifle and shells from the high shelf.

Maybe he'd be smarter to just leave and send someone back after Kent, but if he left Kent alone, he might get away. Or he could wake up at any moment and come after Fred again.

Twice before he could make his trembling hands work well enough to load the blasted rifle he imagined he heard Kent coming after him. He almost stopped breathing. His heart raced in his chest, faster with each sound. But each time the sound came from a tree brushing against the back deck in the cool spring breeze.

At long last, he managed to load the shells in the clip. He slipped extras into his pocket, grabbed a length of rope from a hook on the wall and a roll of duct tape from the workbench. Releasing the safety on the rifle, he crept back into the house.

Every muscle in his body screamed with pain, and his lungs still ached. He'd have given anything for a soak in a tubful of hot water followed by a good night's sleep. But he tiptoed back down the hall into his bedroom and set to work.

Kent started to come around while Fred worked with the rope, but before he became a threat again, Fred secured his arms and legs, lashed him to the headboard, and wrapped the silver tape over the rope for good measure.

When he felt certain Kent couldn't get away, he hobbled back into the kitchen and tried once more to reach Enos. Still no answer.

He glanced at the clock on the wall. Midnight. Too early for Grady to be home yet. Which left Ivan as Fred's only other choice. But even if he could reach Ivan, the blasted boy wouldn't believe a word Fred said. He never did—even with evidence in front of his eyes. Fred would rather wait an hour and try to reach Enos again. He had his rifle, and Kent wouldn't be able to work loose before then.

Grabbing one of the kitchen chairs, Fred dragged it into the bedroom behind him. He found Kent half-sitting on the bed, struggling against the tape and rope.

When he realized he couldn't get away, he sent Fred a hostile glare. "What the hell do you think you're doing?"

"Keeping you here until I can reach the sheriff." Fred settled the chair against the wall, his backside in the chair, and the rifle on his knee.

"I didn't kill her."

"Maybe not," Fred admitted. "But you tried to kill me."

Kent struggled again, then collapsed against the headboard. To Fred's surprise, tears filled his eyes. "She tried to kill herself tonight."

Fred's heartbeat slowed ominously, and his stomach tightened in apprehension. "Who? Hannah?"

Kent nodded miserably. "I found her on her bedroom floor. She left a note."

Fred sat up a little straighter. "A confession?"

"God, yes." A sob wrenched from Kent's throat, and the tears spilled onto his cheeks. "I rushed her to the hospital, and they were able to revive her, but she's ruined. *Ruined.* Do you understand? She had *everything* going for her. She had her whole life ahead of her . . ." He broke off with another wrenching sob. "You're the only one who knew."

"You destroyed the note?"

A miserable nod.

"And you figured if you got rid of me, you could save Hannah. How were you going to explain the suicide attempt?"

"Grief over Lenore's death." The words came out a whisper, almost too low for Fred to hear.

Fred could only stare at him.

"You'd have done the same thing if it were your kid." Kent's voice came out stronger this time. "I know you would."

Fred shook his head slowly. "No."

"It'll *ruin* her," Kent insisted, and when Fred didn't respond, he shouted, "It'll ruin her *life*."

Fred looked away and watched the clock. Kent could cry all he wanted; he could explain until he was blue in the face—Fred didn't care. Fred might usually be an easygoing sort, but Kent had lost all claim to sympathy and understanding when he decided to break in and do away with him. Some things, even Fred had trouble forgiving.

thirty

"Dad? Dad? Are you home?"

Dimly Fred became aware of Margaret's voice through the sleep-induced fog. He blinked his eyes open and stared around his bedroom for a moment, trying to figure out where he was and what he was doing. Slowly everything came back to him.

Kent was still tied to the bed. His head drooped to one side, and his arms hung limp. Fred watched until he saw the other man's chest rise and fall. Thank heaven he was alive. The fight, loss of blood, and his emotional outburst afterward must have finally taken their toll.

He looked far worse in the clear light of day than Fred had imagined the night before. Blood matted his hair and left two thin red trails down his cheek. Splotches of dark red decorated Kent's clothes, the sheets, and Phoebe's handmade quilt. Even Fred's pajamas had a fair smattering of blood down the front. It looked as if someone had died in here.

"Dad?"

Fred tried to sit up straight, but his muscles protested even the slightest movement. Slowly, he lowered the rifle to his side and tried to bend his knees. "I'll be right out, sweetheart." He tried to sound chipper, but his voice came out sounding like a croak and his throat burned, almost as if Kent's hands were still fastened around his neck.

"Where are you?"

"I'm in the bedroom. Getting dressed." He didn't want her

to come in. He didn't want her to see this—it looked bad enough to Fred and he *knew* what happened.

Still holding the rifle, he limped to the dresser and checked his reflection in the mirror. He looked far worse than he'd feared. He held back a groan and looked about for something he could use to wash his face and neck.

"Dad?" She tapped softly on the bedroom door. "Are you all right?"

"I'm fine, sweetheart." Fred swabbed his face with a handkerchief, but it did no good. The blood had dried long ago. He needed access to the bathroom, but Margaret stood in his way.

"You're just getting dressed now?"

"I slept in."

"You *what?*" He could picture her leaning an ear against the door. "You never sleep in. Are you sure you're all right?"

"I'm fine," he lied. "I'll be out in a minute. Why don't you wait for me in the living room?" He didn't sound fine, even to himself. His voice rasped and cut out on a couple of words.

Margaret rattled the doorknob. "I'm going to come in there. Are you decent?"

"Not yet. I'll be out in a second."

Kent stirred on the bed, stared around the room trying to get his bearings, and let out a load groan.

"Dad? I'm coming in there. Something's wrong."

Fred watched, horrified, as the doorknob turned and Margaret opened the door.

Kent strained against his bonds and let out a pitiful wail. "Help me."

Margaret stared, mouth agape, eyes wide, first at Kent on the bed and the bloodstained bedclothes, then at Fred, standing beside the dresser holding his rifle. She gasped, ran to Fred's side, and touched his blood-splotched face. "Are you okay? Where are you hurt?"

Everywhere. But Fred didn't want to admit it. He tried to sound hearty and robust. "I told you I'm fine."

"You've got *blood* all over you."

"It's not mine."

"Not yours?" She flicked another glance at Kent, drew

back a step, and stared at Fred with narrowed eyes. "What in the hell is going on here?"

"He went crazy and attacked me," Kent shouted.

Fred lifted the rifle to remind Kent he still had it. "Kent broke in last night and tried to kill me."

"Kill you? Why?"

Kent struggled to pull his arms free. "Your old man's crazy. Probably has Alzheimer's or something."

Fred's patience snapped. He'd had just about enough of Kent. He lifted the rifle another notch. "Will you shut up before I decide to use this on you?"

"See?" Kent demanded.

But Margaret ignored him. She kept her eyes glued on Fred's. "Did *he* kill Lenore?"

Fred shook his head. "No. Hannah did."

Margaret shut her eyes for a second. "Oh, my God."

"It was an accident," Fred assured her and explained quickly what Hannah had told him the day before. "She promised she'd tell her dad and ask him to go with her when she talked to Enos. Instead, she decided to take a bottle of sleeping pills."

Dread flashed across Margaret's face. She touched one hand to her breast and whispered, "My God, is she . . . ?"

"No. She's fine. Kent says he got her to the hospital in time to save her. But that's what got him so worked up, I guess." Fred's knees buckled. He lowered the rifle and leaned against the dresser. "Until now, I was the only other person who knew the truth. Kent figured if he could get rid of me, Hannah would be home free."

Just the memory of it worked Kent up all over again. "This will ruin her life. Her entire *life*. Don't you understand that? She's just a kid. She has everything to look forward to—"

Margaret's face tightened. She glared at Kent with an expression so hostile that Fred wouldn't have wanted to be on the receiving end of it. "So you tried to kill my dad? Are you insane?"

"I think he planned to make it look as if I'd died peacefully in my sleep," Fred said. "He figured nobody would question it—probably chalk it up as a heart attack or something."

"Peacefully?" Margaret gave the room another once-over. "It didn't work."

In spite of everything, Fred chuckled. "Do me a favor, sweetheart. Try calling Enos for me, would you? I'd like to get Kent out of here."

She stared at him, incredulous. "You haven't called him yet?"

"He wasn't home. He took Jessica to the doctor in Denver. He rubbed the back of his neck with the palm of one hand and held back a groan. "If you can't reach Enos, find Grady."

She didn't move. "How long has he been here?"

"Since eleven or a little after."

Her eyes widened. "You've been alone with him *all night*?"

"I don't get many visitors that time of night."

"Why didn't you call *me*?"

"What would you have done?"

"I would have come over. At least there would have been two of us. Or I could have found Grady or Ivan to come and get him. Good grief, Dad—"

Fred didn't want to argue with her. He wanted to get Kent out of his bed, change the sheets, take a hot bath, and catch a catnap. "Well," he said. "What's done is done. Can't change it now."

"Sometimes I wonder about you," she muttered, and she turned toward the door. "I truly do."

"I thought I kept life interesting."

She rolled her eyes at him.

Fred fixed her with a paternal stare—the one that had worked wonders when the kids were small. "Are you going to call Enos, or should I?"

The look didn't seem to have the same effect on her as an adult. "Oh, I'll call him, all right. Don't worry about that." It sounded more like a threat than a promise, but she disappeared through the door and hurried into the kitchen.

He could hear her voice a few seconds later, rising and falling as she told someone what had happened. Good. He no longer cared who came after Kent—as long as someone did.

He crossed to the chair again and dropped onto it. But his

backside hurt from spending so many hours in the same position, and pain zinged up his knee when he bent it.

Less than five minutes later, Fred heard the squeal of tires in his driveway and Enos's quick, heavy footsteps as he ran up the front walk and onto the porch. Margaret must have been waiting for him—he didn't even have to knock.

Margaret led Enos toward Fred's bedroom. "They're in here," she said. "Prepare yourself—you are not going to believe this."

Enos stepped into the room, sized up the situation with a scowl, and sighted in on Fred. "Good billy hell, Fred. I can't even leave you alone for half a day, can I?"

"I don't want to hear it," Fred grumbled.

To his surprise, Enos laughed. He crossed to the bed, cut away the tape and untied Kent's ropes. Pulling a pair of handcuffs from his duty belt, he snapped them over Kent's wrists. "You're under arrest for attempted murder."

"I didn't do anything," Kent shouted. "I came here to talk to that crazy old fart, and *he* attacked *me*. Look at me. I'm injured."

"Yeah? Well, Fred's always doing that." Enos flicked an amused glance at Fred. "I guess you should have known better than to sneak into his house in the middle of the night for your conversation." He led Kent into the hallway, reciting his rights as they walked. Halfway to the living room, he stopped and looked back over his shoulder at Margaret. "Can you stay here for a few minutes? I'll turn Kent over to Grady and come back to take your dad's statement."

She nodded, blushed a delicate shade of pink, and tucked a lock of hair behind her ear. All at once she looked sixteen again. "Can I take the sheets off the bed for him?"

"Go ahead," Enos said, trying to sound businesslike and failing miserably. "But don't wash them. We may need them for evidence."

Fred couldn't imagine why Margaret needed to be present for Enos to take his statement, but he didn't say a word. He just settled back in his chair and watched as Margaret set to work. When the telephone rang a few seconds later, he pushed back to his feet and limped into the kitchen to answer.

"Hello?"

"Dad?"

Joseph. Of all people. Calling to kick Fred when he was down. He must be able to sense Fred's moods.

"Yes."

"I'm just calling to let you know I have an airline reservation for next weekend. I'll be arriving early Saturday morning. Do you think Maggie could pick me up at Denver International?"

Fred closed his eyes and rubbed his forehead. He wasn't in the mood for this. Not right now. Thank goodness he'd come to his senses and decided to stay in Cutler. Joseph would drive him around the bend in less than a month.

"I've talked to Zane Neville at High Mountain Realtors," Joseph said. "He's agreed to get an appraiser to meet me there on Saturday afternoon."

"I won't let him in the door."

Joseph paused. "What?"

"I said, I won't let him in the door, so don't bother."

"Oh, now, Dad—"

"I mean it, Joseph. I'm not moving. I'm not selling. I'm not doing a blasted thing but staying right here in my home until the day I die." Which, considering how badly Fred ached at the moment, could easily come sooner than Joseph expected.

"I thought we had this all settled—"

"*You* had it settled," Fred snapped. "I never said I'd move."

Joseph let out a heavy sigh, and Fred could almost hear his brain cranking through the telephone wire.

"Let me make this clear once and for all," Fred said. "If you're coming to Cutler next weekend for a visit, you're more than welcome. If you're coming to put my house on the market, don't waste your money or your time."

"Dad, you're getting old. It's dangerous for you to stay there alone."

Fred bit back a smile. Joseph had no idea just how dangerous life in Cutler could be. "It's true," he admitted. "I'm getting older. But I'm not feeble. I'm not losing my mind. I'm perfectly capable of looking after myself."

"Maybe you are *now*," Joseph insisted. "But what will happen in a few years?"

Fred didn't want to think about that. "If it becomes a problem, we'll deal with it then."

Joseph let out another put-upon sigh just as Margaret pushed open the kitchen door and looked inside. A second later, Enos's heavy footsteps announced his return.

Margaret nodded at the telephone. "Who is it?"

Fred motioned Enos inside and mouthed his response. "Joseph."

Margaret stepped into the room and held out her hand. "Let me talk to him."

Fred hesitated for a second. He didn't know what Margaret would say after what she'd just seen in the bedroom.

"Oh, for heaven's sake. I'm on your side." She tugged the phone from his hand and leaned against the counter. "Joe? I've been meaning to call you. It's about this idea you had for Dad."

Fred held his breath.

Enos crossed the room to stand beside him. "Joseph, huh?"

Fred nodded.

"No," Margaret said, shaking her head as if Joseph could see her. "That won't work. I need him here."

Fred let out the breath he'd been holding. His lips curved in a smile.

"I *need* him here," Margaret repeated. "Webb moved out this morning."

Fred's next breath caught in his sore throat. Enos looked as if someone had gut-punched him.

Margaret just smiled softly. "Oh, you know. Things have been rough for a long time. We've only been staying together because of the kids."

Fred pulled out a chair from the table and lowered himself into it. Enos followed his example. They sat that way, glancing at each other and looking away, both trying to take it all in and make sense of the new order of things, until Margaret replaced the receiver on the wall.

She met Fred's astonished gaze with a slow smile. "I did it.

I asked him to leave. I was going to tell you about it when I got here, but you distracted me."

Fred could hardly breathe, and he knew Enos wasn't faring much better.

"Are you getting a divorce?" Fred croaked.

She shrugged. "Not right away. We'll just see how things go for a while, I guess. Six months, maybe. We'll see if he can control his drinking and hold down a job that long."

Fred nodded as if he comprehended everything.

"Now, I've *got* to get your bed made. I'll be back in a minute," she said and bolted from the room.

Enos pulled in a ragged breath and watched her leave. He wore that soft expression he'd never used for anyone else. But there was something else in his eyes this time. Fred couldn't miss it. His eyes were full of fear.

He touched Enos's shoulder with a gentle hand and smiled. "Worried?"

Enos managed a thin smile. "A little, I guess."

"I don't think she's going to rush into anything, son. If they divorce, I can't imagine her remarrying any time soon."

Enos swallowed and managed a thin smile. "I hope not. I don't think I could go through it all again."

"I hope you don't have to," Fred said. "But I'm not going anywhere. I'll be here to take care of her."

He leaned back in his seat and locked his aching arms behind his head. He turned a smile toward the kitchen window, as if Phoebe were standing there to share the moment. And she probably was. Fred knew she wouldn't have missed this for anything.

And neither would he.